The last thing a fourteen-year-old boy expects to find along an Ozark river bottom is a tree full of monkeys. Jay Berry's grandpa had an explanation, of course—as he did for most things. The monkeys had escaped from a circus, and there was a handsome reward in store for anyone who could catch them. Grandpa said there wasn't any animal that couldn't be caught somehow, and Jay Berry started out believing him.

But by the end of "the summer of the monkeys," Jay Berry Lee had learned a lot more than he ever bargained for—and not just about monkeys. He learned about faith, and wishes coming true, and knowing what it is you *really* want

This novel, set in rural Oklahoma around the turn of the century, is a funny and heartwarming family story about a time and place when miracles were really the simplest things.

WILSON RAWLS was born on a small farm in the Ozarks, in the heart of the Cherokee Nation. He spent his youth prowling the hills and river bottoms with an old blue tick hound—his only companion. He made up his own stories and it wasn't until his family moved to Tahlequah, Oklahoma, and he discovered the public library, that Mr. Rawls had access to real books. His first novel, *Where the Red Fern Grows*, continues to be popular with young readers and adults alike, and was made into a motion picture.

ALSO AVAILABLE IN LAUREL-LEAF BOOKS:

A DAY NO PIGS WOULD DIE, *Robert Newton Peck*

THE NIGHT SWIMMERS, *Betsy Byars*

THE OUTSIDERS, *S.E. Hinton*

THAT WAS THEN, THIS IS NOW, *S.E. Hinton*

RUMBLE FISH, *S.E. Hinton*

TEX, *S.E. Hinton*

WOULD YOU SETTLE FOR IMPROBABLE?, *P.J. Petersen*

HARRIET THE SPY, *Louise Fitzhugh*

THE LONG SECRET, *Louise Fitzhugh*

SPORT, *Louise Fitzhugh*

Summer of the Monkeys

WILSON RAWLS

LAUREL-LEAF BOOKS bring together under a single imprint outstanding works of fiction and nonfiction particularly suitable for young adult readers, both in and out of the classroom. Charles F. Reasoner, Professor Emeritus of Children's Literature and Reading, New York University, is consultant to this series.

Published by
Dell Publishing
a division of
The Bantam Doubleday Dell Publishing Group, Inc.
666 Fifth Avenue
New York, New York 10103

The trademark Laurel-Leaf Library® is registered in the U.S. Patent
and Trademark Office.
ISBN: 0-440-98175-1

RL: 4.9

Reprinted by arrangement with
Doubleday & Company, Inc.
Printed in the United States of America
October 1977

20 19 18

KRI

Summer
of the
Monkeys

1

Up until I was fourteen years old, no boy on earth could have been happier. I didn't have a worry in the world. In fact, I was beginning to think that it wasn't going to be hard at all for me to grow up. But, just when things were really looking good for me, something happened. I got mixed up with a bunch of monkeys and all of my happiness flew right out the window. Those monkeys all but drove me out of my mind.

If I had kept this monkey trouble to myself, I don't think it would have amounted to much; but I got my grandpa mixed up in it. I felt pretty bad about that because Grandpa was my pal, and all he was trying to do was help me.

I even coaxed Rowdy, my old bluetick hound, into helping me with this monkey trouble. He came out of the mess worse than Grandpa and I did. Rowdy got so disgusted with me, monkeys, and everything in general, he wouldn't even come out from under the house when I called him.

It was in the late 1800s, the best I can remember. Anyhow—at the time, we were living in a brand-new country that had just been opened up for settlement. The farm we lived on was called Cherokee land because it was smack dab in the middle of the Cherokee Nation. It lay in a strip from the foothills of the Ozark Mountains to the banks of the Illinois River in northeastern Oklahoma. This was the last place in the world that anyone would expect to find a bunch of monkeys.

I wasn't much bigger than a young possum when Mama and Papa settled on the land; but after I grew up a little, Papa told me all about it. How he and Mama hadn't been married very long, and were share-cropping in Missouri. They were unhappy, too; because in those days, being a sharecropper was just about as bad as being a hog thief. Everybody looked down on you.

Mama and Papa were young and proud, and to have people look down on them was almost more than they could stand. They stayed to themselves, kept on share-cropping, and saving every dollar they could; hoping that someday they could buy a farm of their own.

Just when things were looking pretty good for Mama and Papa, something happened. Mama hauled off and had twins—my little sister Daisy and me.

Papa said that I was born first, and he never saw a healthier boy. I was as pink as a sunburnt huckleberry, and as lively as a young squirrel in a corn crib. It was different with Daisy though. Somewhere along the line something went wrong and she was born with her right leg all twisted up.

The doctor said there wasn't much wrong with Daisy's old leg. It had something to do with the mus-cles, leaders, and things like that, being all tangled up. He said there were doctors in Oklahoma City that could take a crippled leg and straighten it out as straight as a ramrod. This would cost quite a bit of money though; and money was the one thing that Mama and Papa didn't have.

Mama cried a lot in those days, and she prayed a lot, too; but nothing seemed to do any good. It was bad enough to be stuck there on that sharecropper's farm; but to have a little daughter and a twisted leg, and not be able to do anything for her, hurt worst of all.

Then one day, right out of a clear blue sky, Mama got a letter from Grandpa. She read it and her face turned as white as the bark on a sycamore tree. She sat right down on the dirt floor of our sod house and started laughing and crying all at the same time. Papa said that after he had read the letter, it was all he could do to keep from bawling a little, too.

Grandpa and Grandma were living down in the Cherokee Nation of Oklahoma. They owned one of those big old country stores that had everything in it. Grandpa wasn't only a storekeeper; he was a trader, too, and a good one. Papa always said that Grandpa was the only honest trader he ever knew that could trade a terrapin out of its shell.

In his letter, Grandpa told Mama and Papa that he had done some trading with a Cherokee Indian for sixty acres of virgin land, and that it was theirs if they wanted it. All they had to do was come down and make a farm out of it. They could pay him for it any way they wanted to.

Well, the way Mama was carrying on, there wasn't but one thing Papa could do. The next morning, before the roosters started crowing, he took what money they had saved and headed for town. He bought a team of big red Missouri mules and a covered wagon. Then he bought a turning plow, some seed corn, and a milk cow. This took about all the money he had.

It was way in the night when Papa got back home. Mama hadn't even gone to bed. She had everything they owned packed, and was ready to go. They were both so eager to get away from that sharecropping farm that they started loading the wagon by moonlight.

The last thing Papa did was to make a two-baby cradle. He took Mama's old washtub and tied a short piece of rope to each handle. To give the cradle a little bit of bounce, he tied the ropes to two cultivator springs and hung the whole contraption to the bows inside the covered wagon.

Mama thought that old washtub was the best baby cradle she had ever seen. She filled it about half full of corn shucks and quilts, and then put Daisy and me down in it.

After taking one last look at the sod house, Papa cracked the whip and they left Missouri for the Oklahoma Territory.

When Papa told me that part of the story, he laughed and said, "If anyone ever asks you how you got from Missouri to the Cherokee Nation of Oklahoma, you just tell them that you rode a washtub every inch of the way."

The day they reached Grandpa's store, Papa was just about all in and had his mind set on sleeping in one of Grandma's feather beds. Mama wouldn't listen to that kind of talk at all. She had waited so long for a farm of her own, she was bound and determined to spend that night on her own land.

Grandma tried to talk some sense into Mama. She told her that the land was only three miles down the river, and it certainly wasn't going to run away. They could stay all night with them, rest up, and go on the next day.

Mama puffed up like a settin' hen in a hailstorm. Nothing Grandma or Grandpa said changed her mind. She told Papa that he could stay there if he wanted to, she'd just take Daisy and me and go on by herself.

Papa knew better than to open his mouth, because once Mama had made up her mind like that, she wouldn't have budged an inch from a buzzing rattler. There wasn't but one thing he could do. He just climbed back in the wagon, unwrapped the check lines from the brake, and said, "Get up!" to those old Missouri mules.

It was in the twilight of evening when Mama and Papa reached the land of their dreams. They camped for the night in a grove of tall white sycamores, right on the bank of the Illinois River.

Papa said that as long as he lived, he would never forget that night. It seemed to him that they were being welcomed by every living thing in those Cherokee bottoms. Whippoorwills were calling, and night hawks were crying as they dipped and darted through the starlit sky. Bullfrogs and hoot owls were jarring the ground with their deep voices. Even the little speckled tree frogs, the katydids, and the crickets were chipping in with their nickel's worth of welcome music.

A big grinning Ozark moon crawled up out of no-where and seemed to say, "Hi, neighbor! I've been looking for you. It gets kind of lonesome out here. Welcome to the land of the Cherokee!"

Papa said Mama was so taken in by all of that beauty, she seemed to be hypnotized. She just stood there in the moonlight with a warm little smile on her face, staring out over the river, her black eyes glowing like black haws in morning dew. Finally, she gave a deep sigh, just as if she had dropped some-thing heavy from her shoulders. Then spreading her arms out wide, she said in a low voice, "It's the work of the Lord—that's what it is. Just think—all of this is ours—sixty acres of it."

Papa said he was feeling so good that he felt he could have walked right out on the waters of the river just as Jesus did when he walked on the waters of the sea.

Mama was a little woman, barely tipping the scales at a hundred pounds; but what she lacked in height and weight, she made up in strength and spirit. Pulling her end of a crosscut saw, and swinging the heavy blade of a double-bitted ax, she helped Papa clear the land.

Papa let Mama pick the spot for our log house. This wasn't an easy chore for her. She walked all over that sixty acres, looking and looking. Finally, she found the very spot she wanted and put her foot down. It was in the foothills overlooking the river bottoms, in the mouth of a blue little canyon.

I grew up on that Cherokee farm and was just about as wild as the gray squirrels in the sycamore trees, and as free as the red-tail hawks that wheeeeed their cries in those Ozark skies. I had a dandy pocketknife, and a darn good dog; that was about all a boy could hope for in those days.

My little sister Daisy grew up, too; but not like I did. It seemed as if that old leg of hers held her grow-ing back. Each year it got worse and worse. The foot part kept twisting and twisting, until finally she couldn't walk on it at all. That's when Papa made a crutch for her out of a red oak limb with a fork on one end. The way Daisy could zip around on that old home-made crutch was something to see. She could get around on it just about as well as I could on two straight legs.

It was always a mystery to me how my little sister could be so happy, and so full of life with an old twisted leg like that. She was always laughing and singing and hopping around on that old crutch just as if she didn't have a worry in the world. Her one big delight was in getting me all riled up by poking fun at me. She never overlooked an opportunity, and it seemed that these opportunities came about every fifteen minutes.

Up on the hillside from our house, under a huge red oak tree, Daisy had a playhouse. From early spring until late fall, practically all of her time was spent there.

I didn't like to mess around Daisy's playhouse. Every time I went up there, I had a guilty feeling—like maybe I shouldn't be there. She had all kinds of girl stuff setting around; corn shuck dolls, mud pies, and pretty bottles. She treasured every tin can that came to our home. In each one, some kind of wild flower peeked out.

At one end of her playhouse, Daisy had built a little altar. She had made a cross by tying two grapevines together and covering them with tinfoil. The face of Christ was there, too. Daisy had molded it from red clay. For the eyes, she had pressed blue shells from a hatched-out robin's nest into the soft clay. She had covered the crown with moss to resemble hair. When Mama discovered that the moss was actually growing in the soft clay, she told everyone in the hills about it. People came from miles around to see the miracle. I never saw anything like it.

It was pretty around Daisy's playhouse; especially, in the early spring when the dogwoods, redbuds, and mountain flowers were blooming. Warm little breezes would whisper down from the green, rugged hills; and the air would be so full of sweet smells, it would make your nose tickle and burn. If you closed your eyes, and filled your lungs full of that sweet-smelling stuff, your head would get as light as a hummingbird's feather and feel as if it was going to sail away by itself.

Daisy was never alone in her playhouse. She had all kinds of little friends. Big fat bunnies, red squirrels, and chipmunks would come right up to her and eat from her hand. She wouldn't be in her playhouse five minutes until all kinds of wild birds would come winging in from the mountains. They would sit around in the bushes and sing so happy and loud that the mountains would ring with their birdie songs. Sometimes they would even light on her shoulders.

I never could understand how my little sister made friends with the birds and the animals. I couldn't get within a mile of anything that had hair or feathers on it. Daisy said it was because I was a boy and was catching things all the time.

One morning in the early spring, Papa came in from doing the chores with an empty milk bucket in his hand. He looked grouchy, and didn't even say "Good morning" to any of us. This was so unusual that right away Mama knew something was wrong.

From the cook stove where she was fixing our breakfast, Mama smiled and said, "Knowing how desperate you are to get the planting done, I'd say it was going to rain."

"No," Papa said, in a disgusted voice. "It's not going to rain. Sally Gooden's gone again."

Sally Gooden was our crazy old milk cow.

"Oh, no!" Mama exclaimed. "Not again!"

"I can't understand that old cow," Papa said, shaking his head. "Just last week I put an extra rail on the pasture fence. It didn't do any good though. She sailed over it as if it wasn't even there."

Turning to me, Papa said, "Jay Berry, you'll have to find her; that's all there is to it. It's wild onion time, and if she gets a bellyful of those things, her milk won't be any good for days. We can't do without milk and butter."

When Papa asked me to do important things like that, it made me feel just about as big as those Ozark Mountains around our log house.

I puffed out my chest and said, "I'll find Sally Gooden, Papa. She's probably down in the river bottoms. That's where I usually find her."

It seemed that Papa and I never could hold a man-to-man conversation without Mama getting all worked up; especially, if we were talking about my going down to the river bottoms.

Mama frowned and said, "That crazy old cow anyhow. Jay Berry, you be careful. I worry every time you go down in those bottoms."

"Worry!" I said, big-eyed. "Why, Mama? What do you have to worry for? I've been all over those bottoms. You know that."

"I know," Mama said, "but I worry just the same. It's no place for a fourteen-year-old boy. Why, it's a regular jungle down there. You can't see ten feet in any direction; and there are snakes, wild hogs, and goodness knows what all."

"Aw, Mama," I said, "you make it sound like I was going to the jungles in Africa, or something. I've chased Sally Gooden out of those bottoms a thousand times and nothing's happened yet. Besides, Rowdy's always with me and he wouldn't let anything get in a mile of me."

I didn't know it at the time, but about an hour later I wasn't so sure but that I was in Africa—the deepest part of Africa.

Sally Gooden was the one thing we had around our farm that I thought was hardly worth putting up with. I always figured that she was a twin sister to the cow that jumped over the moon. She could stand flatfooted and jump out of a well. It seemed as if I spent about half of my time looking for her, and I figured my time was very valuable.

We kept a bell on the jumping old thing, but that didn't do any good. Every time she heard me coming, she would get behind a bush and stand as still as a fence post. Sometimes I swore that she held that bell in her mouth just to keep me from hearing it. I don't think I ever could have found her if it hadn't been for Rowdy. He could sniff her out every time.

Right after breakfast I called Rowdy and we lit out for the bottoms to look for the Lee family's milk supplier. It didn't take Rowdy long to sniff out Sally Gooden. She was down by an old slough that emptied into the river. It was cool and shady along the banks of the slough and there was plenty of green grass. She was just standing there under a big sycamore, chewing her cud, and looking as innocent as the day she was born. I was just about to warm her up with a switch when an idea popped into my head.

Looking at Rowdy, I said, "It's a cinch she's not going anywhere. Her milk bag is so full now she'll have to walk spraddle-legged. Let's leave her alone for a while and do a little looking around."

Rowdy's long skinny tail started fanning the air. He whined and licked my hand. That was his way of saying, "If you want to do a little looking around, pal, it's all right with me."

Now if there ever was a place that needed looking into, it was the Cherokee bottoms. A jillion little game trails twisted their way through jungles of wild cane and matted masses of elder. Like the crawl of a black snake, they wound their way beneath tall white sycamores, black gums, birches, and box elders. Every chance I had, I was down in those bottoms and was doing a pretty good job of leaving my barefoot tracks in the dust of each trail and of carving my initials in the smooth white bark of every sycamore tree.

In the cool silence of those Cherokee bottoms, I could find all the wonders of a storybook world. Sometimes I was Daniel Boone; then there would be spells of Davy Crockett, Kit Carson, the Last of the Mohicans, and Tarzan of the Apes. My favorite hero was Daniel Boone. With hawk feathers sticking in the top of my old straw hat and with my face painted with pokeberry juice, till I'm sure that it would have scared a hoot owl to death, I laid ten thousand Indians to rest in that sycamore heaven.

Old Rowdy was always there, and he was always in the lead, ever alert for any danger that might lie in my way. He could scent a diamond-back rattler or a copperhead long before I saw it, and he'd let me know that it was there. If there were any wild hogs around, he could scare the daylights out of them with his deep voice.

Sometimes Old Rowdy would hop up on a sycamore log, raise his head high in the air, and bawl. I always smiled when he did it because I knew what he was doing. That was his way of telling every living thing in those Cherokee bottoms to look out, for a mighty hunter and a bluetick hound were on the prowl.

I loved every bone in Old Rowdy's body, but what I liked about him most of all was the way he could understand me. Sometimes I figured that he could understand me ever better than grown folks could. At least, he would never say "No" to anything I suggested.

We were following a little game trail deep in the heart of the bottoms, when all at once Rowdy stopped and raised his head in the air. Standing as rigid as a black locust stump, and with his long ears fanned open, he started sniffing the air. I could tell by Rowdy's actions that he had scented something, but was having trouble locating it. Just then a warm summer breeze whispered down from the hills and fanned its way through the tall-timbered bottoms. That was all it took for the sniffing of Old Rowdy to zero in.

"What is it, boy?" I whispered.

Rowdy looked at me and whined.

"Go get it, boy," I said in a low voice.

With no more noise than the shadow of a winging hawk, Rowdy turned and padded from sight in the folding green. Standing as still as the sycamores around me, I waited and listened. I didn't have to wait long. The bell-like tones of my old dog's voice jarred the silence around me. He was bawling treed, and his deep voice was telling me and the whole wide world that he had something up a tree.

To let Rowdy know that I was coming, I reared back

and whooped as loud as I could, "Who-o-e-e, tell it to him, boy. Sing him a hound-dog song."

Ducking my head and running as fast as my legs could carry me, I started boring my way through the underbrush.

Rowdy had something treed in a huge bur oak that was a solid mass of green. As I walked around the big tree, I peered into the dark foliage.

I said, "What is it, boy? A squirrel?"

Not being able to see anything, I backed off to one side, picked up a stick, and threw it up into the branches. From a shadow close to the trunk of the big tree, something moved out on a limb. I couldn't see what it was until it walked into an opening.

At first, I thought my eyes were playing tricks on me. I just couldn't believe what I was seeing. It was a monkey—an honest-to-goodness live monkey. I was so surprised I couldn't move or say a word. All I could do was stand there with my eyes bugged out, and stare at it.

The monkey was staring at me, too. He just sat there on a limb, boring holes through me with his bright little eyes. Then he opened his mouth like he was going to scream his head off, but he didn't make a sound. All he did was show me a mouthful of needle-sharp teeth. He looked so cute and funny, I couldn't help laughing out loud.

Rowdy had seen the monkey, too; and was having a hound dog fit. He was trying his best to run right up the trunk of the bur oak tree; and all the time his deep voice was telling that monkey it was the end of the road.

I don't know whether the monkey got mad or scared. Anyhow, he reared up on his hind legs and let out a cry. All around me the bottoms came to life with noises I had never heard before; grunts and squeals, barks and cries, and everything else.

I didn't get scared until I remembered that about the only place you could find wild monkeys was in the jungles somewhere. The very thought of jungles brought up visions of all kinds of man-eating things like lions, tigers, and gorillas. Then I really got scared. My old heart started turning somersaults; and something that felt like a thousand-legged centipede jiggled its way up my spine.

"Let's get out of here," I yelled at Rowdy, and tore out down a game trail like a scalded cat.

Any second I expected something to jump out of the bushes and eat me up. Old Rowdy could usually outrun me, but it was all he could do to stay up with me.

I came tearing out of the bottoms into one of our fields. At the far end, I saw Papa hitching one of our mules to the corn planter. I headed for him, kicking up the dust.

About five feet from Papa, I threw on the brakes and said in a loud voice, "Papa, Rowdy treed a monkey."

Papa just stood there for a second looking at me, then he smiled and said, "Jay Berry, when a boy's growing up, it's all right for him to see things. I did myself, but you're getting to be a pretty big boy now and I think it's time you quit seeing things. Rowdy probably treed a squirrel."

"No, he didn't, Papa," I almost shouted. "It wasn't a squirrel. It was a monkey—an honest-to-goodness live monkey. I saw it plain as day."

Looking at me kind of hard, Papa said, "Now hold on just a minute. I can't remember that you've ever seen a monkey before."

"I haven't seen a live one, Papa," I said, "but I have seen pictures of them. You remember that little thing Grandma gave me a long time ago. That little thing that had three monkeys on it who couldn't see anything, or hear anything, or say anything. Well, that thing that Rowdy treed looked just like they did. I'm sure it was a monkey all right."

I guess papas have a way of knowing when boys are telling the truth.

Papa frowned and looked off toward the bottoms. "Maybe you did see a monkey," he said, "but it's sure hard to believe. I've never heard of any monkeys being around here."

"Well, there's one here now, Papa," I said. "He's right down there in the bottoms, sitting on a bur oak limb, big as you please."

Papa didn't even act as if he heard what I had said. He just stood there with a thoughtful look on his face, staring off toward the bottoms.

After what seemed like an hour to me, he chuckled and said, "Why, that explains it. Sure, that's it. It has to be."

"What explains what, Papa?" I asked.

"That monkey," Papa said, still chuckling. "You know all those rich people that come up here in the summer to fish on the river. Well, the way I see it, one of them had a pet monkey and it got away from him."

I was just about to go along with what Papa had said when I remembered all those strange noises I had heard.

"Papa," I said, "I believe there was something else down there. I heard a lot of different noises. Do you reckon it could have been more monkeys?"

"Aw," Papa said, turning to pour seed corn into the hopper of the planter, "you probably got scared and just thought you heard something. Besides, if there were monkeys all over the country, I couldn't do anything about it. I have to get this corn planted. We can do without monkeys, but we can't do without bread corn."

I was aching all over to have Papa go with me to look for the monkey, but I knew it wouldn't do any good to ask him. He thought so much of that little old farm of ours, he wouldn't have stopped working to watch a herd of elephants march down the road.

Just as Papa was putting the check lines over his shoulders, he said, "Oh, by the way, did you find Sally Gooden?"

"Yes, sir," I said. "She's down by that old slough. I guess when I saw the monkey I got so excited I forgot all about her. I'm sorry. I'll go get her."

Papa smiled and said, "No, now that I know where she is, I'll look after her. Your mother needs some things from the store; and I think she has a little job she wants you to do."

"Yes, sir," I said and started at a trot for the house.

I didn't have the least bit of trouble getting Mama to believe in my monkey. She already believed that the bottoms were full of things that could gobble me up.

"Monkey!" Mama said, looking all worried. "I don't doubt it. There could be anything down in those bottoms. Monkey! Why, I never heard of anything like it. I don't know. I just don't know."

I saw right away that if I didn't say something to ease Mama's mind she was liable to start laying down the law about my going to the bottoms.

"Aw, now, Mama," I said, "I can't see why you have to get all worked up like that just because I saw a monkey. Papa said it was probably a pet that belonged to a fisherman, and it got away from him."

"Jay Berry," Mama said, "your father doesn't know everything, but I hope he's right. I certainly do. All we need around here now are some lions and tigers, and a few more wild things. We may as well be living in the jungles. I wish more people would move into the country. It's not safe the way it is. It's too wild and untamed."

To get Mama's mind off all those wild things, I changed the conversation.

"Papa said you wanted me to go to the store," I said.

"I do," Mama said, "but I expect I'd better get a piece of paper and write down the things I want. With that monkey running around in your head, you'd probably forget half the things I need."

I waited while Mama got pencil and paper and made a list of the things she needed.

Cramming the list down in one of my overall pockets, she said, "Now you hurry back from the store. I intend to set some hens today and I need you to put fresh straw in the nests."

"I will, Mama," I said and bolted for the door.

2

It was about three miles to the store and I nearly ran
Rowdy's legs off getting there. I was pretty sure that
when I told my grandpa about the monkey, he'd know
what to do about it. My grandpa was one of those old,
slow-moving, boy-loving kind of grandpas. We had
been pals for as long as I could remember. He'd do
anything he could for me, and I'd do anything I
could for him.

If you were looking at the outside of my grandpa,
you wouldn't see very much. He was just about as big
around the middle as he was tall. He didn't have much
hair either, just a little around the edges; and it was as
grey and stiff as a wild hog's whiskers. He wore glasses,
chewed Star tobacco, and needed a shave about three
hundred and sixty days a year. It was the inside of my
grandpa that really counted. He had a heart as big as
a number four washtub; and inside that wrinkled old
hide of his was enough boy-understanding for all the
boys in the world.

On entering the store, I saw Grandpa over behind
the counter, setting canned goods on a shelf. He didn't
hear me when I came in. Of course, I was barefooted
and didn't make any more noise than a lizard walking
on a rail fence.

I eased right up behind him and said in a voice
much too loud, "Grandpa, Rowdy treed a monkey."

I saw my old grandpa flinch—just about like I always did when a wasp dabbed his fiery little dagger in me. He took his time about turning around. Ducking his head, he looked at me over his glasses; then he looked at Rowdy.

Rowdy was just sitting there on his rear, looking at Grandpa. His long ears were sticking straight up and his tongue was hanging out about a foot.

Grandpa must have liked what he saw. He grinned a little and said, "Now, let's do that all over again—only this time don't talk so loud."

"You mean you want me to go back outside, Grandpa, and come in again, just like I did?" I asked.

"No, no," Grandpa said, waving his hand. "You don't have to go back outside. Just say that all over again."

"Oh," I said. I swallowed a couple of times and tried hard to control my voice. "Rowdy treed a monkey."

Grandpa nodded his head and said, "Uh-huh, that's what I thought you said. I wanted to be sure though. Are you sure it was a monkey?"

"Sure as I need a haircut, Grandpa," I said. "It was a monkey all right. It had a skinny tail, four long legs, a baby-looking face, and hair all over it. Papa thinks it was a pet monkey that belonged to a fisherman and it got away from him."

Grandpa thought a second, then shaking his head, he said, "No, I don't think it belonged to a fisherman. Is one monkey all Rowdy treed?"

"That's all I saw, Grandpa," I said, "but I believe there was something else around there. I heard a lot of noises."

Grandpa's bushy eyebrows jumped straight up.

"Noises?" he asked. "What kind of noises?"

"I don't know what kind of noises they were, Grandpa," I said. "I've heard all kinds of noises in the bottoms and I usually know what's making them, but I've never heard anything like that before. It sounded like cries and squeals, barks and grunts, and everything else. It scared me into a running fit."

Grandpa got all excited. He took off his glasses and I saw a twinkle in his friendly old eyes.

Then very seriously he said, "I'm pretty sure those noises you heard were more monkeys. It sure sounds like it. From what I understand, there were probably about thirty of them."

My eyes got as big as bur oak acorns.

"Thirty!" I exclaimed. "Boy, that's a lot of monkeys, Grandpa. Are you sure?"

"I can't be positive," Grandpa said, "but I'd be willing to bet my last bucket of sorghum molasses on it."

"Grandpa, do you know something about those monkeys?" I asked.

Rearing back and looking as important as Rowdy did when he had treed something, Grandpa said, "Sure I know something about those monkeys. That's what grandpas are for, isn't it? To know things for boys."

I grinned and said, "Yes, sir. I guess so."

It didn't surprise me too much to find out that my grandpa knew something about the monkey. I was firmly convinced that he was the smartest man in those Ozark hills anyhow. He knew a little bit about everything. He knew where all the best fishing holes were, and the right kind of bait to use. He knew the best places to hunt, and the right time to go hunting. It did seem though that all the good things my grandpa knew about were things that I liked.

Pointing to the counter, Grandpa said, "Sit down and I'll tell you about it. Believe me, this monkey business is a good thing. It's a real good thing for you."

"Good for me," I said, as I climbed up on the counter. "What's good about it, Grandpa?"

Shoving his hands in his pockets and looking down at the floor, Grandpa said, "Well, let's see now. To begin with, you've been wanting a pony and a .22, haven't you?"

"I sure have," I said. "I've been wanting a pony and a .22 ever since the day I was born. Every boy in the hills has a pony and a gun, but me. But things like that cost so much money, it doesn't look like I'll ever have them."

"Oh, I wouldn't say that," Grandpa said. "If things go right, you could be riding and shooting before you know it."

"Aw, Grandpa," I said, feeling sorry for myself, "how am I ever going to get enough money to buy a pony and a .22?"

"By catching those monkeys," Grandpa said, "that's how you're going to get it. They're worth a lot of money."

"You mean their skins, Grandpa!" I said. "Are monkey skins worth anything?"

"No! No!" Grandpa said. "Don't even think about skinning them. No, sir, that's the last thing in the world you want to do. They'll have to be taken alive, and not harmed in any way."

"Taken alive!" I said. "Why, Grandpa, how in the world am I going to do that. I don't know anything about catching monkeys. I've caught coons and possums and skunks and everything else, but not monkeys."

Sticking out his chin, Grandpa said, "Well, I'm no expert monkey catcher either, but we're going to catch them just the same. There's a big reward being offered for those monkeys."

When I heard Grandpa mention the reward, I flew completely out of gear.

"Reward!" I said, jumping down from the counter. "How much is it?"

"Now, wait a minute," Grandpa said, holding up his hand, "and don't rush me."

He paused before going on.

"About a week ago, two men stopped here at the store," he said. "Those fellows belonged to a circus train that was wrecked over on the railroad. From what they told me, it must have been a pretty bad wreck. One of the cars jumped the track and busted wide open. There were some valuable monkeys in that car, and a lot of them got away."

Grandpa caught his breath, and said, "A few of the little fellows were killed in the wreck, but not many. The ones that lived were scared to death and they took off through the hills. Now that circus was just coming out of winter quarters, and had a pretty tight schedule laid out for the season. They didn't have much time between stops, but the crew did manage to lay over for a few days. They caught all but about thirty of the monkeys; and I'm pretty sure those were the ones you and Rowdy ran into."

"Grandpa," I said, "if those monkeys are the ones that got away from the circus train, how do you suppose they got way over here? It's eight miles from our place over to the railroad."

"I've been thinking about that," Grandpa said. "You know, this time of the year it's hot and dry in the hills. I expect that the monkeys were having a tough time finding food and water. Now all animals have an instinct that tells them where they can find food and water. Those monkeys probably just kept going until they wound up over here in these Cherokee bottoms. There's food of all kinds for them over here —wild grapes, berries, nuts, acorns, roots, and all kinds of green stuff."

"I'll bet you're right, Grandpa," I said.

Rubbing his hands together and looking as pleased as a fox in a henhouse, Grandpa said, "Just wait until you hear about the reward. All of those monkeys but one are worth two dollars apiece. How does that sound to you?"

"Two dollars apiece!" I cried. "Boy, Grandpa, that's a lot of money. How come they're offering such a big reward for a bunch of little old monkeys?"

"They're not just little old monkeys," Grandpa said. "They've been trained for acts in the circus; that's why they're so valuable. It takes a long time to train a monkey, but you haven't heard the half of it yet. You're overlooking something very important."

"Overlooking something?" I said. "What am I overlooking, Grandpa?"

As if he were put out with me, Grandpa snorted and said, "Well, use your head and think a little. Remember everything I told you about those monkeys and do a little figuring."

Grandpa knew that I wasn't too good with figures, and he was all the time making up some kind of an old arithmetic problem for me to work on. It always made me feel bad when he did this because I never intended to be anything but a hunter or an explorer; and I couldn't see where arithmetic had anything to do with that.

"Grandpa," I said, "with all of this talk about monkeys and money, I can't even see good; much less do any thinking. What is it that I'm overlooking?"

Grandpa snorted like Sally Gooden did when she had seen a booger.

"That last monkey," he said. "I told you they were offering a two dollar reward for all of the monkeys, but one."

"Oh," I said, looking sheepish. "I forgot all about that monkey. Why is it so important?"

"Important!" Grandpa said. "That's the most important monkey of the whole works. He's worth his weight in gold. They're offering a hundred dollar reward for him."

When I heard Grandpa mention that hundred dollar reward, I lost my breath completely. My throat got as dry as the ashes under Mama's old washpot, and I had a heck of a time swallowing.

I finally got hold of myself and said in a loud whisper, "A hundred dollars for one monkey! Suffering cornmeal Johnnie! Grandpa, that must be some monkey!"

Grandpa chuckled and said, "From what those fellows said, that monkey is so smart he's almost human. He's different than the other monkeys. Let's see now, what kind of a monkey did that fellow say he was? Oh, yes, he's a chimpanzee, or something like that. Anyhow, they're offering a hundred dollar reward for him."

I couldn't get over it.

"A hundred dollars!" I exclaimed. "A hundred dollars for one monkey! Why, if I could catch all of them, I'd have more money than the United States bank has in it."

"Just about," Grandpa said, chuckling. "And I think we'd better keep this monkey business to ourselves. If word gets out, every farmer in these hills will quit farming and start hunting monkeys. We can't have that at all."

"We sure can't," I agreed. "I won't say a word to anybody. This is the first time in my life that I've had a chance to earn any money; but what's bothering me is catching those monkeys. How am I going to do that?"

"Right now I don't know," Grandpa said, "but we're going to catch them just the same. There never was an animal that couldn't be caught. All we have to do is figure out a way."

Grandpa put his thinking cap on and started mumbling and grumbling. I couldn't understand one word he was saying.

It always tickled me when Grandpa got something heavy like that on his mind. He did all sorts of things. Sometimes he'd start walking up and back, then again he might start shuffling around in a little circle. He had a habit of pulling at the lobe of his right ear, rubbing his nose, or digging at the wiry whiskers on his chin.

I had learned a long time ago that when my grandpa had his thinking cap on, the best thing for me to do was to be patient, and above all, not to say anything. So I just stood there with monkeys, dollars, ponies, and .22s running around in my head, and waited while Grandpa cut all kinds of didos.

I could almost feel the idea when it hit Grandpa. Looking very pleased with himself, he smiled and said, "I think I've got it figured out. You know you can always figure things out if you use your head a little bit."

I didn't like the way Grandpa looked at me when he said "use your head a little bit" but I didn't say anything.

Walking over to the hardware part of the store, Grandpa picked up six small steel traps and a piece of bailing wire.

Coming back, he looked at me and said, "I've got

some old meal sacks in the storeroom. Go back there and get one of them."

I flew to the storeroom and got the sack, wondering what in the world Grandpa was going to do. Spreading the sack out on the counter, Grandpa took a pair of scissors and started cutting long strips, about two inches wide, from the soft material. Taking one of the traps, he mashed the spring down with his hands.

"Now take that wire and wrap it around the spring, good and tight, so it'll hold the spring down," he said.

Taking the wire in both hands, I started wrapping the spring as Grandpa had told me. I was so excited and nervous I couldn't do anything right. Once I almost wrapped one of Grandpa's fingers to the spring.

"Take it easy," Grandpa barked. "I don't want my fingers cut off with that wire. We've got plenty of time. Those monkeys won't run away."

"I'm sorry, Grandpa," I said, rubbing his work-callused finger with my hand. "Thinking about all those monkeys, and all that money, has got me so worked up I can't do anything right. Why, if I could catch all of them, I'd have more money than that Rockerfellow man."

Grandpa laughed and said, "I don't know about that. I understand he has an awful lot of money."

Once the spring was securely wired, the jaws of the trap were free and useless. Taking one of the cloth strips, Grandpa started wrapping the jaws.

I saw right away what his idea was. With all that soft padding on the jaws of the trap, it probably wouldn't hurt a monkey's paw at all.

Just to let Grandpa know that I was using my head a little bit, I said, "Boy, Grandpa, that sure is a good idea. Why, with the jaws of the trap wrapped like that, a monkey wouldn't even know it was on his foot."

"I think he'd know it was on his foot all right," Grandpa said, "but once he gets in it, I don't think there's much he can do about it."

After the jaws of the trap had been wrapped, Grandpa unwound the wire from the spring and released it.

Holding the trap in his hands and inspecting his work, he grunted and said, "It looks like a pretty good job to me. What do you think about it?"

"It looks all right to me, Grandpa," I said. "I don't see how it could ever hurt a monkey's foot."

Laying the trap down on the floor, Grandpa mashed the spring down with his foot and set the trigger.

Stepping back, he stood for several seconds looking at it; then he grinned and said, "Just to be sure that it won't hurt a monkey's paw, I think it should be tested out, don't you?"

"Tested out?" I said. "How are we going to do that, Grandpa?"

With a twinkle in his eyes and a silly little grin on his face, Grandpa said, "The only way I can think of is for you to poke your finger in it."

I didn't even answer Grandpa. I didn't have to. My actions spoke for me. Closing both hands, I put them behind me and stepped back.

Grandpa grunted and said, "What's the matter? Don't you think I know what I'm doing?"

"Sure, Grandpa," I said, "I think you know what you're doing all right; but I had my finger in a trap once, and believe me, it hurt. Why couldn't we just poke a stick in it?"

"No," Grandpa said, eying the trap and rubbing his nose, "it wouldn't do any good to poke a stick in it. We wouldn't know any more then than we do now."

For several seconds we both stood there in silence, looking at the trap. Rowdy knew that something was going on and got curious. He eased over and took a look at the trap himself. One look was all he wanted. He started backing up like a crawdad. Then, sticking his tail between his legs, he disappeared behind some boxes.

I couldn't help smiling at Old Rowdy's actions. He had gotten a paw in a trap once, and had never forgotten it.

Grandpa broke the silence by saying, "Well, we're

not getting anywhere just standing here. It still has to be tested out. Now I'm going to poke my finger in it, but if that thing hurts, you might have to help me get it off my finger. Do you understand?"

I nodded my head to let him know that I understood, but I didn't like it at all.

"Well, here goes," Grandpa said.

Closing both eyes, he reached over and tripped the trigger with his finger. The trap snapped and Grandpa jumped. I closed both eyes and gritted my teeth. I didn't open my eyes again until I heard Grandpa chuckling.

"That's just about the best monkey-catching trap I've ever seen," he said. "It didn't hurt a bit. I hardly felt it."

All excited, I helped Grandpa get the trap off his finger. Then, working together, we wrapped the jaws of the other five traps.

Handing the traps to me, Grandpa said, "Well, it looks like you're in the monkey-catching business. Let me know how you come out."

I told him I would, and thanked him with all my heart for helping me.

Calling to Rowdy, I started for home.

Just as I reached the door, Grandpa said, "Hey, are you sure your mother didn't want something from the store?"

My heart almost stopped beating.

Digging Mama's list from my pocket, I said, "Boy, Grandpa, I sure am glad you reminded me. If I had gone home without the things Mama wanted, she'd have made me wear a girl's bonnet for a week. That's what she usually does when I forget something."

Taking the list, Grandpa smiled and said, "Well, that's what Grandpas are for, isn't it; to look out for boys?"

I didn't say anything—I didn't have to—my old grandpa knew how I felt about him.

While Grandpa was putting the things Mama wanted into a gunny sack, I thought of something.

"Grandpa," I asked, "where am I going to set my traps?"

"I believe I'd go right back to where you saw the monkey," he said. "If they're not in that bur oak tree, they're around there somewhere. Rowdy will find them."

On hearing Grandpa say his name, Rowdy whined and his tail started fanning the air.

Grandpa looked at him, grinned, and said, "Say that again, pardner, I didn't understand you. Do you want something?"

Rowdy really told Grandpa that he wanted something. His deep voice made the tin cans dance on the shelves.

Grandpa grunted, and walked to the rear of the store. When he came back, he had a meat rind in his hand.

Handing it to Rowdy, he smiled and said, "Here you are, old fellow. That'll be one monkey you owe me."

Rowdy pranced out of the store, looking as proud as he did when he had treed a possum.

"Grandpa," I asked, "do you think I should use bait when I set my traps?"

"Bait?" Grandpa said. "Now, I hadn't thought of that. Yes, I believe I would."

"I don't know what monkeys like to eat," I said. "What kind of bait would you use?"

"Well, let's see," Grandpa said. "I'm not much of an authority on monkeys, but I think I've read where they'll eat most anything. Do you have any apples?"

"We have a whole barrel of apples," I said. "Papa got them from an Arkansas peddler."

"Fine," Grandpa said. "Just set your traps in the dirt at the foot of the tree, and hang an apple above each one. I think that'll do the job."

Just before Grandpa handed me Mama's groceries, I saw him slip something into the sack. I let on like I hadn't seen this because I knew what it was. It was a sack of candy for Daisy and me; and was one item that would never find its way to Papa's bill.

"Here you are," Grandpa said, handing me the groceries. "The next time you're up this way I hope to see a sack full of monkeys."

Putting my traps in the gunny sack, I said, "You will, Grandpa, and one of them will be that hundred dollar monkey. He's the jasper I want to catch."

3

On my way home, I whistled and sang. I was so happy
I made up a little song. It went something like this:

> "There are monkeys in the bottoms
> In those tall white sycamores.
> There are monkeys in the bottoms,
> Worth a million or more.

> "So come along, Old Rowdy,
> And let's get on the trail
> Of a hundred dollar monkey.
> We'll catch him by the tail."

Rowdy didn't seem to like my singing at all. He
wouldn't even look at me. He just jogged along with
his head down as if I wasn't even there.

I was the happiest boy in those Ozark hills; and I
figured I was pretty close to being the richest boy, too.
All I had to do was catch those monkeys. Right then
that didn't seem like any chore at all.

Several times I stopped and tried to do a little
arithmetic in the dust of the country road. Smoothing
out a place with my hand, and using my finger as a
pencil, I tried hard to figure out how much money
the monkeys were worth. I didn't have too much trouble adding up a column of two dollar monkeys. It

was that hundred dollar monkey I had trouble with. Every time I added him to the pot, something went wrong. I'd get so rich and excited I couldn't figure anything right.

Rowdy didn't help the situation in the least. He couldn't understand what I was doing down on my knees in the middle of the road, fiddling around in the dust. He would get curious and come sniffing around to see what was going on. All he did was walk around in my figures and mess things up until I couldn't tell what the monkeys were worth. I finally gave up and decided I'd let Daisy figure it out for me. She was good with arithmetic.

The road from Grandpa's store ran by our farm. As I came walking along, singing my head off, Papa called to me from the field where he was planting corn. I climbed the rail fence and walked over to him.

Papa smiled and said, "Say, it looks like you were right about those monkeys. Right after you left for the store, I went to get Sally Gooden, and I think I saw a monkey in every sycamore tree down there. I can't understand it. As far as I know, we've never had any wild monkeys around here."

"They're not wild monkeys, Papa," I said. "They got away from a circus train that was wrecked over on the railroad. Grandpa told me all about it. He said that there were about thirty of them. They're worth a lot of money, too. The circus people are offering a reward for them."

"So that's where they came from," Papa said, looking relieved. "I'm glad to hear that. I was beginning to wonder what was going on around here. Did you say they're offering a reward for the monkeys?"

"They sure are," I said, "and it's more money than I ever heard of. They're willing to pay two dollars apiece for all of those monkeys but one; and they'll pay a hundred dollars for that one."

I really bore down on it when I told Papa about that hundred dollar monkey.

Papa just stood there for a second, staring at me;

then, uttering a low whistle, he turned and looked toward the river bottoms.

"Say-y-y, that is a lot of money," he said. "I didn't know monkeys were worth that much money."

"I didn't either, Papa," I said. "It beats anything I ever heard of. All of that money for a bunch of little old monkeys!"

Papa frowned and said, "There must be more to this than we know about. I can understand a fellow paying two dollars for a monkey, but whoever heard of anyone paying a hundred dollars for one."

"Papa," I said, "Grandpa says those monkeys have been trained for acts in the circus, and it takes a long time to train a monkey. That's why they're so valuable."

Papa was like me. He couldn't get that hundred dollar monkey off his mind.

"I don't care how long it takes to train a monkey," he said, "a hundred dollars is a hundred dollars. Why, you can buy a good mule for that much money, and if you talk just right, they might even throw in the harness."

"There's a catch to this reward business, Papa," I said. "The monkeys have to be caught alive, and not harmed in any way."

"I see," Papa said, nodding his head. "I figured there was a catch somewhere. When it comes to making money like that, there's always a catch. It would be simple to shoot those monkeys; but taking them alive, I don't know about that. It could turn out to be a tough job.

"I don't care how tough it is, Papa," I said. "If you'll let me, I'd sure like to give it a try. I believe I can catch those monkeys—every last one of them."

Papa thought a second, and said, "It may not be as easy as you think it is. How would you go about catching them?"

"With these," I said, reaching in my gunny sack for the traps. "Grandpa fixed them for me. He thinks they're the very thing for catching monkeys and not hurting them."

Papa took one of the traps and looked it over. Then he laughed and said, "Leave it to your grandpa to figure out something like this; but, by golly, it does look like a good idea. Yes, sir, it sure does. It might work at that."

Handing the trap back to me, Papa said, "You know, this time of the year there's not much to do around the farm, just planting; and I can take care of that. You go right ahead and have a go at those monkeys. Maybe you can catch them; you've caught everything else in these hills."

"I'll catch them," I said, very determinedly. "You just wait and see. By tomorrow night, I'll have a sack full of them; and one of them will be that hundred dollar monkey. He's the jasper I'll be looking for."

"We'll see," Papa said, laughing.

Glancing up at the sun, he said, "Now, you'd better get to the house and help your mother set those hens. I'd like to finish planting this field before sundown."

I thanked Papa for going along with me on my monkey-catching business, and strutted off toward the house.

So far everything was working out fine, but there was one more stump in the way. That was Mama. I was well prepared for her though. After all, I'd been living around Mama for fourteen years; and a boy can learn a lot about his mama in that length of time. I knew just what to do, and just what to say to wear her down.

Papa had already told Mama about seeing the monkeys; but when I told her about the reward and that I intended to catch them, she did just what I had expected her to do. She flew straight up.

"Jay Berry," she said, in a hard voice, "you're not going down in those bottoms to catch any monkeys. Now, that's all there is to it. I won't have it at all. Why, I'd go crazy."

Putting one of my half-dead, broken-leg looks on my face, I got ready for one of those Mama and boy go-arounds.

"But, Mama," I argued, "just think how much

money those monkeys are worth, and you know that I never get a chance to make any money—just ten or fifteen cents now and then for an old possum hide or something. Why, if I could catch all of them, I could get myself the pony and .22 I've been wanting so long. You wouldn't keep me from doing that would you?"

I saw a hurt look spread over Mama's face. This made me feel bad, but I had been wanting a pony and a .22 so long I didn't want to give up.

Mama came over to me and started straightening my suspenders.

It seemed like my old suspenders were always twisted. Grandpa said I got into my britches too fast.

"Jay Berry," Mama said, "I know how you've been wanting a pony and a gun, but I worry so much when you're down in the bottoms—just you and that old hound dog. Why, I never know what's liable to happen. Besides, it would be practically impossible to catch a monkey in those bottoms. Monkeys like to climb, and some of those sycamore trees are a hundred feet tall. You'd probably fall out of one and break every bone in your body."

Reaching for my traps, I said, "Mama, I'm not going to do any tree climbing. I'm going to trap the monkeys."

Mama frowned and took one of the traps. She looked it over and said, "This is some of your grandpa's work, isn't it?"

"Uh-huh," I said. "He fixed them for me."

Shaking her head, Mama said, "I don't know. Sometimes I wonder who the boy is, you or your grandpa. Have you talked to your father about this monkey-catching idea of yours?"

Seeing that Mama was giving in a little, I started talking a hundred miles a minute.

"He said it was all right with him, Mama," I said. "There's not much to do around the farm right now—just planting—and he said that he could take care of that."

Handing the trap back to me, Mama sighed and said, "Well, between your father and your grandpa, it looks like I can't say 'No.' But, Jay Berry, there's one thing I want understood. You are not going to those bottoms, monkey hunting, unless your father is close by in the fields. If something did happen to you, maybe between him and Rowdy, we could at least find your body."

Mama could take a little bit of something like that and make it sound like the funeral had already started. She was good at things like that.

"Mama," I said, very seriously, "do all mamas worry like you do? I'm fourteen years old, almost a grown man, and you've been worrying about me ever since I was born. It makes me feel no bigger than a jumped-up minute."

Mama smiled and said, "I'm pretty sure that all mothers worry about their boys. Right now you're a little too young to understand, but someday you'll be married and probably have a boy of your own; then, I think you will understand."

"Oh, no, I won't, Mama," I said, shaking my head. "I'll never get married. I can't understand women."

Mama got kind of mad when I said that.

"Don't be silly," she snapped. "That wasn't a very nice thing to say. Now, you go get that straw. I want to set those hens."

Feeling as good as if I had just waded the Mississippi River, I breathed a sigh of relief and lit out for the barn to get some straw.

Besides Sally Gooden, there was one other thing we had around our farm that I thought we could surely do without—that was setting hens. Mama and Daisy could do anything in the world with the hateful old things, but I couldn't. Every time I got close to one of the cranky old sisters, she puffed up ten times bigger than she actually was and started squawking and pecking. By the time we had the old gals taken care of, my hands were hurting all over.

Mama and I were back in the house and I was rubbing some Raleigh salve on my henpecked hands when I thought of my little sister.

"Mama, where's Daisy?" I asked. "I want to tell her about the monkeys."

"I think she's up in her playhouse," Mama said. "I saw her going up the trail a while ago."

Taking the sack of candy that Grandpa had given me, I started up to Daisy's playhouse. I was almost there when I heard her laughing and talking. Leaving the trail, I eased around and peeked through the bushes to see what was going on. A small sunbeam had bored its way down through the overhead green, and the playhouse was bathed in a warm radiant glow.

Daisy was sitting on the ground with her back against the trunk of the huge red oak. Her crutch was lying beside her. As usual, her little friends were all around. Chipmunks were scampering and birds were singing. A churring squirrel was perched on an arm of the cross. His flicking tail was keeping perfect time to the music of the hills. A big fat bunny was curled up in Daisy's lap just as though he belonged there.

As I watched, a tiny little wren dropped down from the branches of the red oak and lit on Daisy's crippled leg. She smiled and started cooing to it. Everything looked so peaceful and happy that I hated to disturb them. Just before stepping out of the bushes, I coughed to let them know I was coming.

The instant I showed my face, you'd have thought a booger man had shown up. The bunny hopped and the squirrel jumped. The birds flew and the chipmunks faded into the ground. It always made me mad when the silly things did that. I would never have harmed one of Daisy's little friends. Old Rowdy wouldn't have hurt any of them either, and that was saying something.

Feeling hurt all over but letting on that I hadn't noticed anything, I handed the sack of candy to Daisy and said, "Guess what's happened?"

Daisy always seemed to be about one jump ahead of me.

Smiling, she said, "I already know about the monkeys, Jay Berry. Papa told Mama and me about them when he brought Sally Gooden in from the bottoms."

Trying to act very important, I shoved my hands down in my pockets and said, "Those monkeys are worth quite a bit of money. I'm going to catch them and get myself that pony and gun I've been wanting."

Every time I mentioned catching something to Daisy, she naturally figured that I intended to kill and skin it.

Frowning, she said, "Jay Berry, I know how you've been wanting a pony and gun, but isn't there some other way you could get them? I've seen pictures of monkeys and they're the cutest little things. I just couldn't stand to think of one being skinned. How would you like it if someone caught you and peeled your skin off. You wouldn't like it, would you?"

"Aw, Daisy," I said, "you girls sure do think funny. Whoever heard of anyone skinning a boy. I'm not going to skin the monkeys. I'm going to catch them alive. They won't be hurt in any way."

Daisy sighed her relief and said, "I'm glad you're not going to hurt them. Every time I walk by the smokehouse and see all those little skins you have stretched there, I just shiver all over."

"Well, you can stop shivering," I said. "I promise that I won't harm one hair on those monkeys."

"How do you know so much about the monkeys anyway?" Daisy asked. "Papa said he couldn't remember any wild monkeys being around here before."

"They're not exactly wild monkeys," I said. "They got away from a circus train that had a wreck over on the railroad. Grandpa told me all about it. He even fixed some traps for me so I could catch them."

"That's just like Grandpa," Daisy exclaimed. "He's always telling you how to catch the little animals. Surely, Jay Berry, you don't get any fun out of it, do you?"

"Aw, Daisy," I said, "what do you think animals are for anyway. Just to look at? They're supposed to be hunted. How else would a boy have any fun in these hills?"

Shaking her head and looking very disgusted with me, Daisy said, "Jay Berry, you should have a talk with the Old Man of the Mountains. I think maybe he could tell you a few things. Being a boy though, I doubt if you would understand a word he said."

There it was again—the Old Man of the Mountains. Daisy had mentioned him several times and I hadn't paid much attention to her. After all, she lived in one of those girl kind of worlds and it was chuck full of strange old men, fairies, angels, spirits, knights in shining armor, and everything else you could think of. I just figured that all girls were like that and it wasn't anything to get excited about. But Daisy had a way of making things sound so real that sometimes I didn't know whether to believe her or not.

Daisy did this by telling stories. She was the best storyteller in those Ozark hills. It wasn't only the stories she told, it was the way she told them. She would get real serious and her eyes would get big and starry-looking. She would talk in a whisper, and go through all kinds of motions. By the time she was finished with her story, my hair would be standing straight up and I wouldn't know what to believe.

"Daisy," I said, "you've been telling me about this Old Man of the Mountains for a long time now. Who is he anyway?"

"Oh, he's just a friendly old man," she said very pertly. "He comes around every once in a while and visits with me."

"He does?" I said. "When was the last time you saw him?"

"Why just this morning," she said, "right here in my playhouse."

"You did?" I said. "What's the old man's name?"

"I don't know what his name is," Daisy said. "I never have asked him. I just call him the 'Old Man of the Mountains.'"

"Where does he live?" I asked.

"Way back in the mountains somewhere," Daisy said.

"Is he a farmer?" I asked.

"Oh, no," Daisy said, "he doesn't do any farming. He doesn't have time."

"Doesn't have time!" I said. "What does he do?"

"He takes care of the hills," Daisy said.

"Takes care of the hills!" I exclaimed. "Why, the hills don't need taking care of. Whoever heard of anything like that."

"That's all you know," Daisy said. "There are a lot of things in the hills that need taking care of. What would happen to all of the little animals, the birds, and the flowers if someone didn't look out for them? That's what the Old Man of the Mountains does. He just walks through the hills looking out for everything."

I laughed out loud.

"Aw, Daisy," I said, "you're just making this up. I don't believe there is an old man of the mountains."

A frightened look flashed in Daisy's eyes. Placing a finger over her lips, she looked all around.

"Sh-sh-sh, don't say things like that, Jay Berry," she said. "Don't ever say you don't believe in the Old Man of the Mountains. He hears everything that's said in these hills, and he'll cause you to have bad luck."

At that moment, Daisy couldn't have said anything that would have more effect on me. With all those monkeys around and a chance to make some money, I sure didn't want to have any bad luck. Besides, there were a few bad luck things that I believed in—things like hearing a screech owl at midnight, tripping over a broom, or dropping the water bucket in the well. Those were sure signs of bad luck.

Now, maybe, there was an old man of the mountains, maybe he could cast a "bad luck" spell, and maybe he would get all fired up if I said I didn't believe in him. Anyhow, I wasn't taking any chances.

"Daisy," I said, "is there really an old man of the mountains, and can he cause people to have bad luck?"

Looking at me as if I didn't have any sense at all, Daisy said, "Why certainly, Jay Berry, there's an old man of the mountains. Everyone knows that."

"Well, I didn't," I said.

With all of that bad luck talk, Daisy saw that she had me worried and she took advantage of it. Getting very serious, she took another look around and started talking in a whisper.

"Sit down, Jay Berry," she said, "and I'll tell you about the Old Man of the Mountains."

I didn't want to, but I sat down by her side and listened while she went into her story.

"Jay Berry," she said, "the Old Man of the Mountains is very, very old. He's as old as these hills. His hair is snow white and hangs way down over his shoulders. He wears a long, white robe, and sandals on his feet. Every time I see him, he has a crooked stick in his hand. He can just point that stick at something and it will disappear."

"Daisy," I interrupted in a low voice, "is this old man a ghost or something?"

"Oh, no, Jay Berry," she whispered, "he doesn't even look like a ghost. He has a kind, gentle face. He looks sad though—like maybe he feels sorry about something. I think he feels sorry for the little animals."

"I thought girls were the only ones that felt sorry for animals," I said. "How come this old man feels sorry for them?"

"Because it's his job to look out for them," Daisy said. "You see, Jay Berry, when God made these hills he needed someone to take care of the animals and birds and flowers. So he gave the job to the Old Man of the Mountains. All he does now is walk around through the hills and take care of things."

"What does this old man do in the wintertime when the snows come and everything goes to sleep?" I asked. "What does he do then?"

Daisy had an answer for everything.

"He goes to sleep, too," she said. "That's the only time he gets to rest. He works so hard through the summer that he's very tired when winter comes; so he just goes to sleep and rests until spring comes again."

Daisy stopped to get her breath before going on.

"He's a wonderful old man," she said. "If you're good and believe in him, you'll always be happy and you'll never have bad luck; but if you're mean and hurt the little animals, you had better look out. He'll just point that stick at you and you're sure to have bad luck."

Daisy had me so shaken up by now, I hardly knew what to believe. Just to be on the safe side, I said, "When will you see this old man again?"

"Oh, I never know when I'll see him," she said. "He just comes around any time he wants to."

"Well, the next time you see him," I said, getting to my feet, "you tell him that I'd like to meet him and shake hands with him."

Along about then, I would have shaken hands with a centipede if I had thought that it would help me catch a monkey.

Shaking her head and looking very sad, Daisy said, "Jay Berry, I don't know if the Old Man of the Mountains would see you or not. You've been a pretty bad boy, you know. You're all the time catching the little animals. The Old Man of the Mountains doesn't like anyone who does things like that."

"But every boy in the hills catches things," I said. "Why, the way you make it sound, this old man never could like a boy—just girls."

"Oh, he could like boys, too," Daisy said. "He could like boys just about as much as he does girls but they'd have to leave the little animals alone, or he wouldn't."

Well, I didn't know what to do. Daisy had me pretty well convinced that there was an old man of the mountains. Now, if he didn't like boys who caught animals and could cause them to have bad luck, I was just in for it. That's all there was to it.

4

For all the sleep I got that night, I may as well have stayed up with the hoot owls. Every time I closed my eyes, I'd start seeing monkeys. They would come by in a long line, one behind the other, leaping and squealing. Each monkey had a price tag hanging from his neck, telling how much he was worth.

I wouldn't get too excited until that hundred dollar monkey came leaping by. Every time he passed he would stop and laugh at me, I'd wake up wringing wet with sweat and having an upside-down fit. When I finally did fall asleep, I had a wonderful dream about owning a beautiful paint pony and a brand-new .22. I was riding like the wind, shooting right and left.

I was the first one up the next morning. In fact, I even beat our old red rooster—and that was getting up early. I was out at the woodpile, splitting kindling, when he came sailing out of the henhouse. Ruffling his feathers, he hopped upon the rail fence, threw his head back, and told everything within hearing distance that it was a beautiful Ozark morning and it was time to start stirring.

Papa came out of the house with a milk bucket in his hand. Yawning and rubbing the sleep from his eyes, he looked at me and said, "You're up kind of early, aren't you?"

"I guess I am, Papa," I said. "I wanted to get my chores done so I'd have a good day at those monkeys. I believe I can have a sack full of them before sundown."

Looking concerned, Papa said, "You know, I've been thinking about this monkey-catching business of yours. I still think there's more to it than you think there is. Those monkeys may be too smart for you."

"Papa," I said, "surely monkeys couldn't be any smarter than coons are, and I've caught all kinds of coons. Why, I've even caught a couple of red foxes, and you know how smart they are."

"I know," Papa said, "but it might be a little different catching monkeys. I just hope you haven't overloaded your wagon. It's not good for a boy to want something with all his heart and then be disappointed. Things like that can hurt for a long time."

The way Papa was carrying on had me a little worried. Then I remembered what my grandpa had told me.

"Papa," I said, "Grandpa says that there never was an animal that couldn't be caught."

"Well, I hope your grandpa knows what he's talking about," Papa said, walking off toward the barn.

I thought Mama never would get breakfast ready, but she finally did and I set a new record for the time it takes a fourteen-year-old boy to eat a meal.

While I was out in our cellar getting some apples, Mama fixed a lunch for me and put it in a paper bag. After putting my traps, lunch, and apples in a gunny sack, I called Rowdy and lit out for the bottoms to make my fortune.

Just as we walked out of our fields into the thick timber of the bottoms, a big fat swamp rabbit popped out of a brush pile and tore down a game trail. Old Rowdy saw the rabbit about the same time as I did. He lunged and let out one of his famous catch-a-rabbit bawls.

For a second, I was so excited I almost forgot myself and was just about to urge Rowdy on, when I thought of that old man of the mountains. By this

time, Rowdy was right on that swamp rabbit's tail,
bawling every time his feet touched the ground.

"No, Rowdy, no," I yelled, "let him go."

Rowdy threw on the brakes, turned, and looked at
me as if he knew that I had lost my mind. That was
the first time I had ever called him back from chasing
something and he couldn't understand it at all. He
just stood there in the middle of the trail, looking very
surprised.

"Come here, boy," I said, slapping my leg with my
hand. "I see right now that if I don't have a talk with
you, you're going to mess everything up."

Rowdy came to me, but not willingly. He couldn't
understand what had come over me. Kneeling down, I
put my arms around him and said, "Look, boy, we're
not hunting for anything today but monkeys; and
whatever you do, don't catch anything else. I don't
care if something runs over you, just let on like you
didn't even see it. Now I know this sounds crazy, but
I mean it. You see, there might be an old man sneaking around in these woods looking out for all the
animals; and if we catch anything, he'll cause us to
have bad luck. All he has to do is point a stick at us,
and we'll have all kinds of bad luck. We couldn't
catch a June bug, much less a monkey."

Even though I tried my best to explain to Rowdy
that I didn't want him to catch anything, I don't
think he understood why. It's hard to explain things
like that to a rabbit-hunting hound.

Side by side, and walking as quietly as tomcats on
the prowl, we moved on into monkey country. It was
so still in the bottoms I could hear my heart thumping. Every nerve in my body was as tight as the iron
bands around a rain barrel.

I went right back to the bur oak tree where Rowdy
had treed the monkey and started looking it over. I
looked on every limb, and in each dark shadow. Not
being able to see anything that even looked like a monkey, I was beginning to get a little discouraged when
all at once, from somewhere close by, something let
out a cry that rang through the bottoms like a black-

smith's anvil. The cry didn't sound scary. It was more like a warning cry.

Not being able to identify what had made the racket scared me a little. My old heart started flopping around. It seemed like every time I got scared a little, my old heart was the first one to know about it. I never could understand why it acted that way. To make things worse, Old Rowdy growled way down deep, and started walking around stiff-legged, like when he was getting ready for a fight.

In a quavering voice, I whispered to Rowdy, "What in the world was that? It couldn't have been a monkey. Monkeys are little bitty things. Whatever made that racket must have been as big as a barn."

That one loud cry was all I heard, and again the silence closed in around us. I sent Rowdy to do a little sniffing around. This was an old game to me, and one I never grew tired of playing. I could follow every movement my old dog made by ear.

Over on my left a twig snapped and there was a padding of soft feet. Then ahead of me a small bush wavered as his ghostly shadow passed beneath. He moved on to my right, and I heard the scratching of his claws on bark as he walked a log. Ending up behind me, I heard his loud snuffings and a rustling in the leaves.

Old Rowdy had made a complete circle around me, and I knew that if the tracks of anything dangerous had crossed the line of that circle, he would have let me know about it.

Rowdy was gone for about five minutes. When he came back, he didn't act like he had seen anything more than a grasshopper. As if he didn't have a worry in the world, he sat down on his rear and started digging at a flea that wasn't even there.

Feeling much better, I started setting my traps like Grandpa had told me. All around the bur oak, about three feet out from the trunk, I dug six small holes in the soft soil. Then one by one, I mashed the trap springs down with my foot and set the triggers. Very carefully I placed a trap in each hole and covered it

with leaves. I didn't tie the trap chains to anything
because I didn't figure that a little monkey could do
much climbing with a trap on his foot.

Then I took six apples and punched a nail down
deep in each one. Tying short pieces of string to the
heads of the nails, I hung an apple to the underbrush
above each trap. When I was finished I had a complete
circle of traps around the trunk of the bur oak tree.

Backing off to one side, I took a good look at my
trap setting. It looked like a pretty good job to me. In
fact, at that moment I felt sure that Daniel Boone
would have been proud of me. The traps were completely hidden. All I could see was those big red apples hanging there. They looked so good I kind of
wanted to take a bite out of one myself.

I was still standing there admiring my work when,
from the corner of my eye, I thought I saw a movement in the branches of a sycamore tree. It was just a
flash and I didn't see it again, but I was pretty sure
that I had seen something.

Picking up my gunny sack, I whispered to Rowdy,
"I'm not sure, boy, but I think I saw something. It
could have been a monkey. Come on, let's hide and see
what happens."

About thirty-five yards away, but still in view of my
traps, I found a small opening in a thick stand of
elders. It was a dandy hiding place, and I proceeded
to make myself comfortable. Taking my lunch and apples from the gunny sack, I laid them to one side and
sat down on the empty sack.

Now, I never did like to wait for anything. It seemed
that half of my life had been wasted away waiting for
things. I had to wait for Christmas, and Thanksgiving.
Then there was a long spell of waiting for spring and
fishing time. Now I was waiting for a monkey.

The longer I sat there, the more uncomfortable I
became. First I got hungry, then I got thirsty. The sack
I was sitting on got hard as a rock and my tail bone
started hurting. I got hot and began to sweat. Deer
flies and mosquitoes came and started gnawing on
me. Just about the time that I had convinced myself

that there wasn't a living thing within a hundred miles of me, up popped a monkey, and out popped my eyes.

I never did know where the monkey came from. One instant there wasn't as much as a jaybird around my traps; then as quick as Mama was with a peach tree switch, there was a monkey. I could have sworn that he just popped up out of the ground. Anyhow, there he was, standing on his spindly legs, staring at those big red apples.

I held my breath, watched, and waited.

For several seconds, the monkey just stood, staring at the apples and twisting his head, as if he were trying to make up his mind about something. Then he started jumping around and squealing and making all kinds of noises.

The next thing that happened all but caused me to have a jerking spell. It started raining monkeys. They seemed to come from everywhere; down from the branches of the bur oak tree, from out of the underbrush, and everywhere else. There were big monkeys and little monkeys, fat monkeys and skinny monkeys.

I was paralyzed. It looked like ten jillion monkeys, leaping and squealing. They bunched up about ten feet from my traps and started chattering as if they were talking something over.

Before the monkeys showed up, Rowdy had been lying at my side. Growling and showing his teeth, he started getting to his feet. He was getting ready to tie into those monkeys and I knew it. I laid my hand on his back and I could feel his rock-hard muscles knotting and quivering.

"Rowdy," I whispered, "for heaven's sake, don't do anything now. Those monkeys are worth more money than we'll ever see the rest of our lives. If you make any noise and scare them away, I'll tie you in the corn crib for a year, and I won't even give you a drink of water."

Of course, I didn't mean that, but Rowdy thought I did. He lay down again and kept his mouth shut.

One little monkey, bolder than the others, left the

bunch and started over toward my traps. I reached for my gunny sack and got ready.

Just when I thought for sure that the monkey was going to walk right into my trap, the same loud cry that I had heard before rang out through the bottoms. As if the cry were some kind of signal, the monkeys stopped chattering and stood still. The one that I had thought was going to get in my trap hurried back to the bunch.

I could tell that whatever had made the cry was much closer now than it had been before, and I didn't feel too good about it.

"Rowdy," I whispered, "you keep your eyes open and whatever it is that's squalling like that, don't let it get too close to us."

The way Old Rowdy was sniffing and looking, I couldn't tell whether he was mad or scared. This didn't help me at all. I put a lot of confidence in Old Rowdy; and if he was scared, then it was time for me to be getting away from there.

I was trying to make up my mind what to do, when I heard the cry again. This time it was so close it made my eardrums ring. My hair flew straight up and felt as if it was pushing the top out of my old straw hat.

The noise was coming from above me. I started looking around in the treetops. On the limb of a big sycamore, I saw something. At first I thought it was a boy. It looked just like a small boy, standing there on a limb. I wondered what he was doing up in a tree, screaming his head off. Maybe he had climbed the tree and couldn't get down. I had done that several times and Papa had had to come and help me down. Then again he might be a crazy boy. Daisy had told me that crazy people did all kinds of things like that.

I forgot about being scared and got kind of mad.

"Rowdy," I whispered, "I don't know if that's a boy or not, but if it is, he's sure messing things up for us. If he keeps on screaming like that, and scares the monkeys away, I'm going to wear him out."

Just then the thing moved out on the limb into some

sunlight and I got a better look at it. I could see then that it wasn't a boy but was some kind of black, hairy animal. It had short stubby legs, and long arms that hung down almost to the limb it was standing on. When I discovered that it didn't have a tail, I didn't know what to think. I had never seen an animal that didn't have a tail of some kind.

It was too far away to tell what color its eyes were, but I could have sworn that they were as red as our old red rooster. Anything that had red eyes always did scare me. Goose pimples jumped out all over me. My old heart started running around inside me like a scared lizard.

"Rowdy," I whispered, in a shaky voice, "that's an animal all right, but I've never laid eyes on anything that looked like that before, and I don't like the looks of it."

I had just about decided that my monkey-catching days were over, and was getting ready to get away from there, when I remembered what my grandpa had told me about that hundred dollar monkey. He had said that it was different than the other monkeys, and that thing I was looking at sure didn't look like those other monkeys.

Just then the big monkey let out another cry, and running to the end of the limb, he leaped high in the air. I was so startled by this I stood up. I thought sure that he had sprouted wings and was flying away. Instead, he lit in the branches of the bur oak tree; and using those long arms, he started dropping down from limb to limb and landed on the ground between the little monkeys and my traps.

This all happened so fast it left me a little bit breathless. I thought squirrels could move around in the timber, but they couldn't do anything that monkey couldn't do. Every move he made was as sure as Daniel Boone's musket, and as smooth as the dasher in Mama's old churn.

All the time this had been going on, the little monkeys hadn't made a sound. They just stood there in a bunch, watching every move the big monkey made.

About that time one of them decided that as long as there were some apples around, he may as well have one. He left the bunch and with his skinny tail sticking straight in the air, he started toward my traps.

The big monkey saw this and went all to pieces. He started jumping up and down, and making deep grunting noises as if he were talking to the little monkey. The little monkey seemed to understand what the big monkey was saying. He squealed like someone had stepped on his tail and scurried back to the others.

It was hard for me to believe what I had seen. Yet it was as plain as the stripes in a rainbow. That big monkey had known that the little monkey was in danger, and in his monkey talk, he had simply told him so.

"Rowdy," I whispered, "did you see what the monkey was doing? He was talking to that little monkey, that's what he was doing. Grandpa didn't tell me that they could talk to each other."

As if he were proud of the fact that he had knocked me out of a two dollar reward, the big monkey then did something that all but caused me to swallow my Adam's apple. Looking straight at my hiding place, he pealed his lips back, opened his mouth, and let out another one of those squalls. When he did, I got a good look at his fighting tools.

I had thought that our old mules had big mouths and teeth, but they were nothing compared to what that monkey had. To me, it looked as if you could have thrown a pumpkin straight down his throat and never scratched the peeling on one of his long teeth.

"Holy smokes, Rowdy," I whispered, "did you see those teeth? You'd better think twice before you jump on him. He could eat you up—collar and all."

Old Rowdy didn't seem to be the least bit scared. If I had said "Sick 'em!" he would have torn out of those elders like a cyclone. He may have taken a whipping, but there would have been a lot of monkey hair flying around while it was going on.

I didn't have to worry about the big monkey jumping on us. Instead, he turned, and still making those

deep grunting noises, he walked up within two feet of
a trap and stopped. For several seconds, he just stood
there, looking at the apple and all around at the
ground. He kept making funny little noises, as if he
were talking to himself.

The strain was almost more than I could stand. My
insides got all knotted up and I felt like I was going to
bust wide open. If the monkey hadn't done something
about then, I think I would have. Instead of stepping
in my trap, he just reached out with one of those
long arms, took hold of the apple, and pulled on it
until the nail came out.

Holding the apple in his paw about like I would if
I were eating one, he opened his huge mouth, took one
bite, and tossed what was left to the little monkeys.

This caused a loud commotion. The little monkeys
started fighting over the apple. I never heard so much
squealing and chattering. In no time there wasn't as
much as a seed left.

I sat there as if I were frozen to the ground and
watched that big monkey walk all around the bur oak,
taking the apples and never stepping in a trap. One
bite from each apple seemed to be all he wanted.
What was left was tossed to the little monkeys.

When the last apple had disappeared, the big monkey did something that made me wonder if I wasn't
seeing things. He started turning somersaults and
rolling around on the ground. At the same time, he
was making the bottoms ring with a peculiar noise
that he hadn't made before.

Now I had never heard a monkey laugh and didn't
even know they could; but as I sat there watching the
capers of that big monkey, it didn't take me long to
figure out what he was doing. He was laughing at me.
I was sure of it. I even remembered the dream I had
had about the hundred dollar monkey—how every time
he came leaping by, he would stop and laugh at me.

The little monkeys seemed to know that something
funny was going on. They started screeching and chattering like a bunch of squirrels in a hickory nut tree.

My neck and face got all hot. I knew I was blushing,

but I couldn't help it. That was the first time I had ever had a monkey laugh at me. I looked at Old Rowdy. The way I was feeling, if he had been laughing, I would have taken a stick to him. But Rowdy wasn't laughing. He was just as serious about catching those monkeys as I was.

All at once the big monkey stopped making a fool out of himself and turned to the little monkeys. Uttering a couple of those deep grunts, he just seemed to rise up in the air like fog off the river and disappeared in the branches of the bur oak tree. The little monkeys followed him—zip, zip, zip—one behind the other.

After the monkeys had all disappeared, it got so still around there you could have heard a grasshopper walking. I looked at Rowdy, and Rowdy looked at me.

"Did you ever see anything like that, Rowdy?" I said. "Grandpa was right when he said that monkey was smart, but I didn't think he was that smart. Why, he knew all the time that we were here. And he sat right up there on that sycamore limb and watched me set my traps. Then he stole all of my apples and laughed at me. Now, how do you like that!"

My first go-around with the monkeys left me a little discouraged—but not too much. After all, my grandpa had taught me practically all there was to know about the trapping business. I figured it was just a matter of time until I'd have them all in the sack.

Trying to act like nothing had happened, I said, "Rowdy, that monkey may not know it, but he's messing around with one of the best trappers in these Cherokee hills. If he comes back one more time, we'll see who does the laughing. Let's try the old mouse-catching trick on him. I think that will stop this laughing business."

Rowdy whined and licked my hand. That gave me a lot of confidence and I felt much better.

Taking three more of my apples, I set them up on a log. Then taking my pocketknife, I cut them in half. Walking over to where my traps were, I lifted them from their hiding places and tripped the triggers with a stick. Untying the strings from the nails and bushes,

I used the short pieces to tie half of an apple to the trigger of each trap.

I wrapped those pieces of apple to the top of the triggers as tightly as I could, and tied the ends of the strings in hard knots. Then I reset the traps and placed them back in the holes. Very carefully, I covered each trap with leaves but left the apples in plain sight.

Backing off to one side, I took another good look at my trap setting. Every time I had set a trap I had been proud of the way I had done it, but on that day I was especially proud. You could see the pieces of apple all right, but you sure couldn't tell there were any traps there. Not one shiny piece of metal could be seen.

"Rowdy," I said, "I don't care how smart that monkey is, if he gets one of those apples, he's going to wind up with a trap on his foot, and that's all there is to it."

All of the time I was resetting my traps I kept looking around in the trees for a monkey. I didn't see one, but I had a feeling that there were ten thousand monkey eyeballs looking right at me.

Feeling about as smart as Old Trapper Dan himself, I said, "Come on, Rowdy, I think the money will start rolling in now."

I didn't go straight back to my hiding place. Instead, I took off in another direction, circled around, and came back to it. I thought that I was being smart doing this, but I felt silly, too; because if that big monkey was sitting somewhere in the top of a sycamore tree, he was probably watching every move I made.

I was so sure that I would catch a monkey this time, I didn't sit down on my gunny sack. I held it in my hand so that I would be ready to sack him up the instant I heard the snap of a trap.

It seemed that Rowdy and I had hardly gotten seated when here came the monkeys: leaping, squealing, and chattering.

"Boy, Rowdy," I whispered, "that sure was fast, wasn't it. They must have been waiting for us. Why, the way they're acting, they must think we're playing some kind of game. They won't think it's a game when I get a few of them in the sack."

It was a little different this time than it was before. The big monkey was the first one to touch the ground, and he was standing very close to one of my traps. The little monkeys were milling around everywhere. They didn't seem to know what was going on, but every time one got close to a trap, that big monkey would fly out of gear like a mama jaybird when I wanted to take a look at her babies.

He would scream like someone had slapped a branding iron on him, and start jumping up and down, and making those deep grunting noises. He would run at the little monkeys and scare the daylights out of them. Finally he succeeded in herding them all to one side where they bunched up and stayed.

If I had known then what that big monkey was going to do next, I wouldn't have stayed there and watched it.

Again he walked over close to one of my traps and stopped. I knew that I was watching a monkey, but he still looked like a small boy, standing there, trying to figure something out. Once he even bent over so that he could get a better look at things. Then he reached up with one of his long arms and scratched his head. When I saw him do that I thought of my grandpa. He was always scratching his head when he had something heavy on his mind.

"Rowdy," I whispered, "I believe that monkey knows the trap is there and he's trying to figure out how he can get the apple and not get caught. I don't think he can do it. I don't care how smart he is, he's not that smart." How wrong I was.

As if he had solved the problem, and was tickled to death about it, the big monkey turned a few somersaults. He stopped and stared straight at my hiding place. Then he let out another one of those squalls before he reached down and picked up a long stick from the ground. Holding the stick out in front of him, still uttering those deep grunts, he started beating at the apple as if he was killing a snake.

I almost jumped out of my britches when I heard the trap snap. I sat in a trance and watched that hundred dollar monkey spring every one of my traps the same way. Every time a trap snapped, he would look straight at my hiding place and squall.

He didn't use his teeth to tear the apples from the triggers. He simply used his fingers and untied the knots in the strings.

There was one thing I could say for that monkey. He wasn't only smart, he was very polite, too. He saw to it that the little monkeys got their share of each apple.

After it was all over and the monkeys had again disappeared in the treetops, I looked to Rowdy for some kind of understanding. I didn't get any help from him. He was just lying there with his long ears sticking straight up, looking at me as if he were the most surprised hound dog in the world.

I was so dumbfounded I couldn't even think straight, much less say anything. For several seconds I sat there staring at the ground and trying to remember everything that had happened. The more I thought about how that big monkey had outsmarted me, the madder I got.

"Rowdy," I said, "I wish I had brought Papa's old shotgun along. I'd sure warm that monkey's hide with some bird shot. It's bad enough that he made a fool out of me, but he didn't have to laugh like that."

I put my lunch and apples back in the gunny sack, and walked over to where my traps were. Mashing the springs down with my foot, I released the sticks from the jaws. I put the traps back in my sack. Then I sat down on a stump to do a little thinking. I could remember every trick my grandpa had taught me about trapping, but I couldn't think of a thing that would catch a monkey. The more I thought about everything, the more disgusted I got.

Talking to myself, I said, "There's only one thing I can do. I'll have to get rid of that smart-aleck monkey. If I can get rid of him, I believe I can catch the little ones. They don't seem to have any sense at all. I'll just go to the house, get Papa's gun, and do away with that monkey once and for all."

Then I thought, "What in the world am I thinking of. I can't do that. Why, it would be like hanging a hundred dollar bill in a tree and shooting it all to pieces. And, there was the Old Man of the Mountains. If I shot one of those silly monkeys, there was no telling what he'd do."

Old Rowdy saved the day for me, or at least I thought so at the time. About fifteen feet from the stump I was sitting on was a big hollow log. Rowdy was over there sniffing around. He never could keep his sniffer out of anything that had a hole in it. He just couldn't do things like that.

The instant I saw the log a plan jumped right out of the hollow end and bored its way into my monkey-troubled mind. I walked over to the log, got down on my knees, and looked back into the hollow. It was perfect. The hole was large and went back about four feet. I was so pleased I could have kissed Old Rowdy, but he never did like to be kissed.

Patting the log with my hand, I said, "Rowdy, you could have sniffed all over these bottoms and not found anything this good. This is just what I've been looking for. I'll put my apples back in the hollow and set my traps out here in front. Now if that smart monkey wants an apple, he'll have to wade through all of my traps to get one. If he can do that, and not get caught, then we're just beat and that's all there is to it."

Rowdy seemed to know that I was pleased about something. He reared up on me and tickled my ear with his long pink tongue.

"Come to think of it, Rowdy," I said, "I'm starving to death for a drink of water. Let's go get a drink first and then we'll really get after these monkeys."

Not far away, at the upper end of an old slough, the cool, clear water of a spring gushed out from under the roots of a huge gum tree. I always figured that the spring belonged to Rowdy and me. We had discovered it on one of our exploring trips. I had even named it "Jay Berry's Spring."

We had a good drink and I washed my hot face in the cool water.

There was never a time that Rowdy and I prowled those Cherokee bottoms that we didn't run into all kinds of surprises, but when I got back to the bur oak tree, I got the biggest surprise of my life. Everything I owned was gone; my gunny sack, lunch, apples, traps, and all.

"Rowdy," I said, looking all around, "I know I left that sack right here by this stump. Now it's gone, and everything we had was in it. I wonder what happened to it."

Rowdy started sniffing around the stump. Then he trailed over to a big sycamore, reared up on it, looked at me, and whined.

"What are you doing that for, boy?" I asked him. "You know that sack couldn't climb a tree."

Regardless of what I said, Rowdy seemed to think the sack had climbed the tree. He started bawling the tree bark. I had never known my old dog to lie, so I looked up into the branches of the big sycamore. What I saw all but caused me to fall over backwards.

Sitting on a limb, with his back against the trunk, was that hundred dollar monkey. He was just sitting there, as big as you please, with a sandwich in one paw, and an apple in the other, eating away and looking straight at me.

He had passed out my apples to some of the little monkeys. They were sitting around on the limbs, chewing away and peering at me with their beady little eyes. I could see my gunny sack with the traps in it draped over a limb.

I felt the anger start way down in my feet. It burned its way through my body and exploded in my head.

"Why you thieving rascal," I yelled. "You can't get away with this. You give that stuff back to me."

I saw right away that the big monkey had no intention of giving anything back to me. He stood up on the limb and started jumping up and down, and laughing fit to kill. This made me so mad I came close to cussing a little.

While hanging around my grandpa's store, I had learned a few cuss words from the men, but I never did use them. I was afraid to. Daisy had told me that if any boy who wasn't twenty-one years old yet cussed, his tongue would rot out of his head. So I just didn't do any cussing. I didn't figure that I could get along without my tongue. But I was so mad at that monkey, I had to do something.

I grabbed up a chunk from the ground and threw it at him as hard as I could. I didn't come close to hitting him, but it made him mad anyway. He let out a squall and threw one of my apples straight at me. I had to jump sideways to keep it from hitting me.

The idea of an old monkey throwing something at me was more than I could stand. I went all to pieces. I had a darn good beanshooter, and was such a good shot I could almost drive nails with it. I jerked it out of my pocket and reached for some ammunition. When I discovered that I didn't have one little rock in my pocket, that really made me mad. It looked like everything in the world was going against me.

Not far away was a washout and the bottom was covered with gravel. I ran over and jumped down in it. Dropping to my knees, I started filling my pockets with small rocks.

"Rowdy," I said, "I don't care what the Old Man of the Mountains, or anyone else, does, I'm not going to let that monkey get away with this. I'll make it so hot for him he'll think that the woods are on fire."

With my pockets bulging with ammunition, I climbed out of the washout and ran back to the sycamore tree. The big monkey was still standing on the limb, jumping up and down, and laughing his head off.

I loaded my beanshooter and pulled the rubbers back as far as I could. Taking dead aim, I let go. Old William Tell himself couldn't have shot any straighter than I did. I plunked that monkey a good one about where his belly button should have been. He let out a squall that could have been heard all over the bottoms, and started scratching at the spot where my rock had stung him. I couldn't have been more pleased.

I reared back and laughed as loud as I could. "How do you like that?" I yelled at him. "It's not so funny now, is it? Well, you haven't seen anything yet."

Chuckling to myself, I loaded up again, took dead aim, and plunked him another good one. I never should have shot that big monkey the second time, because it made him awfully mad. Turning to the little monkeys, he uttered a few of those deep grunts and then every one of them started dropping down from the sycamore tree.

This was the last thing in the world I expected the monkeys to do, and I didn't like what was happening at all. I started backing up, one step at a time.

"Holy smokes, Rowdy," I said, "they're coming after us. I didn't think they'd do that, did you?"

By the time the big monkey had reached the last limb on the sycamore tree, I had a pretty good head start on him. He stopped there for a second, opened his big mouth, and showed me those long teeth again. I wouldn't have been more scared if someone had thrown a crosscut saw at me. I dropped my beanshooter and let out a squall that didn't even sound like me.

"They're going to eat us up, Rowdy," I yelled. "Let's get out of here!"

5

I was so scared I didn't look for any game trails to follow. I just ran the way I was pointed.

Old Rowdy wasn't scared. He would have stayed there and fought those monkeys until the moon came up, but he figured that as long as I was leaving, there was no use in hanging around so he took off with me.

It was tough going through the saw briers and underbrush. My clothes got hung up a few times, but I didn't stop to untangle them. I just moved on, leaving little pieces of my shirt and overalls hanging on the bushes. I never did look around to see if the monkeys were after me, but I could almost feel the hot breath of that big monkey right on the back of my neck. By the time I had reached the rail fence around our fields, I looked like the scarecrow in Mama's garden. I flew over the top rail and ran out into our field a little way. I stopped then and looked back for the monkeys. They were nowhere in sight.

"Rowdy," I said, "I believe those monkeys would eat a fellow up, don't you?"

From the other end of the field where he was working, Papa saw me when I came flying over the rail fence.

"Jay Berry," he hallowed, "what's going on down there? Are you all right?"

"I'm all right, Papa," I hallowed back. "I'm just having a little monkey trouble, that's all."

Papa motioned with his hand for me to come to him. After all the bragging I had done about what a good monkey catcher I was, I hated like the dickens to go and face him, but I couldn't just run away. He wouldn't have liked that at all. Feeling terrible, I walked over to him.

As I walked up, Papa frowned and said, "What were you running from, Jay Berry? And look at your clothes. Why, they're torn all to pieces. What happened anyway?"

I couldn't even look at Papa.

Poking a finger in one of the holes in my britches, I said, "I was running from those monkeys, Papa. I guess I got hung up in the bushes and tore my clothes a little."

"Running from the monkeys?" Papa said. "Were they after you?"

"I think they were, Papa," I said. "I didn't look back to see if they were chasing me, but I'm pretty sure they were after me all right."

"Aw," Papa said, chuckling, "monkeys aren't dangerous. You probably just thought they were chasing you."

"I don't know, Papa," I said. "I wouldn't put anything past those monkeys. They're the smartest things I've ever seen. They sure made a fool out of me."

"Made a fool out of you?" Papa said. "How did they do that?"

"The little devils stole everything I had," I said, "my traps, my gunny sack, apples, lunch, and all. I guess they've even got my beanshooter by now. When I ran off, I dropped it, too."

"I was afraid something like this was going to happen," Papa said. "I think I've read where monkeys can be pretty smart; especially, if they've been trained."

"It's not the little monkeys, Papa," I said. "They don't seem to have any sense at all. I believe I could catch every one of them. It's that hundred dollar monkey that I'm having trouble with."

"I thought all monkeys looked alike," Papa said. "How can you tell that hundred dollar monkey from the others?"

"Oh, that's easy, Papa," I said. "He doesn't even look like the little monkeys. He's much bigger, and looks just like a little boy when he's standing up; and is he ever smart. I don't believe anyone could catch him in a trap."

"If he's that smart," Papa laughed, "why don't you just forget about catching him, and try to catch the little ones? If you could catch all of them, you'd still have a lot of money."

"It's not that simple, Papa," I said. "That big monkey is the leader of the pack. He tells the little monkeys what to do, and they mind him. He won't let one of them get close to a trap."

Papa frowned and looked at me like he couldn't believe what I had said.

"Are you trying to tell me that those monkeys can talk to each other?" he asked.

"They sure can," I said. "As sure as I'm standing here, they can talk to each other. Why, that big monkey even laughed at me. He can turn flips and somersaults, and do things that you wouldn't believe he could do."

"Aw, Jay Berry," Papa said, "you're just imagining things. Monkeys can't talk to each other. Whatever gave you that idea anyway."

It was getting harder and harder to explain things to Papa. It seemed that the more I talked, the crazier everything sounded; but I wanted him to believe me, so there wasn't but one thing I could do. Starting at the very beginning, I told him everything that had happened, from my first go-around with the monkeys until I had sailed over the rail fence.

Papa listened to me, but I could see a lot of doubt in his eyes. He just stood there with a frown on his face, looking at me, and then at Rowdy. Now and then he would turn and stare off toward the bottoms. Finally, as if he had made up his mind about something, he shook his head, pursed his lips, and blew out a lot of air.

Taking the check lines from his shoulders, he wrapped them around the handles of the corn planter and said, "Well, corn or no corn, I'd like to see an animal that's as smart as all of that. Come on. Let's go and have a look at this educated monkey. "

If I had found a pony and a .22 lying in the middle of the road, I wouldn't have been more pleased. As long as my papa was with me, I wouldn't have been scared of the devil himself if he'd had horns on both ends. Besides, Papa was as stout as a grizzly bear, and I just knew that if he ever got his hands on that big monkey we would sack him up.

Just as we entered the thick timber of the bottoms, Papa reached down and picked up a club. "I don't think those monkeys will jump on us," he said, "but just in case they do, I think I'll be ready for them."

"That's a good idea, Papa," I said. "I think I'll get one, too." I walked over to an old high-water drift and picked up a club twice as big as the one Papa had.

Papa laughed and said, "What are you going to do with that? Stick it in the ground and climb it in case that big monkey gets after us?"

"That wouldn't do any good, Papa," I said. "It wouldn't do any good to climb anything. Those monkeys can climb better than squirrels can. You ought to see how fast they can get around in the timber."

When we reached the sycamore where I had last seen the monkeys, I got another surprise. My gunny sack was gone again. We walked all around the big tree and really looked it over. There wasn't a monkey or a gunny sack in it.

"Are you sure this is the tree?" Papa asked.

"Oh, I know it's the tree, Papa," I said. "See that limb way up there. That's where my gunny sack and traps were. Now they're gone. I guess that big monkey took them with him."

"Oh, I don't think he could do anything like that,"

Papa said, "but if he did, he couldn't get very far carrying a sack with steel traps in it. Come on, let's look around a little."

Papa didn't know that hundred dollar monkey like I did, or he wouldn't have said anything like that. I was pretty well convinced that the big monkey could do anything a human being could do.

We walked all around through the bottoms, looking up into the trees for a monkey. We looked and we looked. Even Old Rowdy looked and sniffed, but we didn't see hair nor hide of a monkey.

About thirty minutes later, Papa wiped the sweat from his brow and said, "It looks like those monkeys flew the coop, doesn't it?"

"They're around here somewhere, Papa," I said. "I know they are. I'll bet right now they're watching every move we make. They're smart, I tell you. They're the smartest things you've ever seen."

"Maybe if we made some noise it would stir them up a little," Papa said. "It's worth a try anyway. You go over there and beat on that old hollow snag with your club, and I'll do some whooping."

I walked over to the snag, spit on my hands, and started whacking away with my club. It sounded like a war drum. Papa started whooping. Rowdy didn't know what was going on, but figured that as long as we were making some noise, he might as well make some, too. He starter bawling for all he was worth.

We made enough racket to scare the hoot owls out of the bottoms, but we sure didn't stir up any monkeys. We listened and listened, but all we could hear was the droning tones of the noise we had made die away in the thick timber.

"Well," Papa said, looking at me, "it sure looks like those monkeys have left the country. What are you going to do now?"

"There's not but one thing I can do, Papa," I said. "I'll just have to go and have another talk with Grandpa. Maybe he can tell me what to do. I still believe those monkeys are around here somewhere."

"That's not a bad idea," Papa said. "If I know your grandpa, he's not going to let a bunch of monkeys get the best of him—not your grandpa."

All the way back to Papa's corn planter I was feeling terrible. What if those monkeys had left the country. There just wouldn't be any pony or a .22, and that's all there was to it.

Papa must have realized how I felt. "I wouldn't feel too bad about this if I were you," Papa said. "If you think those monkeys are still around here, I don't think you have anything to worry about. I'm pretty sure that your grandpa will come up with something."

"I sure hope he does, Papa," I said. "It makes me sick to think how close I came to making all of that money and then to wind up without a nickel. If it hadn't been for that smart-aleck monkey, I would probably be worth a million dollars by now."

Papa laughed and said, "I'll tell you what I'll do. If you haven't located those monkeys by the time I get this field planted, I'll take a couple of days off and we'll both look for them. I'd still like to see that smart monkey."

When Papa said that, it was just like lighting the lamps in a dark room for me. I began to feel better and everything started looking good again.

Just as Papa unwrapped the check lines from the handles of the corn planter, he said, "As long as you're going to the store, I think you should tell your mother where you're going. She won't worry so much if she knows you're not down in the bottoms."

"Yes, sir," I said, and started for the house.

I didn't think I'd have to do any explaining to Mama and Daisy about my monkey trouble, but I should have known better. After all, they were women folks.

They were both sitting out on the well curb, shelling early peas, when Rowdy and I came walking up. Mama looked at me, dropped the peas she had in her hand, and you would have thought that it was the first time in her life that she had ever laid eyes on me.

"For heaven's sake, Jay Berry!" Mama exclaimed. "What on earth happened? How did your clothes get torn like that?"

"Why nothing happened, Mama," I said, trying to look as surprised as she was. "I was just running and got my clothes hung up in the bushes and tore them—that's all."

Before Mama could say anything else, Daisy had to put in her nickel's worth. She giggled and said, "Jay Berry, you look just like my old rag doll did the time Rowdy got hold of her."

It had been a terrible day for me. To have a monkey laugh at me was bad enough; but to have a girl laugh at me, even though it was my little sister, was a little too much.

"Mama," I wailed, "you'd better make her stop giggling like that. It's not funny."

Mama was so interested in my torn clothes she ignored my plea altogether.

"Jay Berry, why were you running?" she asked. "Was something after you?"

I decided right then that if I could get out of it, I wouldn't tell Mama everything that had happened down in the bottoms. I was afraid she might put a stop to my monkey hunting, and that was the last thing in the world I wanted.

"Aw, Mama," I said, "what makes you think something was after me. You're all the time thinking things like that. Every time I go to the bottoms you think something's going to eat me up. You don't see any blood on me, do you?"

The scared look vanished from Mama's face, and everything would have been all right if it hadn't been for Daisy. She just couldn't leave well enough alone.

"Did you catch any monkeys, Jay Berry?" Daisy asked.

"No," I growled, glaring at her. "I didn't catch any monkeys. But I'm going to."

"Where are your traps and gunny sack?" Daisy asked.

Boy! Boy! Boy! I loved my little sister very much, but she sure could ask some silly questions. I decided that I'd act like I didn't even hear what she had asked me.

"Mama," I said, "it looks like I can't catch those monkeys with traps so I'm going back to the store and have another talk with Grandpa. Maybe he can tell me another way I can catch them. Do you need anything from the store?"

"No," Mama said. "I don't need anything today, but what did happen to your gunny sack and traps? Did you lose them?"

I never did lie to my mama, but right then I sure wanted to tell her one, but I didn't.

"The monkeys got away with them," I said as if it were something that didn't amount to anything. "Well, I'd better be on my way to the store. I'd like to get back before dark."

Daisy didn't give me a chance to get started to the store. She popped up and said, "Did you say the monkeys got away with your traps and gunny sack, Jay Berry? How did they do that?"

"They stole them," I said, almost shouting. "That's how they did it. They stole everything I had. Now are you satisfied?"

Daisy laughed so loud it scared our old hens and they all started cackling. She grabbed up her crutch and headed for the house, squealing with laughter.

"Now, Mama," I cried, "there she goes again, and you won't say a word to her. You better make her stop. If I laughed at her, you'd jump all over me."

"Jay Berry," Mama said, looking at me real hard, "I think you'd better go on to the store before you get into it; but first you go in the house and change clothes. I wouldn't want people to see you looking like that. They'd think we were starving to death."

"Aw, Mama," I said, "people aren't going to think we're starving to death just because I have a few holes in my britches. Every boy in the hills tears holes in his britches."

"Now look, young man," Mama said, "I'm in no mood for an argument. If you want to go to the store, you'd better change your clothes, or you're not going."

Grumbling to myself, I went in the house and changed my clothes.

Grandpa was sitting on the porch of the store when Rowdy and I came walking up the road. He was just sitting there in his old rocking chair, with a fly swatter in his hand, looking off across the country.

As I walked up, Grandpa peered at me over the tops of his glasses and smiled. "You can take those monkeys out to the barn and put them in the corn crib," he said. "They'll be safe there."

I grinned a little, but I didn't want to.

"Aw, Grandpa," I said, as I sat down beside him, "you know I don't have any monkeys. I didn't catch a one."

"Didn't catch any!" Grandpa said, trying to look surprised. "Why, I figured that you'd have a sack full of monkeys by now. What happened? Couldn't you find them?"

"Oh, I found them all right," I said. "It's just like you figured it was. The bottoms are full of monkeys. All kinds of monkeys."

"That's fine," Grandpa said. "That's what I wanted to hear. Did you see that hundred dollar monkey?"

"See him!" I said. "I'll say I saw him. I saw so much of that monkey I don't care if I never lay eyes on him again. He's the smartest thing that ever climbed a tree. I believe he's smarter than the President."

Grandpa laughed and said, "Oh, I don't think he's that smart, is he? For the good of the country, I hope he isn't. What happened anyway?"

Taking a deep breath, I told Grandpa everything that had happened down in the bottoms. I didn't leave out a thing.

Grandpa started fidgeting in his chair like something was biting him. He jerked out his old red hand-

kerchief and made a big to-do about blowing his
nose. I couldn't see very much of his face for the handkerchief, but what little I could see was as red as a
busted watermelon. Grandpa was having a hard time
holding back a good laugh. It always made me feel
good to see my grandpa laugh because he laughed all
over. But right then, I wouldn't have enjoyed hearing Santa Claus laugh. I was miserable.

Grandpa finally got hold of himself and said, "I
figured that monkey was smart, but I didn't think he
was that smart."

"I didn't either, Grandpa," I said. "It's a cinch that
I'll never catch him in a trap; and as long as he's
around, it doesn't look like I'll be able to catch any of
the little monkeys either. I don't know what to do
now."

Grandpa got that serious look in his eyes. "You
know, it's always a good idea to have more than one
iron in the fire," he said. "You watch the store for a
few minutes. I'll be right back."

"Do you have another plan, Grandpa?" I asked.

"Sure, I have another plan," Grandpa said. "That's
what grandpas are for, isn't it? Don't worry about
catching those monkeys. Before you know it, we'll have
every one of them in the sack."

Grandpa was the best boy perker-upper in the world.
The way he was talking had me feeling like I was already sitting in the saddle and shooting at everything that moved. I watched Grandpa shuffle off
toward the barn and disappear inside. He wasn't gone
long before I saw him coming back, carrying the odd-
est-looking outfit I'd ever laid eyes on. It was a long
pole with a net on one end.

As Grandpa walked up, I said, "Grandpa, what in
the world is that thing?"

Hefting the long pole in his hand, Grandpa chuckled and said, "To be truthful, I don't know what it
is. I don't think it has a name. I guess right now
is as good a time as any to give it a name. Let's just
call it a monkey-catching net."

"A monkey-catching net!" I said, big-eyed. "Aw,

Grandpa, you couldn't catch a monkey with that thing, could you?"

"Well," Grandpa said, still chuckling, "you'll have to admit one thing, if you ever got a monkey in this outfit, he would sure be a caught monkey."

On taking a closer look at the odd contraption, I could see that the pole part had eyes on it like the guides on a fishing rod, and two strings ran down from the loop of the net through the eyelets almost to the end of the pole. On the end of each string was a good-size celluloid ring—one was blue and the other was yellow.

"Grandpa," I said, "what are all of those strings and rings for?"

"That's what works the outfit," Grandpa said. "Watch now."

Poking the pole out in front of him, Grandpa pulled the yellow ring and the net opened. "Now let's say there's a monkey out there and you want to catch him," he said, making a long swipe at an imaginary monkey. "Now he's in the net. Watch closely. Here comes the good part."

He pulled the blue ring and the net closed.

"See how it works," he said. "What do you think of it?"

Once I had seen how the net worked, I was so pleased I couldn't say a word. I just stood there staring at that wonderful monkey-catching net.

"Well," Grandpa said, rather impatiently, "what do you think of it?"

"I think it's a dandy, Grandpa," I said. "That's the slickest working thing I've ever seen. You're right. If I ever get a monkey in it, he would sure be a caught monkey, wouldn't he?"

"Do you think you could ever get close enough to a monkey to slap the net on him?" Grandpa asked.

I thought a minute and said, "I don't think I could ever catch that hundred dollar monkey in it, Grandpa. He's too smart to be caught that easy, but I might be able to catch the little ones. They're not half as smart as that big monkey, and they don't seem to be scary at all."

"That's all right," Grandpa said. "You catch the little ones first, and then we'll figure out something for that hundred dollar monkey. We're going to catch him, too, you know."

Grandpa handed me the net, and just to get used to it, I made a few swipes with it. At first I had a little trouble with the ring-pulling part. I was closing when I should have been opening, but I finally got it and and everything looked fine to me.

"Grandpa, I believe this is a better idea than those traps were," I said. "All I have to do now is figure out how I'm going to get a monkey in this thing."

Grandpa grunted, and taking the net from me, he laid it down on the ground. Motioning as he talked, he said, "I believe if I were you I'd work it this way. Right about where the end of the handle is, I'd dig a hole big enough for you and Rowdy to hide in. It might be a good idea to put some brush over the top of the hole so those monkeys can't see you from the treetops. Then I'd take leaves and cover the handle and net until a monkey couldn't see a thing.

"Be sure the net is open. Lay your apples in the center of the loop. Then crawl down in the hole and wait. When a monkey steps in to get an apple, just lift up on the handle, jerk the blue ring, and you'll have one for sure."

I saw right away that Grandpa's idea was a jim-dandy, but there was one thing that was bothering me. "Grandpa," I said, "that's a good idea all right but I think we're overlooking something—that hundred dollar monkey. He sits up in those sycamore trees and watches everything I do. If he sees me digging that hole and hiding that net, he won't get in a mile of it. He won't let any of those little monkeys get close to it either. How am I going to get around that?"

Grandpa frowned and started scratching his head. "Well, you could go down there tonight and dig that hole," he said. "Monkeys don't stir around at night. They go to sleep. Then in the morning you'd have to be there before they wake up. That way they wouldn't know what went on."

"By golly, Grandpa," I said, "you sure think of everything, don't you. That's just what I'll do. I'll go down there tonight and dig the hole. Then in the morning all I'll have to do is hide the net, put out my apples, and wait for those monkeys. I really believe we'll out-fox them this time. I sure do. Don't you?"

Grandpa laughed and said, "I don't know. We'll just have to wait and see. Now that we've got everything figured out, maybe you'd better be high-tailing it for home. And, if this doesn't work out, I wouldn't let it bother me. Just remember there never was an animal that couldn't be caught."

I was feeling so good I could have hugged my grandpa's neck, but ever since I had grown up to be a man, I had quit doing things like that.

Just as I picked up the net, I thought of something. "Grandpa," I asked, "where in the world did you ever get a thing like this anyway?"

Grandpa laughed, then he walked over and sat down in his old rocker. He picked up his fly swatter, reared back, and said, "That's a long story. It happened way back when you were just a little bitty thing. One year a fellow from the college in Tahlequah came up here and stayed all summer with your grandma and me. He was one of those butterfly professors."

"Grandpa," I interrupted, "did you say this fellow was a butterfly professor?"

"I think there's another name for them," Grandpa said, "but I don't know what it is. It's a big word and would break your tongue to say it. Anyhow, when this fellow came up here, he brought that net with him. All he did that summer was lope around through the country catching butterflies in that net. He must have caught a million butterflies."

I laughed out loud. "Grandpa," I said, "what in the world did that fellow want with all of those butterflies?"

"He studied them," Grandpa said, "just like you would study a book. I never saw anything like it. He would spend hours looking through a big magnifying glass at the butterflies and then he'd write things down on paper. After he had given them a good looking-over, he would pin them to small white cards. He put those cards in small glass-topped boxes."

"Grandpa," I said, "I've caught a lot of butterflies, but they're such pretty little things I never did stick pins in them. I always turned them loose. Why, that professor must have been crazy, or just plain mean."

"Oh, I don't think he was a mean fellow," Grandpa said, "but there could have been something wrong with him. I know one thing—if it hadn't been for your grandma, I would have run that professor clean out of the country."

"Run him out of the country!" I said, very surprised. "Why did you want to do that?"

"Because I was going broke," Grandpa snapped. "That's why. I came close to losing everything I had that summer. From the day that professor got here until the day he left, I never sold as much as a can of snuff."

"Never sold anything?" I said, more surprised than ever. "How come you didn't sell anything? Did this professor have something to do with it?"

"He sure did," Grandpa growled. "He had everything to do with it. You know, most of my trade is with these Cherokee Indians, and you know how superstitious they are about crazy people. They think if a person has lost his mind he is dead already, and his soul has gone on to the happy hunting grounds. They won't get close to a crazy man, and won't come around where one is. The way the professor was carrying on, every Indian in these hills thought he was crazy, and they wouldn't come within a mile of my store. So—I didn't sell anything."

"I know how these Indians feel about crazy people, Grandpa," I said, "but how come they thought the professor was crazy."

"Oh, there were a lot of reasons," Grandpa said. "In a way, you couldn't blame them. This professor was an odd-looking duck. He was as long as a fence rail and as bony as a whalebone corset. He had a little beard that stuck straight out from his chin about five inches. It was so sharp on the end you could have split a stump with it. I never saw a man with so much hair on his head, and I don't think he ever combed it as it was always bushed out like the tail of a scared tom-cat."

I laughed and said, "Why, Grandpa, no wonder the Indians thought that professor was crazy. If I saw a man who looked like that, I'd think he was crazy, too."

Grandpa nodded his head, and said, "It wasn't only the way the professor looked. I think the way he acted and his clothes had a lot to do with it. He wore shirts that didn't have any sleeves at all, and his pants were cut off about to here."

With his finger, Grandpa made a slash across his legs above his knees.

"Every time the professor got after a butterfly, he would start running and waving that net, and yelling and making all kinds of racket. The Indians saw him loping around through the country and figured that he had lost his mind. If it hadn't been for your grandma, I would have taken a club to that professor."

"What did Grandma have to do with it, Grandpa?" I asked.

Grandpa frowned and started digging at the whiskers on his chin.

"This professor was a talker," he said. "He could talk a fish right out of the river. Your grandma thought he was the smartest man in the world. He got her all interested in those butterflies, and she wouldn't listen to my running him off."

I laughed and laughed and laughed. Great big tears boiled out of my eyes and ran all over my face.

Still laughing and wiping tears, I said, "Grandpa, I sure would like to see one of those butterfly professors. That would be better than going to a circus."

Grandpa grunted and said, "If I have anything to do with it, you'll never see one around here. There's not

enough room in the country for me and another one of
those butterfly professors. One of us would have to
leave."

I was still laughing when Grandma hallowed from
the house, "Jay Berry, is that you?"

"Yes, Grandma," I hallowed back. "It's me."

"Before you go home," Grandma said, "you come by
the house. I have some things I want to send to your
mother."

"All right, Grandma," I said.

On hearing Grandma, Grandpa got all nervous. He
got up from his chair and started fidgeting around.

Looking at me, he said, "I don't believe it would be
a good idea to let your grandma know too much about
this monkey-catching business of ours. When it comes
to hunting and fishing and things like that, women
can't see things like men can."

"I know just what you mean, Grandpa," I said. "I
have enough trouble with Mama and Daisy. Every
time I leave the house, Mama thinks I'm going to get
eaten up by something; and if I even catch a little old
lizard, Daisy thinks I'm the meanest boy in the world.
The other day she told me that if I didn't quit catching things, God was going to send a bolt of lighting
down out of the sky and split me wide open."

Grandpa laughed and said, "Oh, I don't think the
good Lord would do anything like that—not to a boy
anyway. He can understand things better than women
folks can. I found out a long time ago not to pay too
much attention to the women. They don't mean half of
what they say anyhow."

"I try not to pay any attention to them, Grandpa,"
I said, "but it doesn't seem to do any good. Why, Mama
has broken so many switches off our peach trees I don't
think they will ever have any more peaches on them."

Grandpa laughed and said, "Peaches are pretty good
things to have around all right, but they're not the
most important things in the world."

"They're not half as important as hunting and fishing," I said.

Looking at his watch, Grandpa said, "Well, it's

getting late, and you'd better be getting for home. I don't want you to be out on the road after dark."

"Oh, I'm not scared of the dark, Grandpa," I said. "I used to be, but not as long as Rowdy is with me. He can take care of anything that wants to jump on us."

Looking at Rowdy, Grandpa smiled and said, "Yes, I guess he could. You know, when I was a boy about your age, I had a dog, too. He was a hound just about like Rowdy, and I felt about like you do. As long as he was with me, I wasn't scared of anything."

"Why, Grandpa," I said, "I didn't know that you had a dog when you were a boy. You've never said anything to me about it before. I bet you could tell me a lot of good stories about some of the things you and your dog did."

With a faraway look in his eyes, Grandpa said, "Yes, I expect I could, but right now with it getting late and with your grandma wanting to see you, I don't think we have time. Someday after we've caught all of the monkeys, I'll tell you about some of the things my old dog and I got into."

"Is that a promise, Grandpa?" I asked.

"Yes," Grandpa said, nodding his head, "that's a promise. Now, you'd better be on your way. I have to lock up the store and get my chores done."

I thanked Grandpa again for all the help he had given me, and started for the house to see what Grandma wanted.

6

I hid my net behind a big lilac bush in Grandma's
front yard, walked around the house, and came in
through the back door. That was the quickest way to
the kitchen and I dearly loved that part of the house.
I could never remember a time when I walked into
Grandma's kitchen that I didn't get something to eat.
I had one of the best little old grandmas a boy ever
had, but she worried about me too much. She was always worrying about my health and my schooling, and
everything else you could think of.

Grandma was a pretty good doctor, too. No germ
could escape her eagle eye. About three times a year
she would take time out from her work and give me
a complete examination. While these examinations
were taking place, I'd have to stand perfectly still with
my head thrown back, and with my mouth open like
any angry turtle.

Grandma would look at my teeth, my tongue, and
my tonsils; and way on down into my throat. After she
had given my insides a good looking-over, then she'd
look me over on the outside. She would peel back my
eyelids and look at my eyeballs, peer down in my ears,
and punch around on me with her fingers.

About the only thing Grandma could ever find
wrong with me would be a few dirty spots. It made no

difference if Rowdy and I had been swimming in the river all day long, Grandma could usually find a little bit of dirt on me somewhere. I never could understand how it was still there.

I didn't mind these examinations so much. It was the standing-still part that always got the best of me. I just never could stand still very long.

Grandma was over at her cupboard putting something in a basket when I walked into the kitchen.

She turned, looked at me, frowned, and said, "I declare, Jay Berry, I believe you're getting skinnier and skinnier. Don't you ever eat anything?"

"Eat anything?" I said. "Why, Grandma, I eat everything I can get my hands on—you know that."

"I know," Grandma said, "but it doesn't seem to be putting any meat on your bones. Why, you look like a fishing pole."

I laughed and said, "Aw, Grandma, I know I'm a little skinny, but I don't look like a fishing pole, do I?"

Grandma smiled and said, "Well, maybe not exactly like a fishing pole, but almost."

"Being skinny doesn't count, Grandma," I said. "It's being hard that counts, and I'm as hard as a flint rock."

I pumped up one of my arms and said, "If you don't believe I'm hard, just feel of my muscle."

Grandma came over and very tenderly pinched my muscle between two fingers. "Well," she said, "it is hard all right, but there's not much of it there. It's not much bigger than a quail's egg."

This hurt my feelings a little bit. Looking down at my arm, I said, "Aw, Grandma, my muscle is bigger than a quail's egg. If it got any bigger, I couldn't carry it around."

Grandma smiled and said, "I'll bet a piece of huckleberry pie and a glass of milk would help build those muscles a little, don't you?"

"It sure would, Grandma," I said. "The huckleberry pies that you bake would put muscles on a grapevine."

Grandma chuckled and said, "I'm not interested in putting muscles on any grapevines, but I would like to see yours puff up a little more."

While I was eating, Grandma said, "How is your little sister getting along?"

My mouth was so full of huckleberry pie I had to swallow four or five times before I had room enough to say anything.

"Oh, I guess she's all right, Grandma," I said. "You know how Daisy is, she's always laughing and singing and hopping around on that old crutch. You couldn't tell if anything was wrong with her or not."

Looking concerned, Grandma said, "Jay Berry, I don't think your little sister is as happy as she lets on. She just doesn't want to worry anyone. I'll bet if the truth were known, she's probably in pain all the time."

I didn't like to talk about Daisy's crippled leg. It always made me feel bad, and there wasn't anything I could do about it. Besides, right then I had too many worries of my own to wrestle with. There were those monkeys to be caught, and a chance to get the pony and .22. I figured that was about all the worries I could take care of at one time.

Grandma said, "I know that your mother and father have been saving their money, hoping to send Daisy to the hospital. Do you know if they've saved any?"

"I guess they've saved a little, Grandma," I said, "but I don't think it's very much. Papa can't seem to get ahold of much money. He gave up his smoking tobacco, and Mama has been saving her egg money. She doesn't order anything out of the catalogue any more. They're saving every dime they can, but I don't think they've saved very much."

Grandma frowned and said, "Times are so hard it's a problem for anyone to save money. Your grandpa and I have been putting a few dollars away to help out, but you know how your grandpa is. He does more credit business than he does cash business, and people can't pay their bills."

I felt pretty good when Grandma told me she and Grandpa were trying to save some money, too. If they were all saving their money, then sooner or later Daisy's leg would be fixed up. In fact, I couldn't see where anyone had anything to worry about but me.

Getting up from the table, I said, "Grandma, I have so many things to do I'd better be getting home. What did you want me to take to Mama?"

Picking up the basket, Grandma handed it to me and said, "I baked some fresh bread today and want to send a few loaves to her. Be careful now, and don't mash them."

"I won't, Grandma," I said, "and thanks for the pie and milk."

"Are you sure you wouldn't care for another piece of pie?" Grandma asked.

I patted my tummy and said, "No, thanks, Grandma, I think that'll hold me until I get home."

I had more than enough room for another piece of Grandma's pie, but with all of those monkeys hopping around in my head, I couldn't think too much about eating.

On my way home, I decided that I'd try out my net on something that was alive. There were plenty of rabbits, chipmunks, and birds to try it on, but every time I poked the net out toward one of them, it would scare them half to death. They took off like they were leaving the country for good.

I finally gave up and decided that I'd wait until I got home to catch something. We had all kinds of things around our farm that weren't scared of anything like a little old net.

Not wanting to answer a lot of questions from Mama and Daisy about my monkey-catching net, I hid it under the front porch before going in the house.

Mama and Daisy were in the kitchen fixing supper. Setting the basket on the table, I said, "Mama, Grandma baked some bread today and she sent you some."

"That was nice of your grandma," Mama said. "Did you thank her for the bread?"

I thought for a second, and said, "I don't know, Mama, if I did or not. She gave me some pie and I thanked her for that, but I could have forgotten to thank her for the bread."

With a hurt look on her face, Daisy said, "Jay Berry, you should be ashamed of yourself. Grandma has been so good to us and you can't even thank her when she gives us something."

"Aw, now, Daisy," I said, glaring at her, "don't make it sound like I had burned the barn down. I didn't do it on purpose. I just have so many things on my mind I can't think straight any more."

"It's those monkeys," Mama said, disgustedly, "that's what it is. I suppose you and your grandpa have it all figured out how you're going to catch them."

"We sure have," I said. "Grandpa really came up with a good idea this time."

"How are you going to catch them?" Daisy asked.

"With a net," I said.

"A net!" Daisy said. "What kind of net?"

"Oh, it's just a net on the end of a long pole," I said. "It opens and shuts."

Daisy giggled. "Jay Berry, you're going to keep messing around with those monkeys and they'll catch you," she said. "That's what's going to happen."

Mama laughed and said, "That's probably what will happen."

"Go ahead and laugh," I said, heading for the door. "It won't be so funny when I catch those monkeys and make all that money. And I'm going to catch them—you just wait and see."

Very disgusted with the women in our family, I went and got my net, called Rowdy, and headed for the barn lot.

"Come on, Rowdy," I said, "let's see if we can catch something with this thing."

I had no trouble finding something I could try to catch in the net. We had seven geese: six hen geese and one old gander. I found them out behind the barn, scratching around in the dirt. It was easy to get along with the hen geese, but it was different with the gander. He was the meanest old goose that ever honked a honk. Daisy had named him "Gandy."

As far back as I could remember, Gandy and I had been bitter enemies. He was a sneaky old goose, always coming up behind me, and trying his best to twist a chunk of meat out of my sitting-down place. I had plotted to do away with Gandy a dozen times, but in some way he always survived every one of my plans.

The nearest I came to doing away with Gandy was the time I came in from fishing and leaned my pole up against the house. I had forgotten and left a nice fat worm wadded up on the hook. Gandy found the juicy tidbit and swallowed it—worm, hook, line, sinker, and all. We had no goose doctors in the country, and all Mama could do was cut the line and let Gandy fare for himself.

For about a month, Gandy walked around with a stiff neck. Every time he honked he would jump straight up about three feet. He was a tough old goose though—I have to say that much for him—because he lived after swallowing the fish hook and got meaner and meaner.

Rowdy hated every feather on Gandy's body. In the summer when it would get too hot for Rowdy to sleep under the house, he would go out in our yard in the shade of the red oak trees and dig himself a sleeping hole down in the ground where it was cool. This would please Gandy very much. He would honk his delight to the four winds, walk around as though he wasn't paying any attention until Rowdy got comfortable and went to sleep. Then he'd sneak in and get Rowdy by the tail or one of his long tender ears. Every time this happened, there would be a terrible fight and goose feathers would fly everywhere.

Gandy had been in so many fights he was scarred up like a back alley tomcat, which didn't seem to help his meanness at all. He would get up in the morning looking for a fight, and when he went to bed he dreamed about fighting. He was just a mean old goose and that's all there was to it.

"Rowdy," I said, eying Gandy, "I think this is a good time to get even with that old goose for all the times he has pecked us, don't you?"

Rowdy seemed to understand that I was planning some kind of trouble for Gandy and was very pleased about it.

Holding the pole out in front of me as far as I could

reach, I pulled the yellow ring, darted in, slapped the net over Gandy, and jerked the blue ring.

At first Gandy wasn't too scared. He thought it was just another fight and started fighting back at the net. He hissed, and he pecked, and he honked. He beat at the net with his wings and flounced all over the place.

Holding onto the pole and grinning like a possum eating briers, I said to no one in particular, "Boy, Grandpa was right. If I ever got a monkey in this thing I sure would have him."

It didn't take Gandy long to realize that whatever it was that had hold of him wasn't going to turn him loose and was much more than he could handle. He got scared then and let out a honk that sounded like a foghorn with a bad cold.

Rowdy must have known that a storm was brewing. He took off for the house as fast as he could run and disappeared under the porch.

By this time, Gandy was sure that his little goose world was coming to an end, and he was very unhappy about it.

I was so pleased about how my net had worked I didn't think about being scared until Old Rowdy ran out on me. Jerking the yellow ring, I started to dump Gandy out of the net. I saw right away that it was impossible. Gandy had gotten his feet and head through the mesh in the net and the rest of him was so tangled up in the cord that I couldn't dump him out. I even tried to shake him out of the net and couldn't.

Regardless of how ugly and mean Gandy was, the hen geese must have thought a lot of him. On hearing his call for help, they started hissing and honking. Then, as if they had all made up their minds at the same time, they lowered their bills within an inch of the ground and here they came to Gandy's rescue.

I was kicking at the hen geese with both feet and trying my best to get rid of Gandy when I heard a noise behind me. Looking over my shoulder, I saw it was Daisy. She took one look at what was going on, and her mouth and eyes flew open at the same time.

"Jay Berry," she shouted, "what are you doing to Gandy?"

"I'm not doing anything to the old fool, but trying to turn him loose," I shouted back.

"Mama! Mama!" Daisy yelled. "You'd better come quick! Jay Berry's killing Old Gandy!"

I heard the back door slam, and Mama came running; wanting to know what in the world was going on.

"Look, Mama!" Daisy shouted, pointing with her hand. "Just look what he's doing!"

Gandy was making so much racket with his hissing and honking and flapping around, it took Mama a few seconds to figure things out. Then she yelled at me. "Jay Berry, what on earth are you doing? You turn that goose loose."

"I'm trying to turn him loose, Mama," I shouted. "Can't you see that?"

Mama could see that Gandy was tangled up in the net. "Well, hold him still," she shouted. "He's going to kill himself."

"I can't hold him still, Mama," I shouted. "He's gone crazy."

Daisy was almost bawling. "You'd go crazy, too," she shouted, "if someone caught you in that silly old net."

"Oh, for heaven's sake," Mama said, "something has to be done."

Closing her eyes and turning her head sideways, she darted in and grabbed Gandy up in her arms—net and all. This scared Gandy more than ever. He figured that he was surely headed for the pot and was telling the whole wide world that he didn't like it at all.

By this time I was so scared I couldn't even run. I just stood there holding onto the pole and waiting for what I knew was coming from Mama.

Working together, Mama and Daisy unwound Gandy from the net and turned him loose. Gandy didn't even wait to get his breath. He ran faster than I had ever seen him run for about ten feet, and then he took to the air. He sailed around the barn, up over the house and the red oak trees. Honking every foot of the way, he sailed on down over our fields and disappeared in the river bottoms.

For several seconds after Gandy had faded from sight, we stood in silence, and stared at the spot where he had disappeared.

With her black eyes shooting fire, Mama turned to me and said, "Jay Berry, I hope you're satisfied. We've just lost the best goose we ever had."

"Aw, Mama," I said, in a quavering voice, "that old goose wasn't hurt. He'll be back. You couldn't make him stay away from these hen geese."

"No, Gandy won't be back," Daisy wailed. "He won't ever come back, and I don't blame him one bit. Jay Berry, I don't know about you. I just don't know."

"I know one thing," Mama said, in a hard voice. "If you don't get rid of that net, young man, you're going to be in a worse fix than Gandy is. Now, you better believe that."

I did believe Mama, too. I believed every word she said.

Just then Papa came in from the field, riding one of our mules. "What's going on?" he asked. "I never heard so much racket."

"It's Jay Berry, Papa," Daisy said. "He scared Old Gandy clean out of the country."

Papa looked at me and said, "I saw that goose, but I didn't think it was one of ours. I thought it was a wild one. He was really traveling. What happened anyway?"

"Aw, nothing happened, Papa," I said. "Grandpa gave me this net to catch those monkeys. I wanted to see how it would work—so I tried it out on Gandy."

Papa looked at the net. As he got down from the mule's back, he laughed and said, "I don't think we have to worry about Gandy not coming back. He's scared now, but he'll get over that and come looking for these hen geese."

"That's what I tried to tell Mama and Daisy, Papa,"

I said, "but you can't tell them anything. They think Gandy is clear over in Arkansas by now."

Papa laughed. "I don't think Gandy has made it to Arkansas yet," he said, "but if he keeps on going like he was the last time I saw him, it won't take him long to get there."

The way Papa was laughing and making a joke out of everything, I didn't think it would hurt if I laughed a little, too. I never should have laughed right then because it made Mama madder than ever.

"Jay Berry," she snapped, "you won't think it's so funny if I make you go to your room and do without your supper."

This scared all of the laughter out of me. If there was one thing I dreaded, it was having to stay in my room. I would much rather have been hung by my heels to a white oak tree.

"Mama," I said in desperation, "you can't make me go to my room now. I have to go down in the bottoms tonight and dig a hole."

I thought Mama would really have a fit when I said that. "Dig a hole!" she said, in a loud voice. "Jay Berry, you're not going down in those bottoms at night to dig any holes. Why, whoever heard of such a thing."

"But I have to, Mama," I pleaded. "That's the only way I'll ever catch those monkeys."

Mama must have seen that I was desperate. "I can't see where digging a hole could have anything to do with catching monkeys," she said, "but if you're so all-fired set on it, you can go down there tomorrow and dig it. But you're not going tonight and that's all there is to it."

"It wouldn't do any good to dig the hole in the daytime, Mama," I said. "That big monkey would see me, and he's so smart I wouldn't have a chance of catching one of them. I have to dig it at night while those monkeys are asleep."

Daisy squealed with laughter as she took off around the barn. "Jay Berry," she said, "if you dig that hole, those monkeys will push you in it and cover you up, sure as shootin'."

"Now, there she goes again, Mama," I cried, "laughing and making fun of me. Why don't you make her stop?"

If there was one thing that could help Mama get over one of her mad spells, it was to hear Daisy laugh.

"Jay Berry," Mama said, "your little sister is not making fun of you. If she wants to laugh, you let her laugh and don't you say anything about it."

Before I could say anything, Papa stepped in and said to Mama, "Now hold on just a minute. I think you women are carrying things a little too far. I can't see anything wrong with a boy wanting to catch a few monkeys." Looking at me, Papa said, "What's this about digging a hole?"

I explained the plan Grandpa had come up with to catch the monkeys.

Taking the net from me, Papa looked at it and said, "What are these rings and strings for?"

"That's what works the net, Papa," I said. "When you pull the yellow ring, it opens, and the blue ring closes it."

Papa started pulling first one ring and then the other. I saw a pleased look spread over his face. "Say, I think you've got something this time," he said. "Did you have any trouble catching Gandy in it?"

"Heck no, Papa," I said. "I had Gandy caught before he knew what was happening. I believe it's the very thing for catching those monkeys, don't you?"

Still jerking at the rings and watching the net open and close, Papa said, "It looks to me if you could catch a goose in it, you could surely catch a monkey. I'll tell you what—let's have some supper and I'll go down in the bottoms with you and help dig that hole."

Mama gasped as if she had swallowed too much air. Looking at Papa like she couldn't believe what she had heard, she snapped, "Maybe we'd better just quit farming and start catching monkeys."

Papa laughed and said, "That may not be a bad idea. We could probably make more money catching monkeys than we can farming."

Daisy had overheard Mama and Papa. She poked her head around the corner of the barn and said, "Jay Berry, if you and Mama and Papa catch those monkeys, I'll hold the sack for you."

This seemed to fix everything. Mama and Papa started laughing at Daisy. I was feeling so good about Papa going with me to dig the hole, I laughed a little, too.

Right after supper, while Papa was putting some coal oil in the lantern, I went to the tool shed and got a pick and shovel.

"It might be a good idea to take the ax along," Papa said. "We may run into some roots while we're digging the hole."

"I hadn't thought of that, Papa," I said. "We'll run into some roots all right. You can't dig an inch down in those bottoms without running into roots. I know, because Old Rowdy and I have tried to dig rabbits out of their holes down there."

All excited, I ran and got the ax.

As we were leaving the house, Mama and Daisy came out on the porch to see us on our way.

Mama was still in a good humor. She laughed and said, "I hope no one sees my husband down in the river bottoms, at night, digging a hole. What would you tell people?"

"I'll just tell them that we're looking for a pot of gold," Papa said. "Then everyone in the country will be digging holes. How will that be?"

Daisy squealed her delight and said, "Jay Berry, you'd better be careful. If you wake those monkeys up, they might get mad and run you clean out of the country."

I wanted to say something back to Daisy but I figured that as long as Mama was in a good humor I had better leave well enough alone. So I just walked on like I hadn't even heard what she had said.

Old Rowdy thought we were going possum hunting and he was raring to go. He came over, reared up on me, and all but busted my eardrums with his deep voice.

It was one of those warm, full-moon nights when it's so bright it's more like twilight in the evening than nighttime. Thousands of lightning bugs were dancing a flickering rhythm all around us. Overhead, I could hear the hissing whistles of feeding bats as they dipped and darted in the starlit sky.

From deep in the river bottoms, an old hooty owl was asking his age-old question, over and over, "Who-o-o, who-o-o, who-o-o are you? Who-o-o, who-o-o are you?"

If Papa hadn't been with me I would have answered him by saying, "I am the booger man. I'm coming to get you."

That usually shut old hooty up.

Feeling big and important, I said, "Papa, it sure is a pretty night, isn't it?"

"Yes, it is," Papa said. "Nights like this are good for planting. The soil gets warm and mellow. Everything you plant will pop up out of the ground before you know it."

Right then I wasn't interested in any old green thing popping up out of the ground. I was interested in monkeys, ponies, .22s, and things like that.

Papa said, "It's going to be a lot darker in the bottoms than it is out here in the fields. Do you think you can find that monkey tree?"

"Oh, sure, Papa," I said. "I could find that monkey tree if I had a cotton sack over my head. You just follow me."

It wasn't as easy finding the tree as I thought it would be. Several times I got on the wrong trail but I finally found it.

Setting the lantern down on the ground, Papa said, "Where do you think we should dig the hole?"

"Oh, anywhere, Papa," I said, looking around. "One place is as good as another, just so it's close to this bur oak tree."

Picking out a small opening in the underbrush, Papa raked the dead leaves and sticks to one side with the shovel and started digging. Every time Papa ran into a root he would rest while I hacked away with the ax.

The rich black soil was soft and easy digging. In no time we had a good-size hole dug.

Climbing out of the hole, Papa said, "How does that look? Do you think it's deep enough?"

I looked the hole over and said, "There's one way to be sure, Papa. Rowdy and I will get down in it and see how it fits."

Papa chuckled and said, "Do you think you can get Rowdy down in the hole?"

"Oh, I won't have any trouble doing that, Papa," I said. "Old Rowdy will do just about anything I ask him to do. There's only one thing he won't do. He won't help me fight wasp nests. He won't have any part of that."

Still chuckling, Papa said, "Well, you can't hardly blame him for that."

I got down in the hole and called to Rowdy.

"Come on, boy," I said. "You may as well get used to this hole because we might be sitting in it for a long time."

During the past few days, I had asked Rowdy to do so many things he had never done before that he didn't know straight up from straight down. Standing on the rim of the hole and peering down at me, he started whining and whimpering and fidgeting around. Then he just hawled off and jumped clean over the hole and looked at me from another angle. I could hear Papa chuckling in the darkness.

"Aw, Rowdy," I said, "what's the matter with you. Surely you're not scared of this little old hole. Why you've had your nose in every hole in these bottoms. Come on now."

Whimpering like he was getting ready to swim the ice-cold waters of the river, Rowdy got down on his belly, slid off into the hole, and sat down by my side.

"I'm sorry, boy," I said, patting his head. "I know I've got you all mixed up but in the morning I think you'll understand what this is all about."

"Well, what do you think?" Papa asked.

"It's just right, Papa," I said, "but there's one more thing we have to do."

"What's that?" Papa asked.

Climbing out of the hole, I said, "Grandpa thinks it would be a good idea to cover the top of the hole with brush so those monkeys can't see me from the tree-tops."

"That won't be hard to do," Papa said, reaching for his pocketknife.

Papa started cutting brush while I carried it over and arranged it over the top of the hole. Knowing how smart that hundred-dollar monkey was, I took the shovel and scattered the fresh dirt that had come from the hole. After everything had been taken care of, Papa held the lantern up so we could get a better look at our work.

"I don't care how smart those monkeys are," Papa said, "they'll never spot that hole. Why, if I didn't know it was there, I'd probably fall in it myself."

At that moment, no big-game hunter in Africa could have felt more sure of himself than I did.

"Papa," I said, "I really believe I'll catch some of those monkeys this time. I really do."

"I do, too," Papa said. "What time do you intend to be here in the morning?"

"I'd like to be here before sunup, Papa," I said.

"In that case," Papa said, "we'd better be getting home so you can get some sleep."

7

By this time, I had the monkey-catching fever so bad,
I didn't think I'd get any sleep at all that night. In
fact, I couldn't see much use in even going to bed.
But I must have been more tired than I thought I was.
I fell asleep and didn't even dream about monkeys.

It seemed like I had barely closed my eyes when I
was awakened by Papa shaking me.

"You'd better get up," Papa said. "It's almost daylight and those monkeys will be waking up."

While I was putting on my clothes, I heard the
rattling of pots and pans. I thought it was Papa messing around in the kitchen until I walked in and saw
that it was Mama fixing breakfast.

"Aw, Mama," I said, as I poured water into the wash
pan, "you didn't have to get up this early. Why didn't
you stay in bed and get your rest? I could have done
without anything to eat till noon."

"You can't hunt monkeys on an empty stomach,"
Mama said. "Besides, it doesn't look like I'll get any
work out of you until you get over this monkey business."

I finished eating breakfast long before Mama and
Papa did, and I started getting my monkey-catching
gear together. I hurried to the cellar and got some
more apples. Then I rushed to the barn for another

gunny sack. Calling to Rowdy, I picked up my net and headed for the bottoms as fast as I could trot.

I was about halfway through our fields when I met Old Gandy waddling home. If he wasn't a mess. His feathers were all ruffled and he was smeared with mud from his head to his tail. He seemed to be dog-tired and wasn't moving any faster than a terrapin could walk.

"Br-r-rother, Gandy," I said, looking him over, "you must have had a terrible night. It looks like those wild geese down on the river really worked you over."

Keeping his eye on the net, Gandy honked his disgust and waddled over to one side as if he didn't care to have a thing to do with me.

Rowdy could see that Gandy was just about all in and he figured it was a good time to aggravate him a little. He bounded over and started barking at him, and for the very first time, Gandy refused to fight back. Honking and flapping his wings, he lit out for home. Rowdy was right after him, nipping at his tail feathers and having the time of his life.

"Aw, come on, Rowdy," I said, "leave the old fool alone. We've got more important things to do than to mess with an old goose."

It was almost sunup when I arrived at the hole Papa and I had dug. I opened my net and very carefully placed it on the ground with about a foot of the handle and the celluloid rings sticking over the rim of the hole. Then I started covering the handle, loop, and netting with dead leaves and grass.

After everything had been completely covered, I placed three big apples in the center of the hidden loop and then backed off to one side to see what kind of a job I had done.

I was very pleased with my net-hiding skill. "Rowdy," I said, "I don't know much about trapping this way, but you'll have to admit one thing, that net is sure hidden."

Even if Old Rowdy couldn't understand some of the things I did, he always acted like he did anyway.

He wagged his tail and seemed to be pleased with everything.

Picking up my sack, I said, "Come on, boy, let's get in the hole and wait for those monkeys."

With Rowdy behind me, we got down on our stomachs, squirmed back under the brush, and dropped down in the hole.

Rowdy and I hadn't been in the hole ten minutes when from somewhere in the bottoms an old woodpecker started banging away on a dead snag. This seemed to wake up everything in the bottoms. Birds started chirping and squirrels began chattering. From across the river, a big old bullfrog started drumming away—brro-o-m, brro-o-m.

"Rowdy," I whispered, "if those monkeys are around, I don't think it'll be long now. Nothing could sleep with all that racket going on. I hope they're hungry and would like to have a few apples for breakfast."

When I first heard the noise, I couldn't make out what it was—although I knew that I had heard it before. It was a slow, scratchy, leaf-rattling noise. Then I noticed that the brush over the top of the hole started shaking.

"Rowdy," I whispered, "something is messing around with the brush up there. You don't suppose it could be that smart monkey?"

Then I saw what it was. It was a big, old, black snake as big around as my arm. There was no doubt but what he had just shed his skin because he was as black and shiny as a new stove pipe. On he came, sticking out his tongue and twisting his way through the brush. When he was directly over the top of the hole, he stopped and peered down at Rowdy and me.

I thought, "Now wouldn't it be something if that snake decided to come down in this hole?"

Things began happening to me. I got as cold all over as I did the time some mean boys threw me in a spring. My skin started crawling around on me. I stopped breathing and my old heart went absolutely crazy.

"Rowdy," I said, in a low voice, "I know that old

black snake isn't poison, but he's still a snake. If he takes a notion to come down in this hole, everything in the bottoms will know that we're down here because I'll probably make a lot of racket."

I wanted to run but I couldn't. The only way out of that hole was right over the snake and I never did like to run over snakes.

Ordinarily Rowdy wasn't scared of snakes; that is, if he was out where he could maneuver around a little. But he didn't seem to like the idea of sharing that hole with the snake any more than I did. He was whimpering and trying his best to crawl under me.

In desperation, I picked up a handful of dirt and threw it in the snake's face. This scared him. He reared his head back, stuck his tongue out at me about a thousand times, then slithered on through the brush and disappeared.

Letting out a lot of air that had long since grown stale, I breathed a sigh of relief and said, "Rowdy, that was close, wasn't it? For a second there, I sure thought we'd have to let that snake have this hole."

The next visitor we had came awfully close to messing up everything. It was a big old hornet. He came buzzing around in the brush and then dropped down in the hole. Gritting my teeth, I closed my eyes, held my breath, and tried to sit as still as a knot on a bur oak tree.

I didn't know why I was holding my breath because I knew that the old saying of how you could hold your breath and nothing would sting you was pure hogwash. I had tried that before and it hadn't worked at all.

Rowdy would have absolutely nothing to do with anything that had wings and stingers. I had taken him on several wasp-fighting expeditions and the little red warriors had really worked him over. He knew all too well that you couldn't hide from them and it was impossible to outrun them. I had to hold onto his collar and squeeze him up tight to keep him from having a runaway.

The hornet buzzed all around us. I just knew that

he was looking me over for a good soft spot to jab his stinger in. Finally, after what seemed like hours, he must have decided that there wasn't anything in the hole worth stinging and buzzed on his way.

Wiping the sweat from my brow, I said, "Rowdy, I've sure learned one thing today. If you want to get everything in these bottoms interested, just dig a hole. That's all you have to do. I wouldn't be a bit surprised if a skeleton didn't come jiggling around next."

Everything went all right for the next thirty minutes, and then I began to have those old doubts again. Maybe Papa was right. Maybe those monkeys had left the country. The more I thought about it, the more convinced I was that my monkey-catching days had come to an end.

I had just about decided to give up and go home when all at once I heard that hundred dollar monkey squall. I perked up like our old hens did when a chicken hawk came flying around.

"Did you hear that, Rowdy?" I whispered. "It was that hundred dollar monkey. We're still in business."

I raised up to where I could peek through the brush and started looking for monkeys. At first I couldn't see a thing. Then I saw one. He was a little brown monkey and was sitting on a stump about thirty feet away.

I was keeping my eyes on him when that big monkey let out another squall. From down in the hole, I couldn't tell where he was, but I knew that he was close-by. Peering up through the brush, I saw him. He was sitting on a low limb of the bur oak tree, directly above my net, looking down at the apples.

I could tell by the big monkey's actions that apples were just what he wanted for breakfast, but he couldn't seem to convince himself that everything was all right.

He stood up on his short legs and started looking things over. Once he looked straight at my hiding place, and I all but crawled down in my skin.

"Rowdy," I whispered, "he's looking for us but I think we've got him fooled this time."

As if he had finally made up his mind, the big monkey squalled again and started moving backward and forward on the limb—all the time uttering those deep grunts.

"Rowdy," I whispered, "he's talking to those little monkeys. I know he is because he did the same thing before. I wonder what he's saying to them this time."

The big monkey must have been telling the little monkeys that everything looked all right to him because here they came. A whole passel of them dropped down from the branches and started grabbing apples.

I couldn't see my net for monkeys. They were standing all over it. Very gently, I took hold of the handle with my left hand and caught hold of the blue ring with my right hand. Using the rim of the hole for leverage, I jerked down on the handle and yanked the blue ring.

Just as I pulled the ring, I heard the big monkey let out a warning cry, but it was too late. The net had already closed.

I couldn't see too well through the brush but I could tell that I had caught something, for the handle of the net was jerking in my hand more than it did when I had Old Gandy wound up in it.

When the net flipped up out of the leaves and grass, it scared the monkeys half to death. Screeching and chattering, they scattered in all directions and disappeared in the timber.

Rowdy and I threw brush all over the bottoms when we came boiling up out of the hole. My eyes all but popped out of my head when I saw that I had caught two little monkeys in my net. I was so pleased I whooped like a possum hunter whooping to his dog.

"I've got them, Rowdy," I shouted. "I got two of them. Look at 'em."

Rowdy was just as pleased as I was. Wagging his long tail, he ran over and started barking and growling at the flouncing monkeys.

The monkeys were so cute and I was so happy that I had finally caught one, I couldn't keep my hands off of them. I wanted to touch one. Working the handle back through my hands until the net was close to me,

I poke a finger through the mesh and tickled one in the ribs.

I wouldn't have been more surprised if I had stuck my finger in the firebox of Mama's cook stove. The monkey squeaked and sank his teeth in my finger. I dropped the net and did a little squalling myself.

Slinging my hand and doing a jig-jig dance, I shouted, "You bit me. What did you do that for? I wasn't going to hurt you."

Rowdy had seen the monkey bite me and he really got mad. He darted in, grabbed one of the monkeys—net and all—in his mouth and started shaking it.

"No, Rowdy, no!" I yelled. "Don't you hurt that monkey."

I yelled too late. It seemed the monkey just turned over in his skin and sank his needle-sharp teeth right in the end of Rowdy's nose.

Rowdy wouldn't have turned loose of a bumblebee any faster than he did that monkey. He bawled and jumped back so fast he almost fell over backwards. Sitting down on his rear, he looked at me and started whimpering.

"Well, don't look at me," I said, "I can't help you. I got bit, too."

It was then that I realized I really had a problem. How was I going to get those monkeys out of the net and into my gunny sack.

"Rowdy," I said, "for all the good this sack is doing us, we may as well have left it at home. I can't get my hands close to those monkeys. They would eat me up."

I decided that I'd just take monkeys, net, and all to the house and maybe Mama and Daisy could help me figure out something.

Holding the net out in front of me as if I were carrying a couple of poison snakes, I started for home. I hadn't gone a hundred yards when the unexpected happened. That hundred dollar monkey dropped down from a sycamore tree and landed smack in the center of the game trail I was walking on. Rowdy and I wouldn't have stopped more suddenly if we had run face on into a white oak tree.

Standing on his short stubby legs and waving his long arms in the air, the big monkey started squalling. He lay down on the ground and rolled over and over. Every little while he would jump up and rush straight at me, showing his teeth, and uttering those deep grunts. He squalled and he screamed. Then he began picking up sticks and chunks and throwing them at me.

Usually when I got scared I could almost outrun my shadow, but I was beyond being scared, I was paralyzed. All I could do was stand there like I was in a trance, hold onto my net, and stare at that big monkey.

Rowdy was between the monkey and me. Every hair on his back was standing straight up. He was growling way down deep and showing his teeth to that squalling monkey.

A full minute went by before it dawned on me that I was still in one piece. When I realized this, I began noticing things. Every time the big monkey ran at me he only came a little way, then he would turn and shuffle back. He was bluffing. I was so sure of it that I got a little of my courage back, but not very much.

"Rowdy," I said, in a croaking voice, "don't jump on that monkey. I don't think he means to harm us. I think he's bluffing, or at least I hope he is."

On hearing my voice, the big monkey went all to pieces. He squalled and here he came shuffling along the ground with his big mouth open and grunting. He came close enough this time to grab the metal loop of my net and start jerking on it.

Every time the big monkey jerked the net his way, I would jerk it back my way. We played tug of war for a few seconds, then he turned his end loose and ran back down the trail a little ways. He lay down in the dirt and started squalling and screaming and cutting all kinds of capers. I thought he was having a fit.

All the time this was going on, I had the feeling that the big monkey was trying to tell me something. I tried hard to figure out what it was but I was so scared I couldn't. Just then here he came again, scooting along on the game trail, screaming and making enough racket to scare a goblin to death. He grabbed my net and started jerking on it again.

It was the same thing all over. We had another jerking session. Again the big monkey turned his end of the net loose, ran back down the trail, lay down, and had another rolling, squalling fit. As I stood there holding onto my net and watching that monkey throw a tantrum, I figured out what it was that he was trying to tell me. He was telling me to turn the little monkeys loose.

"Rowdy," I said, "I believe that silly monkey wants me to turn these little ones loose. But he can just keep on wanting. After all I've gone through to catch them, there'll be whiskers on the moon before I let them go. Why, I'll fight him all over these bottoms."

All at once the big monkey stopped squalling and the bottoms got as still as a graveyard. In the silence, an uneasy feeling came over me. Great big drops of sweat popped out on me. I could almost taste the tension.

Never taking my eyes from that big monkey, I said in a low voice, "Rowdy, I don't like this a bit. I have a feeling that something is going to happen."

I had no more than gotten the words out of my mouth when something did happen. Another monkey dropped down out of nowhere and lit on the ground not over ten feet from me. Not making a sound, it just stood there staring at me.

I was having an eyeball fight with that monkey when another one came from somewhere and plopped himself down on the other side of me. The first thing I knew there was a complete circle of monkeys all around Rowdy and me. They started walking around us stiff-legged, with their tails standing straight up, and looking at us sideways.

"Rowdy," I said, "I believe these monkeys are up to something. You've been wanting to jump on them, and from the looks of things, I think you're going to get the chance."

Old Rowdy wasn't scared. He kept looking at me and waiting for the "Get-um" sign.

I couldn't stand it any longer. Something had to be done. I jerked off my old straw hat, threw it at one of the monkeys, and shouted, "You get away from here. Get now!"

I may as well have been telling Sally Gooden not to jump over the pasture fence. The monkeys didn't even act like they had heard what I said. They just kept circling around and around and around. I could see that the circle was getting smaller and smaller.

I almost unscrewed my head from my neck following those circling monkeys with my eyes.

"Rowdy," I said, "we've got to do something. We can't just stand here and let these monkeys play ring-around-the-rosy with us."

Just then that hundred dollar monkey started grunting that monkey talk again. The little monkeys must have understood what he was saying, for they stopped circling us. They just stood there on their spindly legs, staring straight at Rowdy and me with no expression at all on their silly little faces.

This was too much for me. Every nerve in my body was twanging like the "e" string on a fiddler's fiddle. I was trying to figure out which way to run when it happened. A small monkey with a long skinny tail dropped down from a branch directly above me and landed right on top of my head. He grabbed a wad of my hair in all four of his tiny paws; then he leaned over and took hold of my right ear with his teeth. I dropped my net and squalled at the same time.

Shouting, "Get-um, Rowdy!" I reached up with both hands, grabbed that monkey by the tail, and started pulling. It was like pulling on the rubbers of my beanshooter. The harder I pulled, the longer that monkey seemed to get. I learned something right then. The long skinny tail of a monkey is the best thing in the world to get a good hand hold on.

Closing my eyes and gritting my teeth, I gave a hard jerk on the monkey's tail. Along with a lot of my hair and skin, he came loose.

I was never so mad in all my life.

I still had a good hold on the monkey's tail, and before he could turn around and bite my hands, I started turning in a circle as fast as I could. About halfway in the middle of the third turn I let loose. He sailed out over the bottoms like a flying squirrel and lit in the top of a good-sized bush.

The little monkey didn't seem to be hurt at all. He let out a squeak and hopped down to the ground. For a second he stood on his hind legs and showed his needle-sharp teeth; then here he came again—straight at me—ready for some more fighting.

He hadn't taken over three steps when all at once he fell over backwards. He got to his feet again, took a few more steps, and this time he fell flat on his face. He was so dizzy from that whirlwind I had put him through he couldn't seem to do anything. This tickled me.

I yelled, "How do you like that, you little devil? If you jump on my head again, I'll sling you clear into Arkansas."

My fight with the monkey had taken only a few seconds. During that time, I had been so busy I had completely forgotten about Old Rowdy. On hearing a loud beller from him, I turned to see how he was making out. Boy, did I ever get a surprise.

I saw right away that Rowdy had made a terrible mistake. He was having the fight of his life. He usually enjoyed a good fight, but from the looks and sounds of things, I didn't think he was enjoying this fight very much. He didn't seem to be making any headway at all.

Rowdy was built just right for good monkey biting and the monkeys had sure taken advantage of this. It looked like every square inch of his hide had a monkey glued to it. His long legs and tail were covered with monkeys. Two of the little devils were sitting right on the top of his head, holding on with all four paws. And they had their teeth clamped on his soft tender ears. More monkeys were lined up on his back like snowbirds on a fence; biting, clawing, and squealing. The hair was really flying.

The monkeys were so quick Rowdy couldn't get

ahold of them. Every time he snapped at one, he would wind up with a mouth full of air and no monkey.

I saw right away that if I didn't do something the monkeys were surely going to have a hound dog for breakfast. Looking around for a good whipping stick, I spied one about ten feet away and darted over to get it. The monkeys must have realized what I intended to do, for just as I stooped over to get the stick, a little monkey flew in from somewhere and landed right in the middle of my back.

I forgot all about the stick and was trying to reach around behind me and get ahold of the monkey's tail when another one darted in and latched onto my leg. I was trying to get ahold of that one when another one came squeaking in and bit me on the hand.

In a matter of seconds, I had monkeys all over me. They were biting, clawing, scratching, and squealing. I was hopping all over the place and making more racket than a tomcat with his tail caught in a mouse trap.

Just when things were looking really bad for Rowdy and me, from high in the bur oak tree, the big monkey let out a few grunts and a loud squall. He must have been telling the little monkeys not to eat us completely up—to save a little for the next time—because they turned us loose and disappeared in the underbrush.

Everything had happened so fast, it left Rowdy and me in a daze. I could hardly believe it. One minute we were fighting monkeys all over the place, and the next minute there wasn't a monkey in sight. We just stood there in the silence about twenty feet apart looking at each other.

Rowdy seemed to be more mixed up then I was. He just couldn't believe that a fight like that could have happened so fast and ended so fast.

I looked over to where I had dropped my net. There it was right where I had dropped it; wide open and not a monkey in it. I couldn't believe it. How on earth could the little monkeys have gotten out of the net?

My first thought was that the yellow ring had gotten tangled in a bush, and while the monkeys were flouncing and dragging the net over the ground, the net had opened.

I glanced down at the yellow ring and almost jumped out of my shoes. I saw that it had been pulled all right and it wasn't tangled in any bush.

Mumbling to myself, I said, "Holy smokes! I'll bet while Rowdy and I were fighting the little monkeys, the big monkey sneaked in and opened the net."

I was still trying to figure out how the monkeys had gotten out of my net when I heard a noise from the bur oak tree. I looked up into the branches. There on a big limb stood the big monkey. He was just standing there looking as proud as a general that had won a war.

When the big monkey saw that I was looking at him, he really made a fool out of himself. Staring straight at me, he started jumping up and down on the limb and uttering those deep grunts. He threw his head back and beat on his chest with his paws; then he opened his big mouth and started laughing. He laughed so loud the bottoms rang with his monkey laughter.

This made me so mad I all but choked.

Shaking my fist at him, I yelled, "You're not such a brave monkey. You sicked those little monkeys on Rowdy and me but you didn't do any fighting. What's the matter? Are you scared? If you'll come down here, we'll fight you all over these bottoms."

The big monkey must have understood what I said. He stopped laughing, and with a few grunts, he started dropping down from the tree. My hair flew straight up.

"Rowdy," I said, as I picked up my empty net, "I don't know about you but I've had all the monkey fighting I want for one day. Let's get out of here."

I didn't have to tell Rowdy but once. He felt about monkey fighting like I did. He was way ahead of me when we tore out down a game trail.

We hadn't gone far when I looked back over my shoulder and saw that there were no monkeys chasing us.

"Rowdy," I said, as I walked over and sat down on a sycamore log, "I think we can stop running now. Maybe we can't whip those monkeys but we can sure outrun them."

Taking my handkerchief out of my pocket, I started dabbing my monkey bites. Rowdy sat down on his rear and started licking his wounds.

"Rowdy," I said, "if you think we're in a mess now, you haven't seen anything yet. Just wait until we go home and have to face Mama and Daisy. Mama will probably whip me and lock you up in the corn crib. If we had a little money and a few groceries, we'd just leave the country and never come back. But, we don't have any money and I don't think either one of us could do without something to eat for very long."

Rowdy seemed to understand what I had said because he stopped licking his wounds and looked toward the house. With a little whimper, he came over and started licking at the monkey bites on my hands.

I patted him on the head and said, "You'd better take care of yourself, boy. You're in worse shape than I am."

The more I thought about going home, the more I dreaded it. I thought about going to the store and seeing if Grandpa could help me in some way, but that wouldn't have done any good. Sooner or later, I would still have to go home.

"Well, Rowdy," I said, "I guess there's not but one thing we can do. We'll just have to take what's coming to us and that's all there is to it. But I don't like it. I don't like it at all."

I could tell by the way Rowdy's tail dropped down between his legs that he didn't like it either.

8

Daisy must have seen Rowdy and me coming up through our fields because she was standing on the porch when we came walking up. With a frown on her face, she peered at us.

Letting out a low whistle, she said, "Holy smokes, Jay Berry, what happened to you and Rowdy? Both of you look like you've been run through a brier patch."

"Aw, Daisy," I said, "didn't anything happen to us. We just had a little fight with those monkeys and they bit us a few times. That's all."

"A few times!" Daisy said. "It doesn't look like a few times to me. It looks like those monkeys just about ate you up this time."

Before I could say anything else, Daisy turned and hollered through the open door of the house, "Mama! Mama! Come and look at Jay Berry and Rowdy! They're chewed all to pieces and there's blood all over them."

This time, Mama must have been peeling potatoes when she heard Daisy yell because she still had one in her hand when she came flying out the door—scared half to death.

"Blood!" Mama said in a quavering voice, looking at Daisy. "Who's bleeding?"

"Jay Berry and Rowdy, Mama!" Daisy said as she

pointed with her hand. "Look at them! They look like they've been run through a brier patch."

With more scare in her eyes than I had ever seen before, Mama looked at me and said, "Jay Berry, are you all right?"

"Aw, Mama," I said, "you know how Daisy is. She's just trying to make something big out of nothing. I'm all right. I just got bit a few times by those monkeys—that's all."

Looking up toward the heavens, Mama closed her eyes and muttered something that no one could have understood.

Daisy came over, took hold of my arm, and started looking at my monkey bites. Shaking her head and making a little clicking noise with her tongue, she said, "Jay Berry, I'm scared. I'm scared half to death."

"Scared!" I said. "What are you scared of? The monkeys didn't bite you."

"I don't care," Daisy said, "I'm scared just the same. We don't know anything about monkeys. For all we know, they may have hydrophobia."

I wanted to say something but I couldn't get my mouth open. My stomach got all knotted up and I shivered a little like I was having a cold chill. I looked to Mama for some help.

Mama couldn't help anyone right then because she was just as scared as I was. She just stood there, staring at me with her face as white as a hen's egg. Her mouth opened and I thought she was going to say something but nothing came out.

People in the Cherokee hills were so scared of hydrophobia they didn't talk about it in loud voices. They usually spoke about it in whispers. When news spread through the hills that a mad animal was prowling, windows and doors were locked. Everywhere the menfolks went, they carried their shotguns and rifles. Until the mad animal was taken care of, children were kept indoors and all stock was brought into the barn lot.

While hanging around my grandpa's store, I had heard some weird tales about animals and people that had gone mad with hydrophobia. How they had frothed at the mouth and their eyes had turned as green as cucumbers. In the dark of night, they would prowl through the country howling and moaning; and biting everything that got close to them. It was enough to scare a fellow clean out of his britches.

Daisy saw that she had me paralyzed with fear and she started carrying on again.

"Mama, there's not but one thing we can do," she said. "We'll just have to chain him and Rowdy to a fence post."

This seemed to shake some of the scare out of Mama. "Chain him to a fence post!" she said, in a loud voice. "Why, Daisy, what on earth are you saying?"

"That's all we can do, Mama," Daisy said. "That's all you can do with anything that's going mad. You have to chain them to something and watch them. If their eyes turn green and they start foaming at the mouth and biting things, then you'll know they're mad. It wouldn't do any good to tie him up with a rope. If he does go mad, he would gnaw right through a rope."

Daisy had me so scared by now that I could almost feel myself frothing at the mouth and snapping at everything that got close to me. I think I would have gone mad for sure if Papa hadn't come walking up about that time.

Frowning, Papa looked at Mama and said, "What's the matter? You look like you've seen a ghost."

Before Mama could say anything, Daisy popped up and said, "It's Jay Berry again, Papa. He's really got himself into a mess this time. He and Rowdy had a fight with those monkeys and got bitten all over. For all we know, they may have hydrophobia."

"Papa," I cried, "they think I'm going mad, and they're talking about chaining me to a fence post."

Papa chuckled and said, "Aw, I don't think we'll have to do anything like that. Those monkeys belong to a circus and came in contact with people every day. They've probably been vaccinated for all kinds of diseases. A big circus like that wouldn't have taken a chance on having a bunch of sick monkeys around."

Papa didn't know it, but he had practically brought me back from the grave. I began to feel a little better but not very much.

Regardless of what Papa had said, Daisy wasn't convinced that I wasn't going mad.

"Just the same," she said, "I'm not taking any chances. I'm going to keep my eye on him, and I'm locking the door to my room every night. If he does go mad, I don't want him sneaking in and biting me."

"Oh, for heaven's sake," Mama said, "now that will be enough out of you, young lady. You shouldn't be saying things like that."

Papa said, "I think the best thing to do right now is to get something on those monkey bites. They could get infected."

"I think so, too," Mama said.

Daisy said, "Mama, you doctor Jay Berry, and I'll take care of Rowdy. He wouldn't bite me even if he was going mad."

Mama went in the house and came back with some clean rags, a bottle of peroxide, and some iodine.

Every time Mama dabbed one of the bites with peroxide I would have a dancing fit. But when she started putting that iodine on me, I yipped and hopped all over the place. By the time she was through, I felt like I had been boiled in a washpot.

All the time Mama was doctoring me, I could hear Daisy cooing and talking to Old Rowdy. He was whimpering and whining, and licking Daisy's hands, and begging her not to put that stinging, burning stuff on him.

Daisy was a little more artistic with her doctoring than Mama was. She wrapped Rowdy's monkey bites with all kinds of bright-colored rags and tied them in bow knots. When she was through with him, he looked like a Christmas package.

Rowdy took one look at himself and was so disgusted with what he saw he scooted under the house.

I couldn't help laughing a little.

The next morning I was so sore and stiff I couldn't

get out of bed and make it to the breakfast table. I was lying there, feeling sorry for myself, and thinking about all that money down in the bottoms hopping around in those sycamore trees when Mama, Papa, and Daisy came into my room.

Papa looked at me and asked, "How do you feel?"

"I don't feel so good, Papa," I said. "I'm as sore and stiff as an old hound dog that has been chasing a fox all night."

Daisy giggled and said, "Jay Berry, if you think you're in bad shape, you should see Old Rowdy. He's so sore and stiff he can't even wiggle his tail. He wouldn't come out from under the house to eat his breakfast."

With a concerned look on her face, Mama reached over and placed her hand on my forehead.

"Why, Jay Berry," she said, "you have a little fever. I think you had better forget about this monkey catching and stay in bed for a few days."

The way I was feeling, I didn't even argue with Mama.

As if my getting eaten up by the monkeys was one of the most wonderful things that had ever happened in our family, Daisy squealed her delight and said, "Mama, if you're going to make him stay in bed for a few days, then I'll get to practice my Red Cross nursing on him again."

When I heard Daisy mention that Red Cross nursing business, I started getting out of bed.

"Oh, no, you won't," I said, "you're not practicing any of that stuff on me. I'm not sick enough to go through that again."

Placing both of her hands on my shoulders, Mama pushed me back down in the bed and said, "You just stay put, young man. Somebody has to doctor you and, besides, your little sister is a pretty good nurse."

I wanted to argue but knew that it was useless. To win an argument with both Mama and Daisy was unheard of. I figured that the misery would last for only a couple of days and I could put up with anything that long.

This Red Cross nursing business had popped up about a year back when I had had the mumps and Daisy had read me a story about a Red Cross nurse. From the day she read that story, Daisy was bound and determined that when she grew up she was going to be a Red Cross nurse. She saved enough money to order some material that was the same color as the Red Cross nurses' uniforms. With Mama's help, she made a uniform, complete with an arm band and a dinky little hat.

It got to be a common sight to see Daisy fluttering around in her nurse's uniform, doctoring everything that was sick and a lot of things that weren't sick at all. She took care of the pigs, chickens, calves, cats, birds, Rowdy, me, and everything else you could think of. She took care of all my busted toes, scratches, stone bruises, and boils. If I came down with a bad cold or the flu, Daisy would put on her uniform and go to work. I never saw anything like it.

"Mama," Daisy said, "do you think we could get Old Rowdy into Jay Berry's room? If I had both of them in the same room, it sure would help a lot. That way I could watch both of them at the same time."

Mama smiled and said, "I don't know about that. If Rowdy is as sore and stiff as you say he is, the only way we could move him would be to carry him, and that old hound is pretty heavy."

Daisy thought a second and said, "Mama, we could put him in the wheelbarrow and roll him in."

"Yes," Mama said, nodding her head, "we might be able to do that."

I felt sorry for Rowdy, but there wasn't a thing in the world I could do about it. I didn't figure they could catch him anyway. But I was wrong.

It wasn't long until I heard the screeching of our old wheelbarrow coming through the house. With Rowdy about half in the wheelbarrow and half hanging out, they wheeled him into my room. Daisy made a pallet for him over in the corner.

The next time Daisy entered my room she was all decked out in her nurse's uniform. It was starched as stiff as a gingerbread man. She had a tray in her hands. To me, it looked like she had all the medicine we had in the house on it. There was liniment, Raleigh salve, iodine, peroxide, castor oil, all kinds of clean rags torn in strips, several boxes of pills, and a glass half full of alcohol with a thermometer in it.

"Good morning!" Daisy said, smiling all over. "And how are my patients this fine morning?"

"Aw, Daisy," I said, "you didn't have to say that. You were here just five minutes ago."

"I know," Daisy said, "but that's the way the nurses do it."

Looking up to the ceiling and talking to myself, I said, "Br-r-other, if I come out of this alive, I'll sure be lucky."

Ignoring my remark, Daisy set the tray on the small table in the room and started looking over her nursing supplies.

"Let's see now," she said, "I think I have just about everything I need right now."

Rearing up on my elbows, I said, "Daisy, if you think I'm going to take all of that stuff, you're crazy. Why, I'd be dead before the sun goes down."

As if she were the best doctor in the whole wide world, Daisy said, "Oh, I don't think you'll have to take all of it, Jay Berry, but I won't know just what medicine you'll need until I examine you."

Taking the thermometer, Daisy gave it a good shaking, walked over, and dabbed it in my mouth. She felt my pulse, changed all the bandages on my monkey bites, and washed my face with a cool rag. Then she lit into Rowdy. She changed all of his bandages, washed his face, and got him a pillow to lay his head on.

I had to admit that Daisy was a pretty good nurse but it always made me feel uncomfortable lying there with her fussing around me that way.

The first time Daisy brought me a glass of water I was thirsty and drank every drop of it. Five minutes later she brought me a second glass and I drank it, too. Five minutes later she brought me the third glass and I drank it just to please her.

It didn't seem like I had hardly drunk the third glass when she came with the fourth one. By this time, I was pretty well waterlogged and refused to drink it.

With a scared look on her face, Daisy stepped back and said, "Jay Berry, are you sure you don't want any more water?"

"Sure, I'm sure," I said. "What's the matter with you, anyway?"

Before I hardly knew what was taking place, Daisy yelled, "Mama, you'd better come here right now."

Mama came running, scared half out of her wits.

Looking at me and seeing that I was still alive, she looked at Daisy and said, "What's wrong now?"

With a sorrowful look on her face, Daisy said, "I think we'd better get the chains, Mama. He just quit drinking water and you know what that means."

"No," Mama said, "I'm afraid I don't know what it means. What does it mean?"

"It means he's going mad, Mama," Daisy said. "That's what it means. I looked up the word 'hydrophobia' in the dictionary and it said very plainly that anything going mad refuses to drink water. And, he just quit drinking."

I figured that it was about time for me to say something or I would surely have to drink the well dry or be chained to a fence post.

"Mama," I all but shouted, "I haven't quit drinking water. I just can't drink any more. She's brought me a glass of water every five minutes for an hour and half. I've had so much water now that I feel like a spring."

Glancing at the glass of water Daisy held in her hand, Mama smiled and said, "I think we can forget about the chains for a while. It may be that you're overdoing this water drinking."

Rowdy put up with Daisy's nursing for one day; then he hopped out the window, went back under the house, and refused to come out for anyone.

It was three days before I saw the sunshine again and I was never so happy in all my life. I was burning up with the monkey-catching fever and couldn't wait to get after them again.

On the morning of the fourth day, I got my net and called to Rowdy. "Come on, boy," I said, "let's go to the store and have another talk with Grandpa."

Rowdy started out from under the house but he never came all the way out—just his head. On seeing the net in my hand, he turned around and went back. I saw right away that between Daisy's nursing and those monkeys, Rowdy had had it.

Getting down on my knees, I peered back under the house. I could see Rowdy way back in the farthest corner.

"Come on, boy," I coaxed, "I'm not going monkey hunting. I'm going to the store. Don't you want to come along?"

I could hear a lot of tail thumping, whimpering, and whining; but Rowdy still refused to come out. I begged and I pleaded. I promised him everything from fried rabbit to a red squirrel stew, but it did no good. Disgusted and feeling terrible, I took off down the road for Grandpa's store.

I hadn't gone far when here came Rowdy, wiggling all over and tickled to death. Once he had seen that I wasn't going to the bottoms where those monkeys were, he was willing to come along.

"You should be ashamed of yourself, Rowdy," I said. "A great big dog like you scared of little old monkeys."

I really didn't mean what I had said to Rowdy because way down deep I was just as scared of those monkeys as he was, but I was still determined to catch every last one of them.

Grandpa must have been expecting me, because just before I got to the store he came out onto the porch and looked down the road. On seeing me, he sat down in his favorite chair and waited for me.

As I walked up, he peered at me over his glasses and said, "Well, how did it go?"

"It didn't go so good, Grandpa," I said, as I leaned the net up against the store.

"Didn't the net work?" Grandpa asked.

"Oh, yes, it worked, Grandpa," I said. "It worked

just like you said it would. I caught two of the little monkeys, but they got away from me."

"Got away!" Grandpa said. "How did that happen?"

"I really don't know how it happened, Grandpa," I said. "One minute I had two in the net, and the next minute they were gone. I was pretty busy at the time and didn't see exactly what did happen."

Grandpa arched his eyebrows, and said, "Busy? What were you doing?"

"I was fighting monkeys, Grandpa," I said, "that's what I was doing. They were eating Rowdy and me up. Look!"

Stepping over close to Grandpa, I showed him the scabbed-over monkey bites on my arms and legs.

Grandpa looked me over, let out a long whistle, and said, "Boy, they sure did get ahold of you, didn't they? Did it hurt?"

"Hurt!" I said. "I'll say it hurt. It made me sick. I've been in bed for three days. I never was so sore and stiff in all my life. If you think a squirrel can bite, you just ought to get bit by a monkey."

"How did all this happen?" Grandpa asked. "Tell me about it."

I told Grandpa everything that had happened from the time I jerked the blue ring on the net until the monkeys got away. I ended up by saying, "I don't believe those monkeys can be caught."

"Oh, yes, they can," Grandpa said. "Just remember what I told you about animals. There never was one that couldn't be caught. And always keep more than one iron in the fire."

"I know, Grandpa," I said, "but I'm afraid if things keep going like they have, we're going to run out of irons and the fire's going out."

Grandpa laughed, got up from his chair, and said, "Come here—I've got something to show you."

I followed Grandpa into the store and watched while he reached up on a shelf and picked up an envelope. Waving it in front of my face, Grandpa grinned and said, "Do you know what this is?"

I shook my head.

"This is a letter from an animal trainer down in Florida," Grandpa said. "He's the fellow that trains animals for that circus. He trained that hundred dollar monkey."

"He did!" I said. "He must be a darned good trainer because that is the smartest monkey in the world. I didn't see him do it, but I'm pretty sure that while those other monkeys were chewing on Rowdy and me, he sneaked in and let those two in the net loose."

"I wouldn't doubt that a bit," Grandpa said. "He's smart enough all right. Did you know that monkey has a name?"

"A name!" I said, very surprised. "Whoever heard of a monkey having a name."

"I never gave it much thought," Grandpa said, "but after I read this letter, I got to thinking—practically all tame animals have names. Take your old milk cow, her name is Sally Gooden. Your Dad's two mules are named Fred and George. My buggy mares are named Molly and Birdie."

"I know, Grandpa," I said, "but that monkey's not tame. He's as wild as a hoot owl."

Grandpa frowned and said, "I don't believe that monkey is as wild as you think he is. Once an animal has been tamed, he doesn't ever forget it."

"What's the monkey's name, Grandpa?" I asked.

"According to what this trainer said in his letter, they call him Jimbo," Grandpa said.

"Jimbo!" I said, laughing out loud. "Whoever heard of a name like that."

"Anyhow," Grandpa said, "that's his name."

"Grandpa," I asked, "what good's it going to do us, knowing his name?"

"It might do a lot of good," Grandpa said. "This trainer says that if you could make friends with that monkey he would probably do anything you wanted him to do."

"Make friends with him!" I said. "Grandpa, I don't think that trainer knows what he's talking about. Why, you couldn't make friends with that monkey in a hundred years."

"I don't know," Grandpa said. "The trainer seems to think you could and he should know. He says to offer him something to eat, call him by name, and talk to him. It might be worth a try. After all, you have everything to gain and nothing to lose."

"Nothing to lose!" I said. "Grandpa, if I got close enough to that monkey to offer him something to eat I could lose my arm. He's got teeth like a pitchfork."

"Oh I don't think you have to worry about that," Grandpa said. "From what you've told me, he's about the only monkey in the bunch that hasn't tried to bite you."

Thinking back to everything that had happened, I realized that Grandpa was right.

"By golly, Grandpa, you're right," I said. "That Jimbo monkey hasn't tried to bite either Rowdy or me; but he sure doesn't mind sicking those little monkeys onto a fellow."

"Do you still think that this Jimbo monkey is the leader of the pack?" Grandpa asked.

"Oh, I know he is, Grandpa," I said. "Those little monkeys won't do a thing until he tells them to."

"That's fine," Grandpa said. "If you could make friends with Jimbo and get him to follow you, the little monkeys would probably follow him and you might be able to lead the whole caboodle right into the corn crib."

Grandpa made everything sound so simple and I was feeling so good I would have been willing to try to make friends with a grizzly bear. But there were a few things in my mind that I needed to get straightened out.

"Grandpa," I said, "I know that Jimbo monkey hasn't tried to bite me, but I still can't believe he's looking for any friends. In fact, I believe he's got it in for Rowdy and me. He sure acts like it."

"Naw," Grandpa said, "I don't think Jimbo has it in for anybody. His trainer says he likes people—especially youngsters. He probably thinks you've been playing games with him."

"Another thing, Grandpa," I said, "what could I say

to that monkey to make friends with him? I don't
know how to talk to a monkey."

"You might try talking to him like you do to Rowdy," Grandpa said. "Offer him an apple and call him
by his name. Don't act like you're trying to catch him.
Just act like you're trying to be friends with him."

"Do you really think it'll work, Grandpa?" I asked.

"You can't ever tell," Grandpa said. "I think it's
worth a try."

I thought a second and said, "Okay, Grandpa, I'll
give it a try. If I thought I could catch those monkeys,
I'd be willing to try anything. I sure want that pony
and .22 and this is the only chance I'll ever have to
make enough money to get them."

Looking up at the sun, Grandpa said, "It's early yet.
I think you have time to try it out today."

"I'm going to, Grandpa," I said, "just as soon as I
get home."

As I turned to be on my way, I thought of something.

"Grandpa," I asked, "how come that animal trainer
wrote to you?"

Grandpa grinned and said, "That's one of those
extra irons I was telling you about. I wrote a letter to
those circus people and got an answer from the animal
trainer."

I smiled and said, "I figured it was something like
that, Grandpa. I don't know how I can ever pay you
back for all you've done for me."

"I'll tell you how you can pay me back," Grandpa
said. "Just catch those monkeys and I'll be well paid.
Now if you can't make friends with that monkey,
don't let it bother you too much. If this doesn't work,
we'll try something else."

"Grandpa," I said, "if I can't make friends with that
monkey it won't be my fault because I'll sure be trying. I just hope no one sees me down in those bottoms
talking to a monkey. Why, they would put me in the
crazy house sure as shootin'."

Grandpa laughed and said, "Oh, I don't think anything like that's going to happen. You wouldn't sound

half as bad talking to a monkey as some of these farmers do talking to their mules."

I laughed and said, "I know what you mean, Grandpa. Sometimes I listen to Papa talking to our mules while he's working them. If I was a mule and somebody yelled 'Gee' and 'Haw' at me all day long, I wouldn't do anything. I'd have a runaway every fifteen minutes."

Grandpa said, "You have to let animals know who the boss is, or they'll take advantage of you."

"Well," I said, "I'd better be on my way. I'm anxious to see if I can make friends with that monkey."

"I am, too," Grandpa said. "Let me know how you come out."

9

I was so anxious to try out this friend-making idea, I trotted all the way home. Instead of going into the house, I went straight to the cellar and filled my pockets with apples. As I was shutting the cellar door, Daisy showed up.

Looking very concerned, she said, "Jay Berry, if you don't stop feeding our apples to those monkeys, we're not going to have any apples left. I was looking at the barrel this morning and it's sure going down."

"Aw, Daisy," I said, "you're always snooping around. We have plenty of apples."

"We won't have," Daisy said, "if you keep feeding them to those monkeys. All you're doing is making them fat."

Burning up, I said, "Daisy, if it'll make you feel any better, you can stop worrying about our apples. I probably won't be needing any more because I'm pretty sure that I'll catch those monkeys this time."

Daisy giggled and said, "Seems like I've heard that before. How are you going to catch them this time?"

"I'm going to make friends with that big monkey," I said. "He's the leader of the pack and once I get on the good side of him, I believe I can catch every one of them."

With a disgusted toss of her head, Daisy said, "Oh, for goodness sakes, Jay Berry, you can't make friends with these monkeys. Every time you get close to them they eat you up."

"You just wait and see," I said. "Don't be surprised if you see me coming in with all of those monkeys."

Daisy giggled again and said, "Jay Berry, if I see anything like that, I won't only be surprised, I'll probably faint."

"You had just as well start fainting then," I said, "because you're going to see it all right."

I wanted to get away from Daisy as soon as I could, but I lost a good thirty minutes having another go-around with Rowdy. He had followed me for a little way, but when he saw that I was going toward the bottoms he sat down on his rear and refused to come along.

I tried scolding and shaming him at first but it did no good. Rowdy just ducked his head and wouldn't even look at me. Then I tried sweet-talking him into going with me but he wouldn't budge an inch. I got around behind him, lifted up his rear end, and tried pushing him. This didn't work either because Rowdy just simply lay down.

I had one trick left and it was a good one because it had never failed. I sat down, buried my face in my arms, and made a lot of choking, sobbing sounds like I was crying. Rowdy couldn't stand this. He came over, whimpering and whining and licking me all over. I loved him up a little, got to my feet, and walked on. Rowdy came along, but his heart wasn't in it. Instead of staying in front of me, he stayed behind with his tail between his legs.

I always felt guilty fooling my old dog that way, but the idea of going anywhere close to those monkeys without him was something I wouldn't even consider.

I waited until I was a good way into the bottoms before I started my monkey calling. Taking an apple from my pocket, I held it out in front of me and called, "Here, Jimbo! Come on, boy! I have an apple for you."

I never felt so silly in all my life. I was blushing all

over and could almost feel a hundred people watching me.

Not seeing or hearing anything, I walked a little way on the game trail, stopped, and started calling again. "Here, Jimbo! Where are you, boy? Come on now!"

The only thing my calling attracted that time was an old hog that nearly scared me to death. With a loud grunt, he took off through the bottoms, popping the brush.

"Rowdy," I said, in a quavering voice, "what's the matter with that crazy old hog? He must think I'm a bear or something."

Grumbling to myself about how scary hogs were, I walked on a little way, stopped, and started calling again. "Come on, Jimbo! I'm over here! Come on now!"

Rowdy couldn't understand what was going on. He knew that I was calling something, but I wasn't using his name, and he was all mixed up. On hearing him whimper, I looked behind me and saw him sitting on his rear in the game trail, with his ears standing straight up, looking at me with a puzzled expression in his friendly old eyes.

Still burned up about that old hog scaring me, I said, "Rowdy, if you keep looking at me like that, I'll send you to the house. It may sound crazy to you, but I'm calling a monkey and I don't know any other way to call one."

I was walking along; calling, looking, and listening for monkeys when all at once I smelled something. It was a sweet-sour odor, and I recognized it right away, for I had smelled it before. Somewhere close by there was a whiskey still, and what I was smelling was the odor of fermenting sour mash.

"Rowdy," I said, "some moonshiners have set up a whiskey still down here in the bottoms. I bet it belongs to those Gravely boys. They couldn't sleep good if they didn't have an old whiskey still stuck around somewhere."

I had found several stills while prowling the hills

and river bottoms, but I always kept my mouth shut about finding them. I had learned that it wasn't a good idea for anyone to start blabbing about the location of a whiskey still. The moonshiners didn't like it at all. I always figured that I had enough trouble of my own, and didn't care to have a bunch of moonshiners chasing me all over the country.

I was standing there, sniffing the air to locate the direction of the whiskey still so I could stay away from it, when I heard that Jimbo monkey let out a loud squall. Then I heard the little monkeys screeching and chattering, and making all kinds of racket.

"Listen to that, Rowdy," I said. "That's the most noise I've heard those monkeys make. They must really be having a good time. I wonder what they are doing now."

Leaving the game trail, I started picking my way through the underbrush in the direction of the commotion. As I walked along, I noticed that the odor of whiskey mash was getting stronger and stronger.

I found the monkeys and the whiskey still at the same time. I was so shocked by what I saw I dropped the apple I was holding in my hand. I just stood there with my mouth open, looking things over, and trying to figure out what was going on.

Jimbo was standing up close to a mash barrel with a tin can in one paw and holding onto the rim of the barrel with the other paw. He was looking straight at us and didn't seem to be either mad or scared.

Taking my eyes off Jimbo, I looked at the little monkeys. They were milling around the whiskey still: screeching, chattering, and chasing each other. They seemed to be having a lot of fun. Some were lying on the ground, rolling over and over, and kicking up the dust. They didn't seem to care the least bit about Rowdy and me being there.

"Rowdy," I whispered, "there's something wrong with these monkeys. They're not acting right."

Just then one little monkey, no bigger than a small cat, climbed up onto the rim of a mash barrel. He stood there for a second squealing his head off; then he leaned over, and kerplunk, he fell in the barrel.

This scared me, because I could just see a two dollar bill drowning itself in a whiskey mash barrel. I was just about to dash over and lend the little fellow a helping hand when Jimbo let out a squall, darted over to the barrel, reached in with his long arm, caught the little monkey by the scruff of his neck, lifted him out, and set him down on the ground.

The little monkey was a mess. He was sopping wet and covered with foam from the fermenting mash. Immediately about a dozen other monkeys darted over and started licking him all over. The little fellow just squatted there on the ground, all humped up, with his eyes closed, and let the other monkeys lick away.

I was laughing and watching what was going on when I realized why the monkeys were acting so strangely.

"Holy smokes, Rowdy," I said, "no wonder these monkeys are acting so funny. They've been drinking that sour mash and they're all drunk. Look at them."

I wasn't too surprised, because I knew that practically all animals were fond of the stuff that went into the making of sour mash.

Rowdy was watching the monkeys and I could tell by his actions that no matter if they were drunk or sober, he wasn't having anything to do with them.

Picking up the apple I had dropped, I said, "Rowdy, you stay here. I'm going to see if I can't make friends with Jimbo. But I'll tell you one thing, if those monkeys jump on me and you run out on me, I'll make you sleep in the corn crib with Daisy's cats for ninety days and nights."

Rowdy couldn't get along with cats at all.

Holding the apple out toward Jimbo, I took a few steps and said, "Come on, Jimbo. Look what I've brought you. Come on now. Let's be friends."

Jimbo didn't make a move. He just stood there, holding the tin can in his paw, blinking his eyes, looking first at me and then the apple.

I was so scared I was shaking like a corn tassel in a high wind. If Jimbo had opened his big mouth and jumped at me, I would have fainted dead away. But I had the feeling that he had recognized his name and was more curious than mad.

Taking a few more steps toward him, I said, "Come on, Jimbo. Here's an apple for you. Come on now. I'm not going to hurt you."

That time I got a little reaction out of Jimbo. Bouncing up and down on his short stubby legs, he pushed out his rubbery lips into the shape of an "o" and grunted at me a few times.

I smiled and said, "I don't know what you're saying, Jimbo, but whatever it is, it sounds all right to me. Just don't get mad now and everything will be all right."

With my confidence built up, I eased over quite close to Jimbo, held the apple out to him, and said, "Look what I brought you, Jimbo. Come on now, let's stop fighting each other and be friends. I'm not going to hurt you."

As if he were trying to read my mind, Jimbo just stood there with no expression at all on his face, looking me straight in the eye. Then dropping the tin can he was holding in his paw, he reached over and took the apple from my hand. I wouldn't have been more pleased if I had found a bottle with a genie in it.

All the time that Jimbo was eating the apple, I kept talking to him. I told him what a smart monkey he was and how much I'd like to be his friend.

Because I had given him an apple Jimbo decided that he wanted to give me something. Picking up the tin can, he reached down in a barrel, filled it full of sour mash, and offered it to me.

I smiled and said, "That's all right, Jimbo. You don't owe me a thing. Besides, I don't think I'd like that stuff."

My refusing to take the can of sour mash made Jimbo madder than I had ever seen him. He threw the can to the ground and started grunting, squalling, and bouncing all over the place. Then he started throwing sticks and dirt at me; and everything else he could get his paws on.

Some of the little monkeys came over to show their dislike of me. They stood up on their skinny hind legs; screeching and chattering, and showing their teeth. By refusing Jimbo's offering of sour mash, you would have thought that I had committed the one sin that was unforgivable by all monkeys.

I backed off to one side and waited until the monkeys quieted down a little. Then I started talking to Jimbo again.

"I don't know what you're getting mad for, Jimbo," I said. "I didn't do anything. Come on now, let's not fight each other. Let's be friends."

There was one thing I could say for Jimbo, he had an awful lot of determination. He picked up the can, filled it full of sour mash, and again offered it to me.

I would no more have refused the can of sour mash that time than Santa Claus would have whipped one of his reindeer. The last thing in the world that I wanted to do was to make Jimbo mad. I didn't figure that I would have to drink it anyway. I figured that if I took it, Jimbo would be satisfied, and everything would be all right.

How wrong I was. Jimbo didn't seem to like the idea of my just standing there, holding the can of mash in my hand. He started getting mad again. Looking me straight in the eye, and waving his long arms in the air, he started grunting and squalling.

It was plain to see that he wanted me to drink some of the stuff.

"All right, all right, Jimbo!" I said in desperation. "Don't get mad again. If it'll make you feel any better, I'll have a little drink with you."

I tipped the can up and took a couple of swallows.

Jimbo couldn't have been any more pleased than he would have been if he had just found a bushel of apples. He grunted, clapped his paws, and turned a few somersaults.

At first, the sour mash tasted so nasty I thought I was going to get sick. Then all at once it didn't taste so nasty any more. My tongue and throat started tingling and tickling, and my stomach got as warm as eggs in an incubator. I burped a couple of times and said to no one in particular, "Well, what do you know! That stuff doesn't taste half as bad as I thought it would."

I sat down on a stump, tipped the can up again, and took about three swallows that time.

From the brush where he was hiding, Rowdy could see that I was getting along all right with the monkeys. He came crawling out of the brush on his stomach, heading straight for me. He always was jealous if I talked to or petted any kind of an animal. He couldn't even stand to see me petting an old hog, or a cat.

I held my breath and watched to see what the monkeys would do. They kept their eyes on Rowdy, but made no effort to jump on him.

In every way that he could, Rowdy was showing those monkeys that he was the friendliest hound dog in the world. His long tail was fanning the air, and he was whimpering and inching along on the ground, one foot at a time. He was a very pleased dog when he finally made it over to me all in one piece and sat down by my side.

To show Rowdy that he also wanted to be his friend, Jimbo found another can, filled it full of sour mash, and set it down on the ground right in front of his nose.

Rowdy always did figure that anything I ate or drank was plenty good enough for him. He leaned over and stuck the tip of his long pink tongue into the sour mash and then looked at me.

"You see, Rowdy," I said, "that stuff doesn't taste half bad, does it? Go ahead and help yourself."

Rowdy must have liked the taste of sour mash, for he lapped up the whole can. Jimbo was the best bartender that ever was. Every time our cans were emptied, he saw to it that they were filled again.

By this time I was feeling so good I wanted to sing. Waving the can of sour mash and tapping the ground with my foot, I sang all the songs I knew and made up a few more.

Because I was singing, Rowdy decided that he, too, would sing a little. Lifting his old head high in the air, he started howling a hound-dog tune.

Not to be left out of any of the merrymaking, the monkeys gathered around us, screeching and chattering. Jimbo danced all over the place, clapping his paws, squalling, grunting, and turning somersaults.

The first thing I knew, monkeys were climbing all over me. They poked around in my ears with tickly little fingers, explored my eyes, nose, and mouth. I had a giggling fit when they ran their arms down the back of my shirt.

Rowdy was going through the same thing I was. Monkeys were all around him, looking through the hair on his body as if they were searching for fleas. They lifted up his long floppy ears and peered down in them. They played with his tail, crawled upon his back, lifted up his lips, and inspected his teeth.

Rowdy was really enjoying his new-found friends. With friendly whimpers, he was lapping every monkey he could reach with his long pink tongue.

I never knew when I went to sleep, but I sure knew when I woke up. It was late in the evening and I was as cold as a bullfrog. My stomach felt as if I had swallowed a handful of cockleburs and I was sicker than I had ever been in my life. My head felt as big as a wagon wheel. It was pounding and throbbing, and felt like it was going to split wide open any second.

I couldn't see very well and what I could see seemed to be all out of focus. There must have been a hundred different trees in the bottoms but they all looked alike to me. Every one of them was leaning way over—sideways.

I thought that if I could close my eyes and give my head a good shake it might straighten things out a little. I tried it and squalled like a stepped-on cat with the pain. My head felt as if it had exploded, and I was sure that my eyeballs had popped right out onto the ground.

I couldn't understand why I was so cold. My teeth were chattering and I had goose bumps all over me. When I finally did discover why I was so cold, I jumped straight up and hollered in a loud voice, "Hey, my britches are gone!"

I still had my shirt and shorts but that didn't cover up very much of me because Mama never did make my shirts long enough. I looked all around for my britches, but they were nowhere to be seen.

Rowdy was lying on the ground about five feet away, sound asleep.

"Rowdy!" I said in a loud voice. "Wake up! You're a heck of a watchdog. You laid there sound asleep, and let someone steal my britches. Wake up now, and help me find them before someone sees me like this."

Rowdy got to his feet, but then he just groaned and lay down again. He didn't seem to care if I found my britches or not.

"I know you're sick, Rowdy," I said, "but you're not any sicker than I am. Now you get up from there, and help me find my britches. It'll soon be dark and I can't be running around in these bottoms half naked like this."

Rowdy got to his feet again but made no effort to walk. He just stood there, stiff as a board, with his head down, and his legs spraddled out.

I started over to see if I could help him, but something went wrong. I couldn't seem to walk straight, and kept angling off to one side. I missed Rowdy by a good five feet, and had to grab hold of a sapling to keep from falling down. I was drunk and that's all there was to it.

After a lot of grunting and whimpering, Rowdy got his feet to working and started over to see if he could help me a little. But he seemed to be in about the same shape I was in. He wobbled all over the place and his rear end kept trying to get ahead of his front end.

"Boy, Rowdy," I said, holding my throbbing head in my hands, "I didn't know that sour mash would make a fellow like this. I thought it had to be made into whiskey first before it could make you drunk."

I had forgotten all about the monkeys, and when they did cross my mind, I started looking for them. I looked all around the whiskey still and up in the trees but there wasn't a monkey around. It was so still in the bottoms that all I could hear was the gurgling of sour mash fermenting in the barrels. The very sound of that stuff gurgling made me sicker than ever.

"Rowdy," I said, "I can't understand where my britches went. I don't think anyone would want them because they were patched all over. I wonder if that Jimbo monkey took them off me and ran away with them. I'll bet anything, that's what happened. Now I know why he kept pouring that sour mash down us. He wanted to get us drunk so he could take my britches."

Up until that time I hadn't given much thought about how I was going to explain to Mama about losing my britches. When I did think about it, I got really shook up. There just wasn't any way that I could explain anything like that to Mama.

As far back as I could remember, Rowdy and I had run along those game trails like two wild deer. But on that day, the trail didn't seem to be any bigger than a twine string. The only way I could stay on it was by holding to the bushes on each side.

Rowdy was behind me and was having all kinds of trouble. He just couldn't seem to keep himself pointed in the right direction.

We finally made it to the rail fence around our field and there we ran into another problem. Rowdy and I had jumped that old rail fence a thousand times, but that day the fence looked like it was twenty feet high.

Rowdy didn't even try to jump the fence. He found a wide place between two rails, low to the ground, and wiggled his way through.

I made it to the top of the fence in pretty good shape, then something went wrong. I got dizzy and fell off. For a few seconds, I thought sure that I had broken my neck.

When I finally reached the gate going into our yard, I thought I had it made, but just as I opened the gate, all my luck ran off and left me. Daisy came around the corner of the house on her crutch; humming a silly little tune. She took one look at me standing there half naked, and by the expression on her face, you would have thought that she had stepped on a snake. Her mouth flew open and she gasped like she had swallowed a butterfly.

"Jay Berry," she said, in a loud voice, "where on earth are your britches? It's not very nice to run around half naked like that. What's the matter with you anyway?"

I didn't say a word. There wasn't anything I could say. I just groaned way down deep, wrapped both arms around the gate post, and held on.

Daisy came over, peered at me, and said, "Jay Berry, you're as white as an egg. Are you sick?"

"Sick?" I said. "Daisy, I'm sicker than I've ever been in my life. I think I'm dying."

When I told Daisy that I thought I was dying, it scared her. She caught hold of my arm and said, "Here, let me help you into the house."

Before I could unwind myself from the gate post, Daisy turned loose of my arm, stepped back, and said, "Phew! What's that I smell?"

I didn't say anything and wouldn't even look at her.

Daisy stuck her nose up close to me and started sniffing. With a frown on her face, she stepped back, and said in a disgusted voice, "Jay Berry, you're not sick. You're drunk. You smell just like an old whiskey bottle."

"I can't help it if I am drunk," I said. "I'm sick just the same."

Looking toward the house, Daisy yelled in a voice louder than I had ever heard her yell, "Mama, Mama, come and look at Jay Berry! He's as drunk as a boiled owl and naked as a jaybird."

Mama must have had a pot in her hands when she heard Daisy yell, because I heard something hit the floor with a loud bang and clatter its way across the floor.

I wanted to run but knew if I ever turned loose of the fence post, I would probably fall flat on my face.

Mama came sailing out of the house, looking more surprised than she did the time she found the young hoot owl I had put under an old sitting hen that had just hatched a bunch of chicks.

In the late evening shadows and with me being hugged up so close to the fence post, Mama didn't see me right away. She looked at Daisy and said, "Daisy, what did you say?"

"Look at him, Mama," Daisy said, pointing her finger at me. "He's so drunk, he's cross-eyed, and he's lost his britches. Can you imagine anything like that?"

"No," Mama said in a slow, cold voice, "I can't imagine anything like that."

"Go smell him, Mama," Daisy said. "He smells just like an old whiskey bottle, and you can see for yourself that he's lost his britches."

With a deep frown on her face and an uncertain look in her eyes, Mama came and looked me over from my head to my feet. Then she grabbed me by the arm, shook me a little, and said in a very hard voice, "Jay Berry, are you drunk?"

"I guess I am, Mama," I said, "but I didn't mean to."

"Didn't mean to!" Mama shouted. "What kind of an excuse is that? Who gave you that whiskey anyway? You tell me now! Somebody is going to get into trouble over this. Did those Gravely boys get you drunk?"

"I haven't seen the Gravely boys, Mama," I said. "That Jimbo monkey got me drunk."

"Oh, for heaven's sake, Jay Berry," Mama said, "you don't expect me to believe that, do you?"

"It's the truth, Mama," I said. "There's a whiskey still down in the bottoms. That's where I found the monkeys. They were drinking sour mash and I guess

I had a few drinks with them. I didn't know that stuff would make you drunk."

"What happened to your britches?" Mama asked.

"I don't know, Mama," I said. "I went to sleep and when I woke up they were gone. I think that Jimbo monkey got away with them."

Just then Daisy let out a squeal and said, "Look, Mama! Rowdy's drunk, too!"

Poor old Rowdy. He could tell by the tone of Mama's voice that the fat was in the fire, and he was trying very hard to disappear altogether. He was trying his best to get under the porch.

Mama looked at Rowdy, and then, looking up the heavens, she closed her eyes and said, "Dear Lord, what have I done to deserve this?"

Grabbing me by my left ear, Mama said, "Come on, young man, you're going to bed. Your monkey-hunting days are over. I've had all I can take."

Mama wasn't any too gentle about putting me to bed. She just kind of wadded me up and crammed me down under the covers. I fell asleep immediately.

I woke up sometime during the night and heard Mama talking to Papa and she sounded as if she was real upset. I heard her say, "As far as I know, he's never lied to me, but I just can't believe that a bunch of monkeys could get a boy drunk. I still think that someone got him drunk."

Papa laughed and said, "No, I don't think so. I know there's a still down in the bottoms because while I'm working the fields and if the wind is right, I can smell the sour mash."

Mama said, "I don't care if there are a hundred stills down there. Whoever heard of a bunch of monkeys getting a boy drunk?"

"It probably happened just like he said it did," Papa said. "Those monkeys found that still and you know as well as I do that most animals love sour mash. It's made of everything that animals like— sugar, corn, malt, and yeast. There's probably more to this than we know. I'll have a talk with him in the morning and find out all about it."

"You had better talk to him," Mama said. "I don't think I can take any more of this monkey business. Why, if that monkey is as smart as everyone seems to think he is, he might catch Jay Berry down on the river and drown him."

Papa laughed and said, "Aw, I don't think anything like that's going to happen."

Mama never should have said anything about Jimbo drowning me because after I went back to sleep, I had a horrible dream. I dreamed that the monkeys caught Rowdy and me down in the bottoms. Then they threw us down a deep well that was about half full of ice-cold water. Rowdy and I were swimming for our lives. I could see all the monkeys looking down at us and laughing. I woke up swimming all over the bed.

10

I woke up the next morning with a pounding headache and twice as sick as I had been the day before. My whole body screamed for water and my throat was so dry I had to jiggle my Adam's apple three or four times before I could swallow. I had such a nasty taste in my mouth it reminded me of the time I had eaten some green persimmons.

When I first opened my eyes I couldn't remember a thing. For a few seconds, I didn't even know where I was. Everything I looked at was going round and round and round. Then, little by little, the spinning stopped and things started coming back to me—the monkeys, the whiskey still, drinking the sour mash, and the loss of my britches. The more I thought about everything that had happened to me, the more ashamed I became. I tried covering my face with a pillow but that didn't blot out a thing.

I was lying there, feeling sorry for myself, and wondering how Rowdy was making out, when Papa and Daisy came into my room.

Papa smiled and said, "How do you feel?"

"I'm sick, Papa," I said. "I'm sick enough to die."

Papa laughed and said, "Oh, I don't think you'll die. You may think you will, but you won't. In a day or two, you'll be as good as new."

"Papa," I said, "I didn't know that sour mash would

make you drunk. I thought that it had to be made
into whiskey first."

Shaking his head, Papa said, "Oh, no! Sour mash
will make you just as drunk as whiskey does and twice
as sick. Once that stuff gets down in your stomach, it
just keeps on fermenting and you'll be sick."

Up until then Daisy hadn't opened her mouth.
She just stood there looking disgusted, and listening to
Papa. Turning to leave the room, she said, "Well, I
guess I'd better get busy because it looks like I have
my work cut out for me."

I was so sick that I didn't pay much attention to
what Daisy had said; but I should have known that I
was in for another one of her Red Cross go-arounds,
and that's all there was to it.

I didn't have to worry about Mama paying me a
visit because she was really put out with me. This
didn't bother me too much because Mama's mad
spells never did last very long. My mama was just
about like any other boy's mama. She would stay mad
at me for a little while and then she'd start feeling
sorry for me and everything would be all right.

Papa said, "I can't understand why you drank that
sour mash. I know that you found stills before and I'm
pretty sure you didn't drink any of the mash."

"I didn't, Papa," I said. "That was the first time I
ever drank anything like that. Everything happened
so fast. The first thing I knew Rowdy and I were
both drinking it like water."

Papa sat down on my bed and said, "Suppose you
start at the beginning, and tell me all about it. I'd like
to know just what did go on down in those bottoms."

I could always talk to Papa much better than I
could to Mama. It seemed that he could understand
me better. I figured it was because he, too, had once
been a boy. I told Papa everything that had happened, but I was so ashamed about losing my britches,
I didn't look him in the eye while I was telling it.

Papa laughed and said, "To me it looks like that
Jimbo monkey wanted to get you and Rowdy drunk so

he could steal your britches. What do you suppose he did with them?"

"I don't know, Papa," I said. "He could be wearing them for all I know. I wouldn't put anything past that monkey."

Papa said, "Well, I can't see where there's been too much harm done, but I don't believe I'd tie into that sour mash any more. It might get to be a habit, and that's not good at all."

"Papa," I said, "you don't have to worry about me. I won't be drinking any more sour mash or any other kind of whiskey as long as I live. If drinking makes a fellow as sick as I am, I won't ever drink it again. I mean that, too."

Papa smiled and said, "You know, if a fellow can learn something through experience when he's young, he doesn't ever forget it."

"I won't ever forget this, Papa," I said, "and if I ever get ahold of that Jimbo monkey he won't forget it either."

Papa laughed and said, "I've always figured that a man can do almost anything if he puts his mind to it and doesn't ever give up."

"I won't ever give up," I said. "I'll catch that monkey if I have to chase him clear to Arkansas."

Getting up from the bed, Papa looked at his watch and said, "Your mother and I are going to the store today. Is there anything you want me to tell your grandpa?"

"Just tell him that I'll be up to see him in a day or two, and that we'll have to figure out some other way to catch those monkeys."

Papa smiled and said, "I don't suppose you want me to tell him about how you lost your britches, do you?"

"Aw, I don't care, Papa," I said. "Mama will tell Grandma all about it, and she will tell Grandpa. As long as we keep it in the family, I don't mind so much; but I sure wouldn't want anyone else to know about it."

Chuckling to himself, Papa left the room. It wasn't

long until I heard our old wagon leave and screech
its way up the road.

I had just about dozed off when, to my surprise,
Daisy came into my room. She was all decked out in
that silly-looking Red Cross uniform and was carrying
a tray with a large bottle of castor oil and an empty
water glass sitting on it. I could see that she had a
book tucked under her arm.

I thought, "Oh, no! If she gives me a dose of castor
oil, and then starts reading to me, I will surely die."

It was the same old thing that I had gone through
a hundred times. Smiling all over, Daisy said, "Good
morning! And how is my patient this fine morning?"

"Oh, for heaven's sake, Daisy," I said. "Please! I'm
too sick to go through any Red Cross business this
time. I don't believe I could stand it. I thought that
you went to the store with Mama and Papa. You always do. How come you didn't go this time?"

"Oh, I wanted to go," Daisy said. "I wanted to go
very much; but, Jay Berry, a good nurse never leaves
a sick patient."

"You didn't have to stay here just because of me," I
said. "I'm not that sick. I never will be that sick."

For all the attention Daisy paid to my protests, I
may as well have been talking to a post oak stump.
Taking her thermometer, she startled shaking it. I just
groaned and crawled way down under the covers.

Daisy started pulling at the quilts, saying, "Jay
Berry, you're acting like a little baby. You sit up here
now and let me examine you."

"Go away!" I shouted. "I'll be all right if you'll
just go away and leave me alone."

For a few seconds there was complete silence. Then
I heard Daisy say, "Well, it says in my nursing book
that when a patient gets unruly, a nurse is supposed
to be stern."

Reaching down under the covers, Daisy grabbed a
handful of my hair. I was squalling like a scared
chicken as I was pulled to the head of my bed, and
propped to a sitting position with a pillow.

"Now," Daisy said, sticking the thermometer into

my mouth, "if you'll just be patient, this will be over in a few minutes."

I was too sick to fight any more. "All right," I mumbled. "If I die, it'll be your fault."

Daisy smiled and said, "Jay Berry, you won't die. You may think you will, but you won't. In a day or two, you'll be as good as new, I hope."

"You're just saying that because you heard Papa say it," I said.

"No, I'm not!" Daisy said. "I'm saying it because I'm a nurse, and nurses are supposed to cheer up their patients."

I knew all too well that once Daisy had gotten into one of her Red Cross nursing spells, it was ridiculous to even think of trying to argue her out of it. So I just groaned, closed my eyes, and sat there while she looked me over.

Counting silently, Daisy took my pulse. Then she looked at my eyeballs, felt of my brow, and tapped around on me with her fingers. She even laid her ear on my chest and listened to my heart beat. From the expression on her face, I seemed to be in pretty good shape until she took the thermometer from my mouth and looked at it.

Frowning and letting out a low whistle, Daisy said, "Boy, Jay Berry, you have a fever. Why, it almost busted this thermometer."

This scared me a little. I knew that I was sick, but I didn't think that I was sick enough to bust a thermometer.

Daisy said, "Let me see your tongue."

By this time, I was getting a little bit on the nervous side. Without any protest, I stuck my tongue out as far as I could.

Daisy looked at it, and making a sour face she said, "Yuck! Jay Berry, your tongue is so coated, it looks just like the inside of Papa's shaving mug."

This really shook me up.

"Is that bad?" I asked.

"Oh, it's not too bad," Daisy said, "but it's bad enough. I think I know what's causing it."

"You do!" I said. "What's causing it?"

Daisy said, "Remember what Papa said about your stomach being full of that old sour mash. As long as it's in there, you'll just stay sick, and your tongue will be coated."

"Daisy," I said, "I'm sick all over but it's not my tongue that's sick. What are you going to do now?"

"I don't know," Daisy said as she reached over and picked up the book she had brought with her when she came into my room.

I saw that it was her nursing book.

Daisy wet her thumb on her tongue and started thumbing through the pages.

"Jay Berry," she said, "I don't know a thing about doctoring a drunk. I've looked all through my nursing book and can't find anything that tells me how. But I know that somewhere in here, I've read where it does tell how to keep a patient's tongue from being coated."

"Daisy," I said, "you don't think that I'm a drunk, do you? Just bcause I got drunk once, doesn't mean that I'm a drunk, does it?"

"I'm not too sure about that," Daisy said, still turning pages and not looking at me. "From what I've heard and read that's the way drunkards get started. They have one drink and then they have to have another one, and another, and another. And pretty soon they're drinking it by the barrel."

"Daisy," I said, very seriously, "if I live through this, you won't have to worry about me ever drinking any more mash or whiskey. I promise that. Why, I'll even cross my heart and hope to die."

With a very sad look on her face, Daisy said, "I hope not, Jay Berry. I sure would hate for us to grow up and have people see you staggering down the street and say 'That's that old drunkard, Jay Berry Lee. He's Daisy Lee's brother.' I don't believe I could stand that. I just wouldn't put up with it. I'd tell people that I didn't even know you."

"Aw, Daisy," I cried, "I'm so sick now, I'm not an inch from the grave and you keep talking about all of those old bad things. I thought you said that nurses were supposed to cheer up their patients, not bury them."

Just then Daisy's face lit up and she said, "Ah, here it is."

She sat down on the foot of my bed and started reading in silence. Finally, after what seemed like a week to me, Daisy sighed, closed her book, and said, "Jay-Berry, I think what you need is a big dose of castor oil."

I always did think that the very thought of castor oil was enough to make a buzzard sick. "Castor oil!" I said. "Why, Daisy, I couldn't take any of that nasty stuff. All you think about is castor oil. If I even mash my finger, the first thing you do is grab that old castor oil bottle."

"Aw, Jay Berry," Daisy said, taking the stopper from the bottle, "castor oil isn't hard to take. If you just close your eyes and swallow, you can't even taste it."

"I can taste the darn stuff," I said. "I can taste it even before I take it."

Holding the bottle about a foot above the glass, Daisy started pouring. The very sight of that slick, slimy-looking stuff gurgling down into the glass was more than my poor old sick stomach could bear. I jumped out of bed, flew to a window, and threw up all over the place.

As I was crawling back into bed, Daisy giggled and said, "Jay Berry, I'm a much better nurse than you think I am. I knew that I'd have trouble getting you to take castor oil, so I did the next best thing. I just let you see some of it. I figured if you saw some of it that would be enough to get you to rid yourself of that old sour mash. It sure worked, didn't it? I bet you're feeling better, aren't you?"

"I guess I am," I said, "but if you really want to do something for me, go and bring me about a gallon of good cool water."

Daisy giggled and said, "Aw, Jay Berry, you couldn't drink a gallon of water, could you?"

"You just think I couldn't," I said. "I believe that I could drink ten gallons."

"Well," Daisy said, "if you think that you can drink that much water, there's no use in bringing it in a glass. I'll just bring the water bucket."

That's what she did, and stood there watching while I drank three dippers of water.

"Boy," Daisy said, "if you and Rowdy keep drinking water like that, we'll be lucky if we have any left around here."

"How is Rowdy getting along?" I asked.

Daisy frowned and said, "I don't know how he's getting along. He won't let me get close to him."

Surprised at this, I said, "Won't let you get close to him? What's the matter with him?"

"I don't know," Daisy said. "He went out to the barn lot and dug him a deep hole down in that damp ground under the watering trough. About every ten minutes he crawls out of his hole, rears up on the trough, and drinks water. Every time I go out there to see about him, he growls and shows his teeth. I can't get close to him."

"Did you have that nurse's uniform on when you went out to see about him?" I asked.

"Jay Berry," Daisy said, "a nurse always has her uniform on when she's doing her work. You should know that much."

I laughed and laughed even if it did hurt my old head.

"Daisy," I said, "Rowdy is no fool. He knows what that uniform means as much as I do. He's sick and he doesn't want you messing with him."

"I don't care," Daisy said. "I'm going out there one more time and if he growls at me, I'm going to take a bucket and fill that hole full of water with him in it."

"You'd better not," I said. "He's liable to chase you up a tree."

Sure enough, it wasn't long until I heard a big racket out in the barn lot. Rowdy was barking and whimpering, and Daisy was yelling and scolding.

Pretty soon everything quieted down and I knew that Old Rowdy had been overpowered and was getting the Red Cross treatment. I felt sorry for my old dog, but there wasn't a thing in the world I could do about it. I just pulled the covers up over my head and went to sleep.

Papa was right when he said that in a day or two I'd be as good as new. On the morning of the second day, I crawled out of bed feeling almost like my old self again. Oh, I was still a little nervous and a bit wobbly on my feet, but otherwise I felt pretty good.

As I walked into the kitchen, the family was just sitting down to the breakfast table. Papa and Daisy started whooping and clapping their hands like they hadn't seen me for ten years.

I knew they were kidding me so I grinned, sat down, and helped myself to a double portion of everything on the table.

Eying my loaded plate, Papa smiled and said, "When a fellow starts eating like that, he sure isn't sick."

"Oh, I feel pretty good now, Papa," I said.

Right away Mama started laying the law down to me about my drinking. She told me that if I ever did anything like that again I could just pack my clothes and leave, and I could take that drunken old hound dog with me when I left.

Daisy giggled and said, "Mama, if Jay Berry does leave home, he won't have to do much packing. Those monkeys got away with about everything he owns. Why, they even got away with his britches this time."

I wanted to argue with Mama and Daisy but I realized that I didn't have a leg to stand on. So I just sat there, mad all over, hating monkeys, and more determined than ever to catch every last one of them if it took me until Gabriel blew his horn.

Mama said, "I guess I'll have to stop my work and make you another pair of britches."

Papa laughed and said, "It looks like I'm going to be minus another pair of my overalls."

Overalls in our family really got a good wearing out. Mama made mine from the backs of the ones that Papa wore. Papa wore out the front and I wore out the back.

"Jay Berry," Daisy said, "Old Rowdy's in pretty good shape now. I finally got him to drink some warm milk and I gave him a good cold bath in the watering trough."

As soon as I had eaten my breakfast, I went out to the barn lot and sure enough there was Rowdy just lying on the ground and looking as if he didn't have a friend left in the world.

I walked over and patted my old dog on his head, and said, "I know how you feel, boy. In fact, I don't see how you made it with Daisy messing with you."

Rowdy was so sad he wouldn't even wag his tail.

"Come on, boy," I coaxed, "I'm going to the store to have another talk with Grandpa about those monkeys, and he might give you a meat rind." That was all it took to get him to come with me.

On my way to the store, I stopped to watch a sight that all but left me breathless. To my right, from far up on a hillside, there was a loud gobbling and a beating of heavy wings. Then up out of that green blanket and into the sky rose a flock of wild turkeys. I blinked my eyes at the burst of fiery bronze as they winged their way through the bright rays of the morning sun. Rowdy and I watched until they faded from sight in the thick timber of the river bottoms.

"Boy, Rowdy," I said, "wasn't that something to see. You just wait until I get that gun. We'll have an old gobbler on our kitchen table for breakfast, dinner, and supper every day until I'm old and gray-headed."

A little farther along, just as Rowdy and I rounded a bend in the road, I stopped and stared in wonderment at the sight directly ahead. Here and there on the long sloping hillside, milky white splotches stood out like spilt buckets of milk in the deep green. The

Ozarks' most beautiful flowers, the dogwoods, were in full bloom. Mixed in with the green and white, the deep glare of redbuds gleamed like railroad flares in the dewy morning.

As I stood there drinking in all of that beauty, I said, "Rowdy, Daisy says that the Old Man of the Mountains is taking care of everything in the hills. If he is, he must have worked a long time painting that picture."

I had been so busy looking at all of that Ozark beauty I had forgotten about the monkeys. When I did think about them, I said, "Holy smokes, Rowdy, we better stop this gawking around and get on to the store. Grandpa will think that we're never coming."

To make up for lost time, I started off in a dog trot.

Grandpa wasn't in his store when Rowdy and I arrived, but I knew that he was around somewhere because the door was wide open. Then I heard a loud banging coming from the barn. I walked over and found him putting a new spoke in one of his buckboard wheels.

As Rowdy and I walked up, Grandpa smiled and said, "Hi!"

"Hi, Grandpa!" I said.

With a sly look on his friendly old face, Grandpa looked all around and then leaning over close to me he whispered, "I've got a jug hid there in the corn crib. Would you care for a little drink?"

I knew that Grandpa was kidding me, so I grinned and said, "Aw, Grandpa, you know I'm not a drinking man."

Grandpa said, "Well, I didn't think you were, but your papa told me that you and Rowdy got on a pretty good tooter."

"I guess we did, Grandpa," I said, "but it wasn't our fault. That Jimbo monkey got us drunk. It seems like every time we get close to those monkeys they make fools of us. Why, they even stole my britches this time and I never will live that down."

Grandpa exploded in laughter. He laughed and he laughed. He laughed so hard that great big tears boiled out of his eyes and ran all over his face.

I even laughed a little myself, but I wasn't laughing about losing my britches. I was laughing at Grandpa.

Rowdy thought that because Grandpa and I were laughing we were happy and so he got happy, too. He wiggled and twisted all over the place.

Grandpa finally got over his laughing spell and reached for his old red handkerchief. He took off his glasses, wiped them, and then blew his nose.

"Now that we've had a good laugh," he said, "I think it's time we started thinking about catching those monkeys. We can't let them get away with stealing a fellow's britches."

"Grandpa," I said, "I haven't done anything but think about those monkeys and my thinker is just about wore out. I don't know what to do now. I've tried everything from a to z, and I haven't caught one yet."

"Oh, I don't think we've tried everything yet," Grandpa said. "There's a lot of space between a and z. Now, here's what you do. You go on home and be ready about daybreak in the morning. I'll come by in my buckboard and we'll make a trip into town."

I was really surprised to hear that we were going to town because I didn't get to go to town but about once in ever so long.

"What are we going to town for, Grandpa?" I asked.

"We're going to find out how to catch those monkeys," Grandpa said. "That's what we're going for."

"Grandpa," I asked, all interested, "do you know someone in town that knows how to catch monkeys?"

"No," Grandpa said, shaking his head, "I don't believe I know of any monkey catchers in town, but I think there's a place where we can find out something."

"What kind of a place is that, Grandpa?" I asked.

"The library!" Grandpa said.

I thought a second and said, "Oh, I know now.

That's the place you were telling me about where they have all of those books; thousands and thousands of books."

"That's the place," Grandpa said. "I don't care what kind of a problem a man has, he can always find the answer to it in a library. Somewhere, in one of those books, we'll find the answer to our monkey-catching problem."

"Boy, Grandpa," I said, "we should have thought about this library a long time ago. It sure would have saved a lot of wear and tear on Rowdy and me."

Grandpa looked at me, then he looked at Rowdy. Smiling, he said, "I can't see any wear and tear anywhere. You both look like you're in pretty good shape to me."

Rowdy had seen Grandpa looking at him and he figured that this was as good a time as any to let his wants be known. His old tail started thumping the ground, then he opened his mouth and let out a bawl that scared the chickens out of the barn.

Grandpa said, "What was that all about, boy?"

Rowdy whined, turned, and bounded for the store. On reaching the porch, he stopped, looked back at us, and bawled again.

Frowning and looking surprised, Grandpa said, "What's gotten into him?"

I couldn't help chuckling a little, for I knew what Rowdy was trying to tell Grandpa.

"Aw, Grandpa," I said, "don't pay any attention to him. He just wants a meat rind."

Watching Rowdy bouncing up and down on the porch, Grandpa said, "He seems to know where the meat rinds are, all right. Maybe we'd better get him one before he has a nervous breakdown."

Rowdy wound up with a big fat meat rind and I got my usual sack of candy. I thanked Grandpa and told him that he wouldn't have to wait for me in the morning, that I would be ready and waiting.

11

My promise to Grandpa about being ready and waiting for our trip to town got sidetracked during the night. I was sound asleep the next morning when Papa opened the door to my room.

"You'd better get up," Papa said. "Your grandpa is here and he's waiting for you."

"Grandpa's already here?" I said, rubbing the sleep from my eyes. "What time is it anyway?"

"It's just breaking daylight," Papa said. "You'd better hurry now. Your grandpa is raring to go."

I flew out of bed and jumped into my clothes. As I stepped into the kitchen, I saw to my surprise that everyone in the family was up. Mama was fixing breakfast and Daisy was setting the table. Papa and Grandpa were drinking coffee.

"Boy," I said, as I poured water into the wash pan, "this early in the morning and everybody stirring around."

Looking at Grandpa, Mama said, "Papa, this is the silliest thing I ever heard of, an old codger like you, going to town to read monkey books."

Grandpa snorted and said, "I can't see anything silly about it. We don't know anything about catching monkeys. Maybe in the library, we can learn from a book something about how to catch them. It's worth a try anyway."

Daisy said, "Grandpa, have you ever been in a library?"

Grandpa squirmed a little and said, "No, I haven't, but I understand that anyone can go to a library, and there's always a first time for everything."

It was twelve miles from where we lived in the hills to the little town of Tahlequah, Oklahoma, and it would take a good part of the day to get there. As soon as breakfast was over, Grandpa looked at me and said, "We'd better be on our way. I have a lot of things to do in town."

Mama, Papa, and Daisy followed us out to Grandpa's buckboard. Rowdy was sitting in the spring seat, looking at us, whimpering and whining. His old tail was wagging so fast that I just knew it was going to come unscrewed from his body.

Grandpa chuckled and said, "Would you look at that? He knows that we're going somewhere and he's bound and determined to go with us."

"Rowdy," I said, in a hard voice, "you get down out of that buckboard. You can't go to town with us. What's the matter with you anyway?"

Rowdy dropped his old head and wouldn't even look at me. His tail was the first part of him to die. Very slowly, it stopped wiggling. To make things worse, he squirmed his rear end around until his tail was hanging over the back of the spring seat. It just hung there all limp and lifeless, and looked like a dead grapevine.

Rowdy's sympathy-getting act melted Grandpa's heart. He glanced at Rowdy and then turned to me and said, "I don't see why Rowdy couldn't go to town with us. Lots of people take their dogs to town."

"Oh, Grandpa," I said, "if we took him to town with us, there's no telling what might happen."

Grandpa said, "I don't see how Rowdy could get into any trouble in town. We're going to stay at the wagon yard, and you could tie him under the buckboard. He'd be all right."

"Grandpa," I said, "I'd like to take Rowdy to town with us. I don't like to go anywhere without him, but

I'm afraid I might lose him in that big town. If that happened, I'd just die."

Rowdy knew that we were talking about him. With a low moan, he lay down on the spring seat and closed his eyes. He must have been holding his breath because I couldn't see one speck of life anywhere in his body. His dying act really stirred everybody up.

"All right," I said, throwing up my hands. "I give up. He can go with us but I don't like it—I don't like it at all. I just hope that everything comes out all right."

Grandpa climbed into the buckboard, gathered up the check lines, and said, "We'd better be on our way. We have wasted a good hour as it is."

Mama came over to me and started laying down the ten thousand laws that all mamas have for their going-away boys: things like being a good boy, minding Grandpa, washing my face, combing my hair, and saying my prayers when I went to bed.

I just stood there and waited until Mama ran out of breath, then I said, "Mama, I can't understand you sometimes. Every time you send me to the store—I don't care if it's for two or three little old things—you always write them down on a piece of paper, but if I'm going away for a day or two, you tell me ten thousand things to do and you never write anything down. Why, Mama, I couldn't remember all of those things if I had ten heads."

Mama smiled and said, "I don't expect you to do everything I ask you to do, but if you do just a few of them I'll be satisfied."

Daisy giggled and said, "Jay Berry, you sure would look funny running around with ten heads. Boy, wouldn't you be something to see."

Everyone, but me, was still laughing at Daisy's remarks when Grandpa said "Get up" to the mares.

Just as we were leaving, Daisy yelled, "Jay Berry, you'd better not forget my ribbon. If you do, you'd better not come home."

I didn't even look back at her.

The road we followed stayed at the edge of the foot-

hills for a short distance, and then it made a right
turn and ran down into the river bottoms. We had
no more than entered the bottoms when things began
to happen. Rabbits, squirrels, ground hogs, and quail
began darting across the road. Once, a mama deer with
a spotted baby leaped across the road and disappeared
in a thick cane brake.

Rowdy was on needles and pins. Every time something would zip across the road, his ears would stand
straight up. He would fidget around on the spring seat,
whimper, and whine. He wanted to chase something
so bad, he could hardly stand it.

I understood Rowdy's feelings. I loved him up a little, and said, "I know how you feel, boy, but just let
on like you don't see a thing. We don't have time to
stop and let you do any hunting."

Grandpa laughed. "I don't believe that I've ever
seen so much game in the river bottoms," he said.
"After we catch those monkeys, maybe we can take a
few days off and really do some hunting."

"I'd like that, Grandpa," I said, "and I know Rowdy
would."

About halfway through the bottoms, the road made
a sharp left turn. Just as we made the turn, a big old
mama coon with three little babies waddled across the
road. This was too much for Rowdy. He just simply
couldn't stand it any longer. Letting out a bellow that
all but busted my eardrums and came close to scaring
the mares out of their harness, he leaped down from
the buckboard and took off after the coons.

I stood up in the buckboard and yelled as loud as I
could, "Rowdy, you'd better leave those baby coons
alone. That old mama coon will skin you alive! You
come back here now!"

Mumbling something about a yelling boy and a
bawling hound, Grandpa finally got the mares settled
down. We sat there waiting to see what would happen.
From far out in the bottoms, we heard a loud commotion. The mama coon was squalling and Rowdy
was howling like he was hung up in a barbed-wire
fence.

With a worried look on his face, Grandpa said, "Boy, they're sure going after it, aren't they? Do you think Rowdy'll be all right?"

"Oh, don't worry about Rowdy, Grandpa," I said, "he's been through this a hundred times. You would think that by now he would learn to leave coons alone. He never does though. He always goes back for more."

It wasn't long until the squalling and howling stopped. About a minute later, Rowdy came tearing out of the brush with a sheepish look on his face and with his tail between his legs. I didn't have to tell him to get in the buckboard. He made one leap and landed in the spring seat. He had a raw, red scratch on his nose.

"Rowdy," I said, as I rubbed his nose with my hand, "I don't believe that you'll ever learn anything. I really don't. You know that you can't whip a coon; especially, a mama coon with babies."

Chuckling to himself, Grandpa tapped the mares with his buggy whip and said, "Well, there's one thing you can say for Rowdy, he sure can make things exciting."

Sitting high on the spring seat with my grandpa and my lop-eared hound, no boy could have been happier. "Grandpa," I said, "I really think we're going to catch those monkeys this time, don't you?"

Grandpa smiled. "I wouldn't be a bit surprised," he said. "If there's a book in that library that can tell us how to catch monkeys, we'll catch them all right. Yes, sir-e-e, those monkeys have won the first few rounds, but they can't win all the time."

For the hundredth time, I began to plan what all I would do when I got my pony and .22.

On reaching the river, I knew we had to cross it but I wasn't prepared for what took place. Grandpa stopped the team. He looked at me and said, "You know, I saw a painting once that showed a little boy and his grandpa crossing a stream with a wagon and team. The little boy was driving. The name of the painting was 'The Big Moment.' How about you and

I painting a picture of our own. You drive across the river."

I was so stunned and scared, I couldn't say a word. I just sat there with my mouth open, staring at Grandpa.

"Come on," Grandpa said, offering me the reins. "There's nothing to it."

I was so scared I had to swallow four or five times before any words came out. "Oh, no, Grandpa!" I said. "I don't think I'd better do any driving. Papa lets me drive our old mules once in a while but I don't know about driving these mares. They're kinda spooky, you know."

"Aw," Grandpa said, offering me the reins again, "come on—drive them across. I tell you, there's nothing to it. A fellow never knows what he can do until he tries."

Half of me was saying, "Take the reins." The other half was saying, "Jump out of the buckboard and run."

I didn't even know I had the reins in my hands until I looked down and there they were. Chuckling, Grandpa tapped the mares with his buggy whip and the buckboard eased into the river. I didn't do any driving at all. I just sat there as stiff as a boat paddle; staring across the river at the faraway bank that looked like it was a hundred miles away.

About halfway across the river, I glanced down at the water and came close to screaming. The water was almost up to the bed of the buckboard. Rowdy must have seen the same thing I had and got scared. He started whimpering and whining and fidgeting on the spring seat.

"Rowdy," I said, in a quavering voice, "if you don't sit still, and stop that whining, I'll put a muzzle on you and leave it on for ten years."

Laughing, Grandpa said, "That's about as deep as it will get. From here on across, it's not so deep."

I glanced down again, and sure enough, I could see that it was getting more shallow. I began to get a little of my courage back, but not very much.

On reaching the other side of the river, I stopped the team and handed the reins to Grandpa. As I turned loose of the leather, I saw that my hands were so wet with sweat they looked as wet as they did when I washed dishes for Mama once in a while.

Grandpa smiled and said, "You see how easy it was? There wasn't anything to it, was there?"

Glancing back across the river, I said, "Wait till I tell Daisy about this. She won't believe it though."

Tapping the mares with his buggy whip, Grandpa said, "If you think it'll do any good, I'll be a witness for you."

About noon, we drove into the town of Tahlequah. Just before we entered the main street, off to my right, I saw several large buildings. They were on a small hill in the middle of about ten acres of beautiful green lawn. Huge red oaks, white oaks, maple, locust, and elm trees were growing here and there on the lawn. In the shade of those beautiful trees, small groups of people were either sitting or lying on the green grass. Practically everyone had a book in his hand. I thought, "The people in this town really like to read books."

"Grandpa," I asked, "what are all those buildings up there?"

"Those buildings are the pride and joy of the Cherokee Nation," he said. "That's their college."

"What are all those people doing under the trees?" I asked.

"Those are students," Grandpa said. "They're probably studying their lessons. They have their classes inside those buildings."

"That wouldn't be a bad place to go to school," I said. "Instead of having to stay in the schoolhouse to study, you could just go outside and sit under a tree. I think I'd like that."

"I hope I live to see the day when you go to college here," Grandpa said. "Do you think you'd like it?"

"I think I would, Grandpa," I said.

Not far from the college, we crossed a bridge over a

small creek. A sign on the bridge said, "Bear Creek."

Grandpa said, "This is the main street. Tahlequah is a nice town, and it's the county seat of the Cherokee Nation."

I had never seen so many buildings. There were little ones and big ones. Some of them were two stories high. They lined both sides of the street and were jammed up so close together it looked like you couldn't have driven a nail between them.

I had never seen so many people. They were milling around everywhere. Some were going into stores and some were coming out of stores. Others were just walking up and down the streets. I could hear little kids bawling, and big kids laughing. A man and his wife passed by. They had so many kids following along behind them they looked like a covey of quails.

Everywhere I looked I could see wagons, buggies, buckboards, and saddle horses. Some were tied to hitching rails and others were moving along the street. Dogs were barking and trace chains were jingling.

I was still gawking when Grandpa slowed the mares down and said, "Well, here we are. This is the Eubanks Hotel and Wagon Yard. I'll get us a room in the hotel and we'll eat our meals there, too."

The large, two-story hotel building was on our left. Its second story had a porch that hung out over the sidewalk. I saw several people sitting in chairs up there. They were just sitting there, as comfortable as could be, looking the town over. I thought, "They sure have a bird's-eye view of the town."

Grandpa made a left turn off the main street at the hotel and passed under a big arch. About one hundred yards behind it was one of the biggest barns I had ever seen. Above its huge open doors was a sign in big blue letters that said, "Eubanks Wagon Yard—Fifty Cents for Teams—Twenty-five Cents for Feed."

"Boy, this wagon yard must be doing a lot of business," I said. "Did you ever see so many wagons and teams?"

"This is the only wagon yard in town," Grandpa said. "They do a good business all right. The fellow who owns this place is a fine man. He's a good friend of mine."

Grandpa stopped the team in front of an empty stall. With a few grunts and groans, he got down from the buckboard.

"Grandpa," I said, "I'd feel a lot better if I had a rope on Rowdy."

Grandpa reached in the buckboard and picked up a short piece of good, stout rope. He smiled as he handed it to me. "I think you have a good idea," he said.

After tying the rope to Rowdy's collar, I hopped down from the buckboard and tied the other end to a wheel spoke. Rowdy never did like to be tied up and right away he started whimpering and whining. I petted him and said, "Look, boy, I don't like to tie you up but there's nothing else I can do."

Grandpa said, "I have to put the team in a stall and feed and water them. After that, I'll get us a room and then we'll go downtown and take care of my business."

"When are we going to the library, Grandpa?" I asked.

"We'll do that the first thing in the morning," Grandpa said. "I'd like to leave town about noon. That way we could get home before dark."

Just then the yard master walked up to Grandpa and shook hands with him. They talked for a few minutes before he came over to where Rowdy and I were. He looked at Rowdy, smiled, and said, "Is this your dog, son?"

"Yes, sir," I said.

"Is he any good?" he asked.

I smiled and said, "He's a pretty good dog."

"If you want to," the yard master said, "you can put him in the tack room. There's a pan of water there and I'll see that he gets some scraps from the table."

"Thanks," I said. "That'll be a good place for him." I took Rowdy to the tack room and made a nice bed of straw for him. He fussed a little about staying there, but not too much.

As I was locking the tack-room door, Grandpa came to me and said, "Come on, let's see what the town looks like."

Before the afternoon was over, Grandpa and I visited just about every place in town. I had the time of my life. Grandpa saw to it that I didn't want for anything to eat.

That evening, we went back to the wagon yard. Grandpa took care of the team and I took care of Rowdy. Then we went into the hotel and ate supper. The food was served family style and I ate so much I came close to making myself sick.

The room Grandpa had gotten for us was upstairs in the hotel. I was so tired I fell asleep the minute I crawled into bed. I didn't wake up once during the night—I didn't even dream.

The next morning when I woke up the sun was way up in the sky. I could hear people talking and the rumble of wagons and teams moving along the street. Grandpa was gone. This scared me but I was pretty sure that he wouldn't just run off and leave me. I jumped out of bed and hurried into my clothes. I didn't even take time to wash my face or comb my hair before I ran downstairs.

A smiling, big, heavy woman poked her head out the kitchen door and said, "Are you Jay Berry?"

"Yes, ma'am," I said.

"I'm Big Gen," she said. "Your grandpa said after you've had breakfast you'll find him out in the barn. Come on in and sit down at the table. I'll fix you a cup of hot chocolate."

When Big Gen started setting breakfast on the table, my eyes got as big as goose eggs. There was a large slab of ham, two eggs, fried potatoes, hot biscuits, butter, and strawberry jam. I looked at the food and said, "Brother, if I hung around here very long, I'd get as fat as Sloppy Ann."

"Who's Sloppy Ann?" Big Gen asked.

"She's our hog," I said as I started eating.

Finished with breakfast, I thanked Big Gen and hurried out to the barn. Grandpa had just finished hitching the team to the buckboard. Rowdy was tied to a wheel spoke. He was wiggling all over and tickled to death to see me.

"There you are," Grandpa said. "I was beginning to think you were going to sleep all day."

"What time is it, Grandpa?" I asked as I bent down to pet Rowdy on the head.

"It's about ten o'clock," Grandpa said. "We'd better be going to the library."

As Grandpa and I drove along the main street I asked him if he knew where the library was.

"Sure, I know where the library is," Grandpa said. "I've never been in it but I know where it is."

About halfway through town, Grandpa made a right turn off the main street. We hadn't gone more than two blocks when Grandpa motioned with his left hand and said, "There it is—that's the Carnegie Library."

The library was a large, red-brick building. It was right in the middle of a beautiful green lawn and was surrounded by large trees. Steep sandstone steps led up between two huge marble columns to the front door, which was standing wide open.

Grandpa drove around the library and came in the yard from behind it. He stopped the buckboard under a large white oak, got out, and tied the team to the tree.

Rowdy hopped out of the backboard. With his tail fanning the air, he started his inspection of the lawn.

"Grandpa," I said, "I think I'd better tie Rowdy up, don't you?"

Grandpa watched Rowdy for a couple of seconds, smiled, and said, "I don't think you need to tie him up. He won't get very far from us and this team."

"All right," I said, "but if he gets after a tomcat, we'll probably find him way over in Arkansas somewhere."

Grandpa laughed and said, "I don't think Rowdy's going to find any cats around this library. It just isn't cat country."

Grandpa and I walked around to the front of the

library. Just as we started up the steps, Rowdy came loping around the corner of the building, up the steps, and heading for the open door. As he came by me, I grabbed his collar and said, "Hold on, boy! You can't go in there. You'll have to wait out here. We won't be in there very long—I hope."

I took Rowdy over to one of the big columns, made him lie down, and told him to stay there. He didn't like it but he stayed there.

Grandpa and I took off our hats and walked into the library. The first thing I saw was about twenty boys and girls sitting at small tables—each one reading a book. Every one of them looked up as we walked in. It was so still in there that when one of them turned a page it sounded like someone was dragging a cotton sack across the floor.

Over to our right was a large U-shaped counter. Standing behind it was a little old gray-haired lady, wearing glasses. She had a pencil in one hand and a book in the other. With surprise written all over her face, she too looked at us.

Grandpa walked to the counter and put both hands on it. He cleared his throat and then, in that deep frog voice of his said, "We'd like to read a book that could tell us how to catch monkeys."

I thought the little old lady was going to jump right out of her shoes. Glaring at Grandpa, she leaned toward him, put her finger over her lips, and said, "Sh-sh-sh!"

Grandpa was so startled he dropped his hat on the floor. He stepped back so fast he bumped into me. In a loud voice, he said, "What are you shushing me for?"

The lady didn't say a word. She just pointed to a sign on the counter right in front of Grandpa. In silence we read the sign. It said, "Quiet—Children Studying."

With a sheepish look on his red face, Grandpa said in a whisper, "I'm sorry. This is our first time in a library."

The lady smiled and whispered, "I understand. Did

you say you wanted a book that could tell you how to catch monkeys?"

"Yes, ma'am," Grandpa whispered as he nodded his head.

The lady stood looking down at the floor for several seconds as if she were in deep thought. I saw the thinking wrinkles as they bunched up on her forehead. Then her face cleared. She went over to a large metal cabinet and pulled out one of its drawers. It was full of small yellow cards and all of them were standing on edge in the drawer.

I was fascinated by the fast delicate way the lady's fingers started flipping the cards. It reminded me of our old white leghorn hens picking up yellow kernels of corn from the ground.

Easing one of the cards out of the drawer, she studied it for a second, turned to Grandpa, and whispered, "You and the boy go and sit down at one of the tables. I think I have the very book you're looking for. It may take me a few minutes to find it."

Grandpa and I whispered our thanks. We walked over to one of the small tables and sat down. I had never been in a place that was as still as it was in that library. If someone had batted an eye, it would have sounded like a firecracker had gone off. I was afraid to even move my bare feet for fear I'd make a noise.

I glanced around the room. Everywhere I looked I saw nothing but books, books, and more books. I didn't think there were that many books in the world. I thought, "Boy, if Daisy were here she would be in book heaven."

From somewhere far back in that book jungle, I could hear the little old lady moving around. The silence and the boys and girls watching us made me feel funny. I began feeling uneasy and out of place.

Finally, after what seemed like an hour, the lady came back to us. She had a book in her hand. She smiled as she handed it to Grandpa and whispered, "I hope you can find what you're looking for in this book."

In a whisper, Grandpa thanked her and we watched

as she walked back to her working stall. Grandpa laid the book on the table and both of us read the title, *Trapping Monkeys in the Jungles of Borneo.*

"Boy, Grandpa," I whispered, "that's what we're looking for."

Just as Grandpa opened the book to the index page, the silence of the library was shattered by the deep voice of Rowdy. He had gotten tired of waiting for me and had come to the open door and bawled. He was telling me that it was time I got myself out of there.

I had always known that my old hound had a beautiful voice, but I had never heard it ring like it did in that silent library. The deep tones rolled out over the floor, slammed against the walls, bounced off the ceiling, and made books quiver on the shelves. Boys and girls all over the place started screaming with laughter.

Like a shot out of a gun, the little lady came from behind the counter and over to Rowdy. She stopped right in front of him. With her hands on her hips, she stood there looking at him. Rowdy thought he had found another friend and was acting like he was very proud of what he had done. He just sat there, mopping the floor with his tail and panting happily.

I all but turned my chair over as I came up out of it. I rushed over and grabbed Rowdy's collar with both hands. I thought the lady would be angry and was going to jump on my dog—but she wasn't. She wasn't the least bit mad. I could see a twinkle in her eyes and she was smiling.

"Son," she asked, "is this your dog?"

"Yes, ma'am," I said.

"I've been a librarian here for a good many years," she said, "but this is the first time I've ever had a hound dog ask if he could come in my library. I'm honored."

"It's my fault," I said. "I should have tied him up. He got tired of waiting for me. He never could wait very long."

Still smiling, the lady said, "I wonder if you could

tell me something. Why does that old man want to read a book about catching monkeys?"

"He's my grandpa," I said. "All summer we've been trying to catch a bunch of monkeys and we haven't had much luck. Grandpa thought maybe here in this library we could find a book that could tell us how to catch them."

I saw a confused look come into the lady's eyes. "Where have you been trying to catch monkeys?" she asked.

"Up on the river where we live," I said. "They got away from a circus train that was wrecked."

"Oh, yes," the lady said, nodding her head. "I remember reading about that wreck."

"I'm sorry for what Rowdy did," I said. "I'll take him to the buckboard and tie him up."

"You do that," the lady said as she glanced at the noisy boys and girls. "I'll see if I can get things back to normal in here."

I took Rowdy to the buckboard, made him get up in it, and tied him to the back of the spring seat. I was telling him what a mess he had made of everything when Grandpa came hurrying around the corner of the library. His face was beaming.

Grandpa started talking before he got to us. "I found what I was looking for," he said, all excited. "I don't know why I didn't think of it myself. We'll catch those monkeys this time for sure. You can bet on that."

"How are we going to catch them?" I asked.

"I'll tell you all about it on the way home," Grandpa said. "Right now, I want to get downtown. We have to make one more stop."

12

As I climbed in the buckboard, I said, "Grandpa, why are we stopping in town?"

"We're going to buy some coconuts," Grandpa said.

"Coconuts!" I said, surprised. "What are we going to do with coconuts?"

"We're going to use them for monkey bait," Grandpa said. "From what I read in that book, if there's one thing that monkeys really like to eat, it's coconuts."

I wanted to ask Grandpa a thousand questions but just then we drove up in front of a large building and stopped.

"This is the Wiley Mercantile," Grandpa said. "It's the biggest store in town. You can buy just about anything you need here—from a wagon and team to a can of snuff."

While Grandpa was tying the team to the hitching rail, I had a talk with Rowdy. I told him that if he'd behave himself and not make any fuss I'd bring him a piece of candy. Rowdy wasn't the least bit happy about my leaving him, but he did lay down in the buckboard.

As Grandpa and I started into the mercantile, Grandpa said, "Old Man Wiley owns this store. He's a fine old man and as honest as the day is long—but I never seem to be able to get along with him. He's always rubbing me the wrong way."

I thought Grandpa's store was big, but compared to the mercantile, it wasn't any bigger than a chicken coop. The storekeeper was standing behind a counter when Grandpa and I came through the door. He was an old man and reminded me of Grandpa. As we stepped up to the counter, he looked over his glasses at us and said, "What can I do for you?"

Grandpa looked over his glasses at him and said, "Do you have any coconuts?"

The storekeeper smiled and said, "You're in luck. I just got in a half bushel of them. They're still in the storeroom. How many do you want?"

Grandpa frowned. Drumming the fingers of his left hand on the counter, he mumbled to himself, "A half bushel." Then he spoke up and said, "I guess I'll just take all of them."

The storekeeper drew back and said, "The whole half bushel!"

"Yes!" Grandpa said. "The whole half bushel."

As the storekeeper turned to go to the storeroom to get the coconuts, he shook his head and said, "Boy, you must like coconuts. A half bushel!"

"I do like coconuts," Grandpa growled. "I've never in my life had all I could eat at one time."

I wanted to laugh but I was afraid to. It's not a good idea to laugh at two old men when their dander's up. There's no telling what they're liable to do.

On hearing someone giggle, I turn around. Over behind the candy counter was a girl about my age. She was looking straight at me. She was the prettiest girl I had ever seen. In fact, I didn't think girls got that pretty. She looked like a doll. Her hair was the color of sycamore leaves after the first frost. It hung down her back in two long braids and was tied with purple ribbons. She had a dimple in one cheek. At first I thought her eyes were blue. Then I decided they were green. Then I didn't know what color they were.

Seeing the ribbons in her hair reminded me of Daisy's ribbons. "Boy-oh-boy, Grandpa," I said, "I almost forgot Daisy's ribbons."

Grandpa laughed and said, "If you had forgotten

those ribbons, neither one of us could have gone home."

I walked over to the pretty girl and said, "Do you work here?"

She didn't say a word. She just smiled and nodded her head.

"I'd like to buy two spools of ribbon," I said. "One pink and one blue."

The girl turned and walked to another counter. I followed her. While she was getting the ribbon, I looked through the glass top of the counter and saw a tray of thimbles. Some looked like silver and some looked like gold.

When the girl came back, I waited while she put the ribbons in a small paper sack, then I said, "How much are those thimbles?"

The girl said, "They're fifteen cents each."

"I'll take one of those gold ones," I said.

"What size do you want?" she asked.

"Size?" I said. "I didn't know thimbles came in sizes."

"Oh, sure," the girl said. "Small, medium, and large."

"It's for my mama," I said, "but I don't know what size she would need."

"Well, let's see," the girl said, holding her hand up in front of her and looking at it. "Is your mother's hand bigger than mine?"

I looked at her hand and said, "I don't know. Mama's hand could be a little bigger than yours."

Holding her hand out to me, she said, "Maybe if you held my hand you could tell better."

This really shook me up. I stepped back and said, "I'm not going to hold your hand. What's the matter with you?"

She giggled and said, "I was just trying to help. Didn't you ever hold a girl's hand?"

"No!" I said. "And I'm not going to!"

She said, "I think your mother would need a medium size."

"All right," I said, "give me one of those."

The girl put the thimble in a tiny box with cotton in it and handed it to me. She said, "Will there be anything else?"

"Yeah," I said as I shoved the little box down in my pocket, "I'd like a dime's worth of jawbreakers."

While the girl was getting the candy, I saw something that really took my eye. It was a snow-white shaving mug with a fancy design on it. Some time back Papa had dropped his shaving mug. The handle had broken off, and it had a bad crack in it. He still used it but I knew he would like another one.

"How much is that shaving mug?" I asked the girl.

"It's kind of expensive," she said. "It costs a quarter."

I knew if I bought the mug I'd be flat broke but that didn't make any difference. I wanted Papa to have the shaving mug. "I'll take it," I said.

As I handed the girl my money, she said, "My name is Patricia. Everyone calls me Patty. What's your name?"

"Jay Berry," I said.

The girl giggled and said, "Jay Berry—that's a cute name."

"Cute!" I said. "I don't see anything cute about it."

"Where do you live?" she asked.

"Up on the river," I said as I picked up my packages.

"Do you have a sweetheart?" she asked.

"No, I don't have a sweetheart," I said, as I turned my back to her to walk away. "I'm not looking for one either."

I heard her giggle.

Grandpa had just paid the storekeeper for the coconuts when I walked up. He looked at the packages in my hands and said, "What did you buy?"

"I got a thimble for Mama," I said, "and a shaving mug for Papa. I got a little candy, too, for Rowdy and me."

"What about the ribbon?" Grandpa asked.

"I got it, too." I said.

Grandpa picked up the basket of coconuts. I hurried and opened the door for him.

Just as Grandpa started through the door, the storekeeper said, "I hope you have all the coconuts you can eat this time."

Grandpa stopped, looked at the storekeeper, and very seriously said, "I don't think that's possible. Maybe you should order another bushel for me."

The storekeeper jerked off his glasses and glared at Grandpa. He said, "There's something wrong with you."

"No," Grandpa said, "there's nothing wrong with me. I just like coconuts, that's all."

The girl in the store giggled.

I looked at her and darned if she didn't haul off and wink at me. I slammed the door. With my face on fire, I followed Grandpa to the buckboard. I thought, "Boy, that girl's got a lot of nerve."

As Grandpa set the basket of coconuts in the buckboard he said, "You can put that package of ribbon in the basket with the coconuts but you'd better hold onto that shaving mug. As rough as that road is, it could get broken."

"All right, Grandpa," I said. I picked up one of the coconuts, laid the ribbon in the basket, and put the coconut on top of it.

As Grandpa and I got in the buckboard, he said, "What did you think of that pretty little girl?"

"I think she's boy crazy," I said. "She wanted to know my name and asked me if I had a sweetheart. She tried to get me to hold her hand and even winked at me. I bet she winks at every boy she gets close to."

Grandpa laughed as he tapped the mares with the whip.

"You know," he said, "the best way to stop a girl from winking at you is to haul off and kiss her. That's the thing to do."

"Aw, Grandpa," I said, "I'm not going to kiss any girls. You know I couldn't do anything like that. Why, I'd rather kiss Old Rowdy."

I opened my sack of a candy and plopped a big jawbreaker in my mouth. "Would you like a jaw-breaker, Grandpa?" I asked as I held one out to him.

Grandpa looked at it and said, "I don't believe I care for one right now. Thanks anyway. I don't think that jawbreakers and this Star tobacco I'm chewing would mix very well."

I laughed and said, "I don't think it would either, Grandpa."

Twisting around on the seat, I laid the jawbreaker in front of Rowdy. He rolled it around on the floor of the buckboard with his tongue until it was good and wet. Then he just lapped it up and swallowed it. I plopped another one in his mouth. He didn't even lick that one. He just stretched his neck and down it went.

With a wagging tail and beginning eyes, Rowdy asked for another jawbreaker.

"Aw, Rowdy," I said, "why do you gulp them down like that? You don't even get to taste them. You're supposed to hold them in your mouth and suck on them, or at least chew them. I'm going to give you one more but that's all you're going to get for a while."

I heard Grandpa chuckling.

Shifting the jawbreaker from one cheek to the other, I leaned back and said, "Grandpa, you were going to tell me how we're going to catch those monkeys."

"I don't think we'll have any trouble catching them this time," Grandpa said. "All we need is those coco-nuts, a roll of chicken wire, a snap latch, and a ball of binder twine. Now that we have the coconuts, I have everything else we need in my store."

"What are we going to do with all that stuff, Grandpa?" I asked.

"We're going to build a big pen out of that chicken wire," he said. "It'll have a top on it and a door with a snap latch. We'll put those coconuts right in the center of the pen and leave the door open. Then we'll tie the binder twine to the door and run it back through the pen and out into the brush a little way. When those monkeys go into the pen after those coconuts, we'll pull the binder twine and latch the door. What do you think of that idea?"

Before I answered Grandpa, I closed my eyes and drew a picture of the pen in my mind. I could feel the excitement as it burned its way through me. "Boy, Grandpa," I said, "that sure sounds good to me. Is that what you read in the book?"

"It sure was," Grandpa said. "The story was about a man and woman who lived in the Borneo jungles. All they did was trap monkeys. They sold them to zoos all over the world. They caught thousands and thousands of monkeys—all kinds of monkeys. They always used a pen—just like the one I was telling you about—to catch them; and they used coconuts for bait. It'll work I tell you. We'll get them this time for sure."

"Grandpa," I asked, "are you going to help me build that pen?"

"I sure am," Grandpa said. "We'll get your dad to help, too. I'm going to lock up my store and do nothing but help trap those monkeys. This monkey business has got to come to an end. It's beginning to bother me a little. I can't remember the last time I had a good night's sleep."

Grandpa had me so excited I almost swallowed my jawbreaker. With both Grandpa and Papa helping me catch the monkeys, I couldn't see any way I could lose. Once again, I could almost see myself riding my pony and shooting my .22. Twisting around on the seat, I reached into the basket and lifted out one of the coconuts. As I held it in my hands, I said, "Grandpa, I wonder why monkeys like coconuts so much."

"I don't know," Grandpa said, "but it said in that book there are two things that monkeys won't ever pass up—coconuts and bananas."

I started turning the coconut over and over in my hands. Just then I saw something that I could hardly believe. In the pointed end of it, underneath the brown hairy-looking fiber, I saw what looked like two small black eyes and a tiny mouth. They made it look exactly like the face of a small monkey. I started laugh-ing. Great big tears started streaming down my face.

Grandpa said, "What's so funny?"

Holding the coconut up for him to see, I cried, "Look, Grandpa. These coconuts even look like a monkey's head."

Grandpa leaned over and peered at the coconut for a second. Then he grinned and said, "Well, I'll be darned! They do have a monkey face, don't they? I never noticed that before."

"They should have called these things monkeynuts, instead of coconuts," I said.

Grandpa threw his head back and roared with laughter. He laughed so loud it scared the mares. They started zigzagging all over the road. Grandpa started sawing on the check lines and hollering, "Whoa-whoa-whoa." He finally got the mares quieted down.

Still laughing and wiping tears from his eyes, he said, "Those monkeys may not know it, but they have a big surprise waiting for them."

"They sure have, Grandpa," I said. "I can hardly wait till we start building that pen."

On reaching the river, Grandpa stopped the team and offered the reins to me. "Would you like to drive across the river again?" he asked.

This time I didn't hold back. I took the reins in my hands.

Grandpa chuckled and said, "You'd better call Rowdy, or he'll have to swim the river."

"Come on, Rowdy!" I yelled. "You'd better get in this buckboard, or you're going to get wet."

Rowdy came tearing out of the underbrush and jumped into the buckboard.

That crossing was easy. The water didn't seem to be half as deep as it was the day before. I didn't get the least bit scared.

We were in the bottoms about a hundred yards from the river, when I realized I was thirsty. "I'm thirsty, Grandpa," I said. "Would you like to have a good cold drink of water?"

"I sure would," Grandpa said. "I've been thirsty

ever since we left town, but where are we going to get a cold drink?"

"I know where a spring is," I said. "The water is as cold as ice."

"Where is this spring?" Grandpa asked.

"It's just a little way down in the bottoms," I said.

Grandpa drove the team off to one side of the road and stopped them under a big sweet gum tree. As we tied the halter ropes of the mares to the gum tree, Grandpa said, "As thirsty as I am, I think I'd walk a mile for a cool drink."

"Oh, it's not that far, Grandpa," I said, as I took off on a game trail. "It's just a little way."

As we walked along the trail, I noticed that Rowdy kept looking up into the trees. I grinned and said, "Look, Grandpa, Rowdy's looking for those monkeys."

"I am, too," Grandpa said. "I'd sure like to see that hundred dollar monkey. Do you think he could be around here somewhere?"

"If he's around here, Grandpa," I said, "we won't see him unless he wants us to. He could be sitting in the top of a big sycamore right now, watching every move we make. He's smart, I tell you."

"I don't care how smart he is," Grandpa said, looking up into the trees, "if we ever get him in that pen, and I can get a rope on him, his smart days will be over."

Grandpa was so serious I couldn't help laughing at him. When we arrived at the spring, Grandpa and I got down on our bellies and had a good drink. Grandpa had a terrible time getting down. He wheezed and he groaned and he grunted, but he finally made it.

As Grandpa got back to his knees, he took his handkerchief and wiped the water from his chin. "Boy," he said, "that sure is good water. How did you ever find this spring?"

As I lay back in the cool green grass, I said, "Oh, Rowdy and I found it. There are springs all through these bottoms, but this has always been my most favorite. I named it 'Jay Berry's Spring.' "

"That's not a bad idea," Grandpa said. "Who knows, maybe a hundred years from now, another old man and a boy will stop here and have a good cool drink from Jay Berry's Spring. You can't ever tell; might even be a highway come by here."

"Aw, Grandpa," I said, "nothing like that will ever happen to me. I'd be lucky if I had a grasshopper named after me."

Grandpa chuckled and said, "That's not a bad idea either. If you could find a purple grasshopper and hang a name on it—like 'Jay Berry's Hopper'—it might stick. You can't even tell."

I laughed and said, "Grandpa, we sure have a lot of fun together, don't we?"

Grandpa smiled and said, "We surely do. You know, an old man like me can teach a young boy like you all the good things in life. But it takes a young boy like you to teach an old man like me to appreciate all the good things in life. I guess that's what life's all about."

I didn't quite understand what Grandpa was talking about, but it sounded pretty good to me anyway. Just then Grandpa's mares started snorting and stomping their hoofs. We could hear their trace chains jingling.

Grandpa cocked his ear and said, "It sounds like something has scared my mares."

"It's probably an old hog or a deer," I said. "The bottoms are full of them. We could have spooked one up when we came to the spring; and it ran by the team and scared them."

The mares quieted down.

As Grandpa got to his feet, he said, "I guess that's what it was. It sounds like everything is all right now, though. Let's have one more drink of this spring water, and then we'd better be going. It's getting along in the day."

When Grandpa and I got back to the buckboard, I said, "Grandpa, look at Rowdy. Something's been prowling around here."

Rowdy was sniffing around the buckboard. He was

walking stiff-legged, and every hair on his back was standing straight up.

Watching Rowdy, Grandpa said, "It sure looks that way. I wonder what it was."

"I don't know," I said, "but whatever it was, Rowdy doesn't like the smell of it at all."

Grandpa stepped over to the buckboard and looked in it. In a loud voice, he said, "Hey, our coconuts are gone! The basket is empty!"

"Gone!" I said, as I hurried over and looked into the basket. "By golly, they are gone! But there's something else in the basket."

Grandpa grunted as he reached down into the basket. He lifted out the dirtiest, most ragged pair of britches I had ever seen in my life. Holding them up in front of him, Grandpa said, "I could be wrong, but it looks like a pair of britches to me."

I would never have recognized the britches if I hadn't seen the patch on the seat of the pants. "Sufferin' bullfrogs, Grandpa," I said, "those are my britches. They're the ones I lost the day those monkeys got me drunk. I recognize that patch on them. Mama sewed it on."

Grandpa tossed the britches into the underbrush. "Phew!" he said, wrinkling his nose. "By the way they smell, those monkeys must have been taking turn-about wearing them."

"I wouldn't doubt it, Grandpa," I said. "Those monkeys are liable to do anything."

Looking into the basket, Grandpa said, "It looks like we have something else here." He reached in and lifted out a wet, soggy, nasty-looking gunny sack. I could hear the jingling of metal when he picked it up.

Wide-eyed, I said, "Holy smokes, Grandpa, that's my gunny sack and traps. I didn't think I'd ever see them again."

Dropping the gunny sack in the buckboard, Grandpa reached in the basket again and said, "Well, what do you know!" He lifted out my beanshooter.

"That's my beanshooter, Grandpa," I said, all excited. "I lost it the day I shot that hundred dollar monkey in the belly."

Grandpa started looking in the underbrush. He said, "Something's going on. I think someone is playing a trick on us. I bet it's your dad."

"I don't think it's Papa, Grandpa," I said, as I looked up into the trees. "I think I know who did this. It's those monkeys—that's who did it."

"Naw," Grandpa said. "Monkeys couldn't do anything like that. I still think it's your dad playing a trick on us."

Just then I saw a sight that took me several seconds to figure out what I was seeing. I couldn't believe it. I couldn't breathe. I couldn't even swallow. I couldn't do anything but stand there with my mouth open and stare. I had seen a lot of sycamore trees in my life, but I had never seen one as beautiful as the one I was looking at. Strung from limb to limb, all through the top of the tree, were the pink and blue ribbons I had gotten for Daisy.

Sitting on limbs, here and there, were the monkeys. Each one of them that I could see was holding a coconut in his paws. They were just sitting there looking at Grandpa and me; with no expression at all on their cute little faces. A gentle breeze was stirring the top of the big sycamore. The ribbons were waving and fluttering. Brilliant flashes of pink and blue gleamed and shimmered in the sun's bright rays. It was an unbelievably beautiful sight.

As if from far away, I heard Grandpa say, "What's the matter? Do you see something?"

"Look, Grandpa!" I cried, pointing at the sycamore. "Look at that! I bet you've never seen anything that pretty."

Grandpa looked where I was pointing. I saw him reach and take hold of the buckboard with one hand as if he were steadying himself. He looked down at the ground, shook his head, and looked again at the sycamore. He took off his hat and scratched the top of his bald head. He cleared his throat and said, "What in the name of heaven is that?"

"It's those monkeys, Grandpa," I said. "They didn't only steal our coconuts, they stole Daisy's ribbons, too. They decorated that sycamore tree with them. Isn't it pretty?"

Grandpa never said a word. He just grunted and kept staring at that beautiful sycamore tree. Just then Jimbo walked out onto a big limb. He was carrying a coconut in one of his paws.

Grandpa threw his head back and said, "What in the world is that thing?"

"Grandpa," I said, "you've been wanting to see that hundred dollar monkey. Well, you're looking at him. That's Jimbo."

Grandpa said, "Why, that's no monkey. It's too big to be a monkey. It looks more like an ape to me."

"I don't care what he looks like, Grandpa," I said, "that's Jimbo; and he's the smartest thing you've ever seen in your life."

Jimbo must have realized that we were talking about him, and he decided to show off a little. Waving the coconut in the air, he started hopping up and down on the limb and uttering those deep grunts.

In a surprised voice, Grandpa, said, "What's that monkey doing now?"

"He's talking to you, Grandpa," I said. "That's monkey talk."

I saw when Rowdy took off down the road with his tail between his legs. "Rowdy!" I yelled. "You come back here!" Rowdy acted like he hadn't even heard me. He just put on a little more speed and disappeared around a bend in the road.

"Where's that hound going?" Grandpa asked.

"He's going home, Grandpa," I said. "He's afraid those monkeys might get ahold of him."

Jimbo had seen Rowdy take off for home, and it pleased him. He opened his big mouth and made the bottoms ring with his shrill cries.

Watching Jimbo, Grandpa said, "If I didn't know better, I'd say that monkey was laughing at us."

"He is laughing at us, Grandpa," I said. "He gets a

big kick out of anything like this. If he were down on the ground, he'd turn a few somersaults for us."

Mumbling something that I couldn't understand, Grandpa reached down and picked up a good-sized stick.

"What are you going to do with that stick, Grandpa?" I asked.

"I'm going to see if I can't wrap it around that monkey's neck," Grandpa said. "I don't like to have people laugh at me—much less a silly monkey."

"Oh, Grandpa," I said, "don't do that. Don't ever throw anything at those monkeys. They'll come down from the tree and jump on us, and eat us up."

"Aw," Grandpa said, looking at me. "They wouldn't do anything like that, would they?"

"Oh, yes, they would, Grandpa," I said. "I know. No one knows what those monkeys would do any better than I do. If you hit Jimbo with that stick, he'll sick those little monkeys on us, and they'll eat us up."

Grandpa must have believed what I was telling him. He dropped the stick and looked at the sycamore again. "They're gone!" he said, in a loud voice. "Where did they go?"

I looked, and sure enough, the monkeys had disappeared. I felt like bawling. "They're gone, all right," I said. "So are our coconuts and my pony and .22. Doggone it—just when it looks like I have a cinch on getting my pony and .22, something like this happens every time. What are we going to do now?"

"We're still going to catch those monkeys," Grandpa said, as he untied the halter ropes from the gum tree. "I'm mad now. Just because we lost those coconuts doesn't mean that we have to give up. No, sir-e-e. We're still going to catch those monkeys."

"How are we going to catch them, Grandpa?" I asked. "We don't have any coconuts for bait."

"We're going to build that pen just like we planned," Grandpa said. "We'll use apples for bait. We'll use everything I have in my store if we have to. We're still going to catch those monkeys."

Before Grandpa and I got into the buckboard, we

took another look at that beautiful sycamore tree. Grandpa chuckled and said, "You know, when you think about it, those monkeys didn't exactly steal our coconuts. They made a trade with us. They traded us your old britches, gunny sack, traps, and bean-shooter for the coconuts. It's as simple as that."

"Grandpa," I said, "now do you believe those monkeys are smart?"

"Yes," Grandpa said, as he climbed into the buck-board, "they're smart, all right. But they're not smart enough. I still believe there never was an animal that couldn't be caught. We'll see. We'll see."

When Grandpa and I came in sight of our house, we saw Mama, Papa, Daisy, and Rowdy standing on the porch.

As we drove up, Papa said, "Is everything all right? When I saw Rowdy coming home alone, I was kind of worried."

Grandpa didn't get out of the buckboard. He just sat there, holding the reins in his hand, and looked at Papa. He shifted a little on the seat and said, "I've never deliberately told a lie in my life; but if I thought I could tell one and get out of this, I would. I'm going to tell you what happened to us, but I don't think you're going to believe it. I saw it happen, and I don't believe it."

Taking his time, Grandpa told Papa everything that had happened to us down in the bottoms.

Papa started laughing. I had never seen him laugh so hard. He stood up and laughed. He bent over and laughed. Then he sat down on the porch, buried his face in his arms, and laughed. Mama started laugh-ing, too. Rowdy got all excited and started bawling. With all of that laughter going on, I laughed a little, too.

Everyone was laughing, but Daisy. She didn't crack a smile. With an angry look in her eyes, she just stood there looking at me.

Grandpa either got mad or disgusted. Anyway, he looked at me and said, "Give me a few days to get things straightened out at the store, and then we'll build that pen. We're going to catch those monkeys and stop some of this laughing." He took off down the road, with the buckboard bouncing, and the dust a-boiling.

Grandpa wasn't out of sight when Daisy said, "Jay, Berry, do you mean to tell me that you lost my ribbons?"

"I didn't lose them, Daisy," I said. "Those monkeys stole them. The ribbons are down there in the bottoms, strung all over the top of a sycamore tree."

Daisy said, "You're always bragging what a good tree climber you are. Why didn't you climb the tree and get the ribbons back for me?"

"Climb the tree!" I exclaimed, "Aw, Daisy, you don't know what you're talking about. I couldn't climb that sycamore. It's the biggest one in those bottoms. Why, it's a hundred and fifty feet to the first limb."

With fire flashing from her blue eyes, Daisy said, "Jay Berry Lee, I don't care if it's five hundred and fifty feet to the first limb, you could get yourself down there and get my ribbons. That's the least you could do."

Mama said, "I think we had better forget about the ribbons. I don't want him climbing any sycamore trees. I'm going to order some things from Sears and Roebuck, and I'll get you three spools of ribbons."

That helped to calm Daisy's feelings a little, but not very much. She was still upset about those stupid ribbons.

"Jay Berry," she said, "I'm not going to speak to you for six months. I'm not even going to pass anything at the table to you. I needed those ribbons. I have five doll dresses completely finished and I wanted ribbons for trim."

Daisy had put me through the silent treatment several times in my life, and I didn't like it at all. I could put up with it for a few days and then it would get on my nerves.

It seemed that while I was going through the silent treatment, Daisy would stay as close to me as she could.

She wouldn't say a word; just stare at me with her mouth clamped shut as tight as a snapping turtle.

The only way I could break the spell was by giving her something, or by promising her something.

"Daisy," I said, "if you won't be mad at me for losing your ribbons, I'll let you have Sally Gooden's next calf."

Daisy's eyes lit up and she said, "You will!"

I nodded my head.

"All right," Daisy said. "I'm going to hold you to that. Let's shake hands on it."

I shook hands with her and watched as she hobbled into the house, as happy as a lark.

Daisy and I took turn-about claiming Sally Gooden's calves. Even in that deal, I always came out on the short end. Every time it was Daisy's turn, Sally Gooden had a heifer calf. Every time it was my turn, she had a bull calf. Bull calves weren't worth fifteen cents.

I wasn't feeling too good when I went to bed that night. It had been a terrible day for me. Along with losing the coconuts, I had given up my calf, and I wasn't any closer to having my pony and .22 than I was the day Rowdy treed the first monkey.

I hadn't completely given up on catching the monkeys. I still had a lot of confidence in my old grandpa. With his help, I figured that, in the long run, I'd come out all right. I always did.

13

That night, not long after I had gone to bed, a storm blew in. Br-r-rother, was it ever a storm. As I had often heard my grandpa say, it was a "ringtail wampus cat." I was sound asleep when the storm broke and I was awakened by an earth-jarring clap of thunder that all but turned my bed over. I was lying there, watching the flashes of lightning through my window and listening to the raging storm when the door of my room creaked open.

It was Daisy. She always was scared of storms.

"Jay Berry," she whispered, "I'm scared. Can I come in for a while—just till this crazy old storm blows over?"

I was scared, too, but I wasn't going to let Daisy know it. I figured that boys didn't even let girls know that they were scared.

"Aw, Daisy," I said, as I sat up in the bed, "I don't know what you're scared of. It's just a little old storm."

"A little old storm!" Daisy said, as she came in and sat down on the edge of the bed. "I think it's going to blow the whole country away. I bet my playhouse is a mess, and I had it looking so pretty."

For several minutes, Daisy and I sat in silence, listening to the storm. Lightning was cracking and thunder was rolling. Every time it thundered, our old log house trembled and the windows rattled. Strong

gusts of wind slammed the rain against the window
so hard I thought it would surely break the glass. I
could hear the big red oaks around our home fighting
back at the storm. Limbs were squeaking and snapping, and leaves were rattling.

Right after a loud clap of thunder that all but shook
the house down, Daisy said, "Boy, Old Thor must
really be mad tonight."

"Thor?" I said, surprised. "What are you talking
about? I never heard that name before."

"Surely, Jay Berry," Daisy said, "you've heard of
Thor, the thunder god. Everybody knows about him."

"Well, I didn't know about him," I said. "I've never
heard of a thunder god with a name like Thor. Where
do you hear things like that anyway?"

Daisy sighed and said, "Jay Berry, I just don't know
about you. I learn things by reading. If you would
read something besides those old hunting and fishing
stories, you might learn something, too."

"Aw, Daisy," I said, "I like to read hunting and
fishing stories. I don't like to read anything else. I
wouldn't like to read anything about an old thunder
god."

"I think you'd like to read the story about Thor,
the thunder god," Daisy said. "It's a real good story."

"What's it about?" I asked.

Daisy scooted a little closer to me. She said, "Well,
it goes something like this. Thor, the thunder god,
is a warrior. He lives way up in the heavens somewhere. He has long red hair and a red beard. He has a
chariot, too. It's pulled by four coal-black horses that
snort fire.

"Every time Thor gets mad, he jumps into that
chariot, whacks those black horses, and takes off
through the heavens. The only weapon he has with
him is a big hammer. All along the way, he throws that
hammer right and left. Every time the hammer hits
something, it turns into a bolt of lightning.

"It makes no difference how many times Thor
throws that hammer, he never loses it because it al-

ways comes back to him. The thunder you hear is the rumbling of those chariot wheels. That's why they call him 'Thor, the thunder god.' "

"Boy," I said, "that does sound like a good story. I think I'd like to read it. Do you still have it?"

"Sure," Daisy said. "It's in one of those little books that Grandma gave us. You were supposed to read those books, too; but you never read a one."

"Aw, Daisy," I said, "I don't like to read books like that. Whoever heard of a boy reading stories like *The Little Red Hen, Little Red Riding Hood, The Three Little Pigs,* and stuff like that? They're girl books— that's all they are—girl books."

"Girl books!" Daisy said. "Jay Berry, I declare! I don't think there's any hope at all for you. I don't think you'll ever learn anything. Every girl and boy should read those stories. After all, they are really good stories."

"I don't care how good those stories are," I said. "I couldn't get interested in reading them—not now. The only thing I'm interested in right now is catching those monkeys."

Just mentioning the word "monkeys" made my hair fly straight up. I all but jumped out of bed. I forgot all about the storm and everything else. "Oh!" I said in a loud voice.

A frightened look came over Daisy's face. "What's the matter, Jay Berry?" she asked. "Are you going to have a fit?"

"No," I said, "I'm not going to have any fit! I just thought of those monkeys. I bet they will get drowned in this storm. It would be just my luck."

"Jay Berry," Daisy said, "I don't think you have to worry about those monkeys getting drowned. All animals know how to take care of themselves in a storm. If you know anything at all about animals, you should know that."

"I do know about animals," I said. "I know all about coons, possums, skunks, squirrels, and things like that; but I don't know anything about monkeys.

If I ever catch the ones that are hanging around here now, I hope I never hear the word 'monkey' again as long as I live."

Daisy giggled. "I bet Old Rowdy feels just like you do," she said.

Just then Old Thor really must have thrown that hammer. A big bolt of lightning zoomed down from the sky, hissing like a mad snake. From somewhere close by, there was a loud crack that sounded like a hundred rifles had gone off, all at the same time.

I knew that somewhere in the hills a big tree had split wide open. My room lit up, so bright I could see the stitches in the patchwork of the quilt on my bed. From a sitting position, I jumped about two feet straight up. Daisy shivered; then she uttered a low moan and started rubbing her crippled leg with her hand.

"What's the matter, Daisy?" I asked. "Does your old leg hurt?"

"It sure does," Daisy said. "Every time it storms like this, my leg hurts something terrible. Sometimes I just have to grit my teeth to keep from screaming."

I felt so sorry for my little sister. I wanted to help her but I didn't know what to do. I didn't know anything about doctoring. I couldn't doctor a sick cat, much less a crippled leg.

"Do you want me to get the liniment bottle?" I asked. "Maybe if you rubbed some of that stuff on your leg, it would help."

"No," Daisy said, "that wouldn't help a bit. It used to, but not any more. Lately, nothing seems to help."

"Why don't you tell Mama that your leg is hurting?" I said. "She can doctor anything."

"No," Daisy said, "I don't want Mama to know. She has enough to worry about. Besides, she needs her rest."

About that time, Thor must have gotten tired of riding around in his chariot because the storm let up. The wind, thunder, and lightning stopped but it was still raining tadpoles and crawdads.

As she got up from my bed, Daisy said, "It looks

like the storm is letting up. I think I'll go back to my room and lie down. Maybe my old leg will stop hurting." Just as she reached the door, she stopped and said, "Oh, I almost forgot. Just before I left my room, I saw the Old Man of the Mountains again."

"You did!" I said. "Where was he when you saw him? Right here in our house?"

"No," Daisy said. "He wasn't in the house. When the storm came, I got up to close the window because the rain was coming in. I looked through the glass and saw him standing out in the yard."

"Holy smokes!" I said. "What was the old man doing, prowling around on a night like this? I'll bet he was sopping wet."

"No, he wasn't wet," Daisy said. "The Old Man of the Mountains doesn't get wet if he doesn't want to."

I started to give Daisy one heck of an argument about this. I didn't figure that anyone, not even the Old Man of the Mountains, could mess around in a rainstorm without getting wet, but I had already decided that he was a spirit of some kind and I didn't know a thing in the world about spirits. Maybe they didn't get wet if they didn't want to.

Remembering that Mama had told me to play along with Daisy when she was telling me one of her stories, I said, "What did that old man have to say this time?"

"He didn't say a word," Daisy said. "He was just standing there, pointing that stick at our house."

When I heard Daisy say this, I all but came unglued. "Does that mean we're going to have bad luck?" I asked. "Maybe that old man is going to burn our house down."

"No, Jay Berry," Daisy said. "The Old Man of the Mountains isn't going to burn our house down. He would never do anything like that. He's too kind and gentle."

"But you said every time he pointed that stick at anything, bad luck was sure to come."

"No, Jay Berry," Daisy said, "not every time. It just depends. If the Old Man of the Mountains is frowning when he points that stick, you had better look out. It means he's unhappy with you, and you're sure to have bad luck. But if he's smiling when he points that stick at you, it's different. It means you're going to have good luck."

"Daisy," I interrupted, "when you saw that old man, was he frowning or smiling?"

"He was smiling," Daisy said. "He was just standing out there in the storm with his long white hair and his robe waving in the wind; pointing that stick at our house. Every time the lightning flashed, I could see him as plain as day. He looked pleased and happy, and had a warm smile on his face. We're going to have good luck, Jay Berry, you can be sure of that."

"I sure hope he knows what he's doing," I said. "I could use a lot of good luck right now—a whole tow sack full of it. I'd like to catch those monkeys before someone else does. As unlucky as I've been, that's probably what will happen. I've worried so much now, I'll probably be white-headed before I'm sixteen years old."

"Jay Berry," Daisy said, "maybe if I told you a story, it would get your mind off all that worrying. I have a real good story in mind. Would you like to hear it?"

"Aw, Daisy," I said, "I don't want to hear one of those old ghosty stories; not on a night like this. The way it's been storming and everything, we'll be lucky if we don't wake up dead in the morning anyway."

Daisy giggled. "Jay Berry," she said, "I've never heard of anyone waking up dead; but if you don't want to hear a good story, that's all right. I'll just save it until the next time."

I didn't say anything to my little sister, but I thought, "If I have anything to say about it, there won't be any next-time story telling."

After Daisy left my room, I had a terrible time going to sleep. I kept thinking about that old man of the mountains and the good luck that was supposed to be coming my way.

When I finally did fall asleep, I had a strange dream. I dreamed that Rowdy and I were lost; way,

way back in the mountains. It was pitch dark and I couldn't see where I was going. I walked and I walked. I kept falling over rocks and logs, bumping into trees, and getting all tangled up in the underbrush. Finally, I got so tired and weak, I just couldn't go on. Rowdy and I lay down under a big, white oak tree and went to sleep.

I started dreaming that I heard someone calling my name. "Jay Berry! Jay Berry! Wake up! Wake up now!" I opened my eyes and there before me stood the Old Man of the Mountains in his snow-white robe. I looked down and saw the sandals on his feet. He was just standing there, tall and straight, with his arms folded; looking at Rowdy and me. His eyes were as blue as a robin's egg. He was smiling.

I got up and stood before him. "Old Man of the Mountains," I said, "my little sister said that you would help any girl or boy that had been good. Well, ever since she first told me about you, I've tried hard to be a good boy. I really have. I haven't caught any of the little animals or birds. I haven't even stepped on a flower, or thrown a rock at a lizard. I've done everything that Mama and Papa have asked me to do, and I've said my prayers every night.

"I think I've been a pretty good boy, don't you? Now I need help. I'm lost and I'm tired and hungry. I want to go home. Please, would you show us which way to go?"

The Old Man of the Mountains didn't say a word. He just smiled, nodded his head, and pointed with his stick. Rowdy and I started walking in the direction he had pointed. It wasn't long until I saw the lamplight in the windows of our home.

I was awakened from that wonderful dream by a loud banging noise. Daisy was pounding on the door of my room with that old crutch of hers. "Jay Berry," she yelled, "you'd better get up. Breakfast is ready, and time is a-wasting."

"All right," I yelled, "you don't have to beat the door down. I'm getting up."

Daisy giggled and I heard the thumping of her crutch as she went on her way.

I hopped out of bed and flew into my clothes. Before leaving my room, I walked to the window and raised it. I expected to see a dark, gloomy, miserable day; but I was surprised. The storm had left everything sopping wet, but there wasn't a rain cloud in the sky.

A bright morning sun seemed to be taking a rest right on top of the highest peak of the Ozark Mountains. It was just sitting there, big and bright, and looked like it was trying to make up its mind what to do next; dry everything out or make the green things grow.

Birds were singing and chickens were cackling. Out in the hog pen, Sloppy Ann was squealing with hunger. Up in the pasture, Sally Gooden mooed her delight with the juicy, green world. From down in our fields, I heard the cawing of an old crow and the scream of a red-tail hawk.

It was one of those perfect Ozark mornings—clean, fresh, and green. I closed my eyes, puffed out my chest, and sucked my lungs full of that fresh-scented air. I could feel the tingling sensations clear down to my toes. It made me feel like I had just been born and had my whole life to live again.

As I stepped into the kitchen, I saw that Mama, Papa, and Daisy had just seated themselves at the breakfast table. "Boy," I said as I made ready to wash my face, "wasn't that a storm last night."

"It was a humdinger all right," Daisy said. "With all that rain, I bet Papa's corn will grow twenty feet tall."

"Aw, Daisy," I said as I dried my face on the towel, "corn doesn't even grow that tall. If it did, you'd have to cut the stalks down with an axe to gather the ears."

Papa laughed. "If I ever grow corn twenty feet tall, I'll gather the ears all right," he said. "I wouldn't care if I had to climb the stalks and ride them down to the ground."

Daisy squealed with delight. "Papa, you'd be just like *Jack and the Beanstalk*," she said. "He grew a bean stalk all the way up to the heavens; then he climbed it."

Still chuckling, Papa said, "That would be an easy way to get to heaven. Just grow a bean stalk and start climbing. I'll bet more people would get to heaven by climbing a bean stalk than ever would by following the golden rule."

Looking hard at Papa, Mama said, "I don't want to hear any more talk like that. It's not nice to joke about going to heaven. It's not nice at all."

Papa didn't say a word. He just smiled.

Finished with breakfast, Papa got up from the table. He said, "Well, it's going to be too wet to do any work in the fields today and, in a way, I'm glad of it. There are a few things around the place I've been wanting to do."

Daisy sighed. "I sure have my work cut out for me today," she said.

Mama smiled at her. "What, young lady, are you going to do?" she asked.

"I know that old storm messed up my playhouse, Mama," she said. "I'll just have to give it a good cleaning."

Looking at me, Mama said, "And what do you have on your mind, young man?"

"I'm going down in the bottoms and see about the monkeys," I said. "They could've drowned, or blown away in that storm. I'm worried about them."

"No, I don't want you down in those bottoms," Mama said, shaking her head. "It'll be damp and cold down there. Everything will be dripping wet. You'd probably get soaked and come down with a bad cold or pneumonia."

"Aw, Mama," I said, "whoever heard of a boy getting sick just because he got wet. I've been wet a jillion times and it never has made me sick."

Before Mama could say anything, Daisy giggled and said, "Jay Berry, I remember one time you got wet and you were sick for a month. I'll never forget that."

"When did that happen?" I asked.

"The time you were fixing the pulley on the well, and fell in," Daisy said. "Surely, Jay Berry, you haven't forgotten that. Boy, there was more excitement around here that day than I've ever seen.

"Rowdy was looking down in the well and bawling so loud you could've heard him clear over in Arkansas. Our chickens and geese were making more racket than they do when a hawk comes around. Sloppy Ann was squealing and Sally Gooden went absolutely crazy. She threw her tail in the air, jumped the pasture fence, and we didn't find her for a week. And, with all that racket going on, Cindy—my poor little cat—got so scared she climbed on top of the house and I didn't think I'd ever get her down.

"Mama was screaming and Papa got so scared he almost fell in the well himself—trying to get a rope down to you. Boy, that was a day to remember."

"There was a lot of excitement around here that day all right," Papa said, "but I don't think we've ever had as much excitement as we did the day Rowdy sat down in that yellow jacket nest. It was three days before things were normal again."

"I wish things like that would happen all the time," Daisy said. "It would make things exciting and I just love excitement."

"That wasn't a very nice thing to say, young lady," Mama said. "What if your brother had drowned when he fell in the well? It could have happened, you know."

"Aw, Mama," Daisy said, "I don't think there was much chance of Jay Berry drowning. I looked down in the well and he was swimming like a muskrat down there."

"It wasn't getting wet that made me sick," I mumbled. "I was scared and my nerves got sick."

Everyone laughed, but me. I just couldn't see anything funny about falling in the well. That was a terrible day for me.

Mama seemed to be in a better mood than she had

been and I figured it was a good time to mention the monkeys again.

"Mama," I said, "I wouldn't be down in the bottoms very long—not over a couple of hours. I just want to see how those monkeys made out in the storm."

Mama looked at me and frowned. "Jay Berry," she said, "if you just have to go monkey hunting again, why can't you wait until later in the day? By then, the sun will have things pretty well dried out."

"Oh, all right," I grumbled. "I guess I can wait that long. Boy, I'll be glad when I get a little older."

"And what are you going to do when you get a little older?" Mama asked.

"I'm going way back in the mountains and live in a hollow tree for the rest of my life," I said. "That's what I'm going to do."

"What are you going to do for something to eat, and who's going to wash your clothes?" Mama asked.

"I'll live off the land," I said, "and I won't need any clothes. Won't anyone see me anyway."

Daisy squealed with laughter. She said, "Jay Berry, it gets mighty cold in those mountains in the wintertime. Maybe you'd better take at least one pair of britches with you."

Mama and Daisy started laughing. My blood just boiled.

Papa saw that I was about to blow up and came to my rescue. "I could use some help in the blacksmith shop," he said to me. "I have to sharpen some plow points. You can work the blower on the forge for me."

It was a relief to get out of the house—away from Mama and Daisy.

I loved to help Papa in our blacksmith shop. There was something about the work that fascinated me: the flying sparks and the ringing anvil, the cherry-red metal and the roaring forge.

Papa and I were about halfway to the blacksmith shop when Daisy poked her head out the back door and yelled, "Jay Berry, I've been thinking—if you go to live naked in a hollow tree way back in the mountains, you'd better be careful. A woodchopper might come along and chop that tree down with you in it."

I turned to yell something back, but before I could open my mouth, she giggled and disappeared in the house. I heard Mama laughing with her.

"Women!" I grumbled. "I don't think I'll ever understand them. They think everything is funny."

"Aw, I don't think you're mad at the women," Papa said. "I think you're mad at yourself. Maybe those monkeys have something to do with it. You've been as grumpy as an old settin' hen lately."

"I know, Papa," I said. "I really couldn't get mad at Mama and Daisy. I love them too much; but I want that pony and gun so bad, I can hardly stand it. If something happened to those monkeys, it'll be the end of the world for me and that's all there is to it. I'll never get another chance to make that much money again—not ever."

Papa didn't say anything right away. He just walked along looking down at the ground. Then in a low, deep voice, he said, "Son, if you really want that pony and gun—really want them—I'm pretty sure that someday you'll have them."

I could hardly believe what I was hearing.

"Do you really believe that, Papa?" I said. "Do you really think that someday I'll have a pony and a gun?"

"I sure do," Papa said, nodding his head. "I believe a boy can have anything in life that he wants once he starts working for it. The main thing is not to give up. It makes no difference how tough things get, just bow your back, keep working, and put your heart and soul into it. As you go along your way, live a good clean life, don't hurt anyone or anything, and always be honest. It doesn't hurt to pray a little, too. If you do all of those things—someday you'll have your pony and gun. You'll get help when you least expect it."

"Help?" I said. "Who's going to help me?"

Papa looked at me and smiled. "I think I'll let you figure that out," he said.

I was still trying to figure out what Papa meant when we opened the door to our blacksmith shop. Rowdy had followed us from the house. When he saw where we were going, he stuck his tail between his legs and went back. He didn't like the flying sparks and the ringing anvil. He just didn't like things like that.

14

Thirty minutes later, Papa and I had our old black-smith shop ringing. About that time, I looked through the open door and saw Daisy come out of the house and start up the trail to her playhouse. Rowdy was with her. He was walking along in front of her, wagging his tail as if he didn't have a worry in the world. Daisy was hobbling along on her old crutch and was carrying a broom. Every few steps she would poke Rowdy in his rump with the broom and he seemed to be liking it. He was wiggling all over and snapping at the broom straws.

I stopped turning the handle on the blower. Papa saw me looking out the door and he, too, turned and looked toward the hillside. For several seconds, Papa just stood there, with the tongs in one hand and a hammer in the other, watching Daisy and Rowdy make their way up the trail.

Papa turned again to the anvil and whammed it with the hammer. "It's tough to be a poor man, son," he said, "it's really tough."

"Papa," I said, "is it true that Daisy's old leg is getting worse all the time? Mama said it was."

Papa whammed the anvil again. "I'm afraid it is, son," he said, "and there doesn't seem to be anything I can do about it right now; but someday I will, or I'll die trying."

"But, Papa," I said, "Grandpa and Grandma are saving money, and so are you and Mama. How much money does it take to get Daisy's leg straightened out?"

"It takes a lot of money, son," Papa said. "More money than all of us have; a lot of money."

Just then I heard Daisy yell from the hillside. I had never heard her yell like that. It was scary.

"Mama, come quick! Hurry, Mama! Hurry!"

Mama came flying out the back door. I could see that she was really scared. First, she looked toward the blacksmith where Papa and I were standing in the open door.

From the hillside, Daisy yelled again, "Hurry, Mama! Oh, hurry!"

Mama tore up the trail faster than I had ever seen her run. "What is it, Daisy?" she yelled. "Are you all right?"

Papa looked at me. I could see the scare in his eyes. His face turned a pasty-white. He dropped the hammer and tongs from his hands and snatched a pitchfork from the wall. He shouted, "Snake!" Then he tore out of the blacksmith shop in a loping run.

When Papa shouted "Snake!" my old heart jumped clear up in my throat. I could just see a big diamondback rattler up in Daisy's playhouse, all coiled up, buzzing and ready to sink his poison fangs into anything that moved; maybe he had already bitten Daisy.

Papa was halfway across the barn lot before I caught up with him. We didn't take time to open the gate. We just jumped the rail fence and headed up the trail to the playhouse.

A little bell kept dinging in my head and seemed to be saying, "Something isn't right. Something isn't right."

When I finally figured out what it was, I said in a loud voice, "Papa, it's not a snake."

"How do you know it's not a snake?" Papa shouted.

"Rowdy, Papa!" I said. "If there was a snake up

there, you could hear him bawling all over these hills. You know that. It's not a snake, I tell you."

Papa slowed down. "I guess you're right," he said, "but I wonder what it is."

"I don't know," I said, "but I know it's not a snake."

When Papa and I came puffing up to the playhouse, we found Mama, Daisy, and Rowdy, all standing in a row, looking at the ground.

Papa was holding the pitchfork out in front of him. "What is it? A snake?" he asked.

No one said a word. It was as still as a sleeping ground hog around there.

I looked down to see what they were looking at on the ground. I couldn't see anything but a few little toadstools that had jumped up through the damp earth.

"What is it?" Papa asked again, in a loud voice. "What's wrong?"

"Look, Papa!" Daisy said as she pointed with her hand. "It's a fairy ring!"

"A fairy what?" Papa asked.

"A fairy ring, Papa," Daisy whispered.

Then I saw it—the snow-white circle of little toadstools in a ring that looked about ten feet around. Each toadstool was about the same height. I looked closer and could see that the little stools were the same distance apart—about eight inches. The snow-white ring, the height of the stools, and the distance between each stool was so perfect I could have sworn that someone had planted them.

All my life I had heard stories of the fairy ring: how rare it was, one of the rarest things ever to be found in the Ozark Mountains, and how lucky it was to find one. I knew there was a legend about the ring but I was so stunned I couldn't remember it. I just stood there with my mouth open.

I looked at Mama. I had never seen such an awed expression on her face, or such a warm, tender glow in her eyes. She knelt down, reached out, and touched one of the little toadstools with her hand.

In a low voice, Mama said, "A fairy ring! Oh, how wonderful! So very few have been found. It's a miracle —that's what it is—a miracle!"

Then I noticed something that I hadn't noticed before. A strange silence had settled over the hills. No birds were singing. No squirrels were chattering. I couldn't hear a thing. It was so quiet.

I couldn't remember a day that you couldn't hear something around our home: a cackling chicken, a grunting hog, or a mooing cow. I kept listening and waiting to hear something—any kind of sound. But there was nothing—absolutely nothing—just silence all around us.

"Isn't there a legend about the fairy ring?" Papa said, in a low voice. "Seems like I heard something about it once."

"There is, Papa," Daisy said. "It's an old, old legend—hundreds of years old—and I believe it, too."

"Tell us about it, Daisy," Papa said.

If Papa had gone all over the world, he couldn't have found a better storyteller than my little sister. They just didn't make them any better.

"All right, Papa, I will," she said.

"According to the legend, fairies make the ring so they'll have a place to dance. Some of the fairies sit on the toadstools and clap their hands while the other fairies dance in the circle.

"Whoever finds a fairy ring is very, very lucky. If you step in the center of the ring, kneel down and make a wish, the wish will come true."

Papa looked at Mama. "Say, I remember now," he said. "Not long after we came here from Missouri, someone found a fairy ring. Don't you remember that?"

"Yes," Mama said, "I remember all about it. There's a story about that fairy ring—quite a story."

"Oh, Mama, tell us," Daisy said. "Please, Mama."

Mama smiled and glanced at Papa and me. She could see by the looks on our faces that we wanted to hear the story, too.

"It happened not long after we moved here from Missouri," she said. "I'll never forget it. You children were just little things at the time."

For a few seconds, Mama stopped talking.

Never taking her eyes from that snow-white ring, she said, "Up the river a way, there's a place called Hanging Rock Bluff. Just this side of Hanging Rock, there's a big hollow called Pea Vine Hollow. At the head of it lived a family by the name of Garland. They had a young daughter by the name of Luann, who was in love with a boy by the name of Johnnie George. They were to be married and had already set the wedding date.

"Luann and Johnnie were such a nice young couple and so well liked that people from all over the hills started making up a dowry for them. They were given a team of mules, a milk cow, chickens, pigs, and all kinds of farm machinery; even a little money. It was going to be a big wedding and everyone in the hills was invited."

Mama paused and again she reached out and fingered one of the little toadstools.

"About a month before Luann and Johnnie were to be married, something terrible happened," she said. "Johnnie George was called away to war. Luann's heart was broken but she went right on with her wedding plans as if nothing had happened. She even made her wedding dress.

"Luann got one letter from Johnnie. He told her that he was serving with Teddy Roosevelt and his Rough Riders. Then months went by and not another word was heard. The Garland family felt so sorry for her. Everyone in the hills felt sorry for her. But Luann wouldn't give up. She told everyone that her Johnnie would come home and they would be married.

"Then one day Old Man George came to the Garland home. He had a letter from the War Department—Johnnie George was missing in action.

"People said when Luann heard Johnnie was miss-

ing she went out of her mind. From that day, she
never spoke one word to anyone—not a word. She
walked around as if she were in a daze, and started
taking long walks in the hills. People said that many
times, on moonlight nights, she would put on her
wedding dress and go walking in the hills all alone—
just walking along with her head bowed. It was so sad.

"One morning, right after a rainstorm, while she
was walking in the hills, she found a fairy ring. She
had heard the old legend and so she stepped into the
center of the ring, knelt down, and made a wish—a
wish that God would send Johnnie George home to
her.

"Three days later, in the twilight of evening, just
as the Garlands had seated themselves at the supper
table, they heard someone singing. All excited, Luann
got up from the table. With tears in her eyes and a
smile on her face, she looked at her mother and said,
'Mama, Johnnie's coming home!'

"Those were the first words that Luann had spoken
in a long, long time.

"The Garlands rushed out onto the porch of their
home and looked down the road. Sure enough, it was
Johnnie George coming. He was wearing his army uniform and had a white bandage around his head. He
was walking along so proud; tall and straight; and
with his shoulders thrown back. At the top of his
voice, he was singing the old mountain song 'It's
Whippoorwill Time.' "

Mama hesitated and said, "Let's see, I used to know
the words of that old song. Let's see—oh, yes—I remember.

"In the twilight of evening
 When everything's still
 A song can be heard
 In the Ozark hills.
 It's whippoorwill time. It's whippoorwill time.

"I know of no music
 That has such a thrill

As the twilight song
Of an old whippoorwill.
It's whippoorwill time. It's whippoorwill time.

"Children stop playing
And old ones stand still
And listen to the song
Of an old whippoorwill.
It's whippoorwill time. It's whippoorwill time.

"In the peaceful silence
While lightning bugs glow
All work is forgotten
For the mountain folk know
It's whippoorwill time. It's whippoorwill time.

"When I leave this old world
And climb that steep hill
I hope I am followed
By an old whippoorwill.
It's whippoorwill time. It's whippoorwill time.

"I know he'll be singing
As I walk along
His song of the hills
The whippoorwill song.
It's whippoorwill time. It's whippoorwill time.

After Mama had finished the song, it was very quiet for a few minutes.

Then Daisy said, "Oh, Mama, it's such a beautiful story. Did Luann and Johnnie get married?"

"Yes," Mama said, nodding her head, "Luann and Johnnie got married. It was one of the biggest weddings ever held in these hills. They live in Pea Vine Hollow and have a wonderful family. I met them once at your grandfather's store."

I looked at Daisy. She was standing there, leaning on that old crutch and looking at the fairy ring. Two big tears were slowly rolling down her cheeks.

Again I noticed that strange silence that had settled over the hills. I looked up into the branches of the big red oak. There on a limb sat a gray squirrel. He wasn't making a sound. He was just sitting there as still as a rock, peering down on us. Even his bushy tail wasn't jumping and that was very unusual.

A little wren flew in from the mountains and lit on a low branch of the red oak. I had never seen a wren that could sit still for very long. They seem to be such nervous little birds and are always hopping around and making a racket. That wren never moved or made a sound. It just sat there on the limb as still as a broken fiddle and seemed to be looking at Daisy.

I glanced to my right just as a chipmunk darted to the top of an old hickory stump. He sat up on his tail end, as stiff as a broom handle, with his small front paws bent downward. He never made a squeak. He just sat there as still as the stump he was sitting on, peering at us with his beady little eyes.

Papa had noticed the silence, too. I could tell by the way he looked around.

I couldn't stand that silence. I knew if I didn't say something I was either going to bust wide open or start bawling.

"Boy," I said, in a quavering voice, "it sure is still around here. Why doesn't somebody say something?"

"Well, if finding a fairy ring means you can make a wish and it will come true," Papa said, "I think we should step in this one and make a wish."

"I do, too; and I think Daisy should make the first wish. She found the fairy ring," Mama said.

"Oh, no, Mama," Daisy said, "you make the first wish. Please, Mama."

"Go ahead, Daisy," Papa said. "Make a wish. After all, you were the one that found it."

"Go ahead, Daisy," I said. "Make a wish. You found it."

I knew what my wish was going to be. That was no problem. I was going to wish that I could catch those monkeys, make all that money, and get a pony and a .22.

Daisy smiled. "All right," she said, "I will."

She closed her eyes and said, "Let's see now. What can I wish for? What can I wish for?" Then clapping her hands together to show her delight, she said, "I know what I'll wish for—I know exactly what I'll wish for."

Just before Daisy stepped into the center of the ring to make her wish, she turned her head and looked straight at me. Her blue eyes were as bright as the morning star and a warm smile tugged at her lips.

When I saw my little sister kneeling in the center of that snow-white circle, and that old crutch laying on the ground beside her, I forgot about ponies and .22s. I wanted my little sister to get that old leg of hers fixed up. I wanted that more than anything I had ever wanted in my life. That was going to be my wish.

Once I had made up my mind, I felt pretty good about it. In fact, I had never felt better in my life. I looked at Mama and Papa. They were watching Daisy as she knelt in the center of the fairy ring.

I had never seen such tender, longing looks on their faces. I was pretty sure I knew what their wishes were going to be. They were going to wish for the same thing I was.

Mama and Papa tried to get me to make the second wish but I out-argued them. I told them that I wanted to be last.

All my life I had been wishing for things. Everything you could think of. I had made a million wishes. But the morning I knelt in the center of the fairy ring, I wished harder than I ever had before. I put all my heart and soul into that wish.

After we had made our wishes and were standing there looking at the fairy ring, Mama said in a low voice, "I've been hoping and wishing for so long. I hope the good fairy grants me this one wish—just this one wish."

"Don't tell anyone what you wished," Daisy said. "If you do, the wish won't come true."

"Well," Papa said, "it looks like we've done about all we can here, and there's a lot of work to be done. All we can do now is wait and see if our wishes come true."

Mama looked up at the sun. She said, "It's time I started fixing dinner."

"I'll help you, Mama," Daisy said. "I can clean my playhouse later today. It's a little too wet now anyway."

We hadn't taken ten steps down the trail when I noticed that Rowdy wasn't with us. I turned around to see where he was, and was just in time to see him step very gently over the little toadstools into the fairy ring. He dropped his old nose to the ground and started sniffing around.

"Rowdy," I said in a hard voice, "you get out of there! You're going to step on those toadstools and mash them in the ground."

Rowdy didn't budge an inch. He sat down on his rear and looked straight at me. He whimpered a few times and his old tail waggled all over the place.

Daisy giggled. "Leave him alone, Jay Berry," she said. "Don't you know what he's doing?"

"Sure, I know what he's doing," I said. "He's trying to figure out what we were doing in the fairy ring. He's just nosy."

"No, he's not nosy," Daisy said. "He's making a wish just like we did. That's what he's doing."

"Aw, Daisy," I said, "what are you saying? Whoever heard of a dog making a wish. Dogs don't do things like that."

Mama and Papa had turned around and were watching Rowdy. Both of them were smiling.

"Jay Berry," Mama said, "maybe Rowdy is making a wish. It sure looks like he is."

Papa chuckled. "That old hound is smart," he said. "I'm not surprised at anything he does. I've seen him do things that I couldn't believe."

"He's smart all right," I said. "If I'm digging fishing worms, he'll start digging holes in the ground. He tries to do everything I do."

Papa laughed. "Does he ever pick up a worm and put it in the can?" he asked.

I smiled and said, "No. I've tried to get him to do that, but he won't have anything to do with worms."

Just then Rowdy came bounding out of the fairy ring. He came to me, reared up, and put his paws on my shoulders.

When Rowdy reared up on me like that, he was just about the same height as I was and there was no way I could dodge his lapping tongue. He lapped me on the neck and ears, and all up and down my face. He even pushed my old straw hat off my head and lapped me a few times up there.

I loved him and squeezed him and scratched behind his ears. He liked that.

"Rowdy, if you did make a wish," I said, "I bet I know what you wished for—a big bone or a meat rind."

Oh, how I loved that old hound dog of mine.

Daisy was smiling. "I don't think Rowdy wished for a bone or a meat rind," she said. "I bet he wished those monkeys would disappear."

Both Papa and Mama were laughing at they started down the trail again, ahead of Daisy and me. Papa was carrying the pitchfork in his left hand and his right arm was around Mama's waist. We heard him say to Mama, "Did you notice how still it was there at the fairy ring?"

"Yes, I did," Mama said, "and I couldn't understand it. I've never seen the hills so quiet. You can always hear something."

"Mama," Daisy said, "I know why it was so still there at the fairy ring."

"Oh," Mama said, glancing back at Daisy, "why?"

"Because the Old Man of the Mountains was there," Daisy said. "That's why."

"Aw, Daisy," I said, "you're always seeing things. I never saw any old man. Did you see anyone, Mama?"

"No," Mama said, "I didn't see anyone, but I did have a strange feeling. Maybe the silence had something to do with it. I felt that something was watching us. Something I couldn't see."

"I think we all felt something," Papa said. "I know I did."

"Jay Berry," Daisy said, "just because you didn't see the Old Man of the Mountains doesn't mean that he wasn't there. He was there all right. He's always there. If you ever believed anything in your life, you can believe that."

Just then an old white leghorn hen came sailing out of our henhouse, flapping her wings and cackling her head off. I knew that she had just laid an egg and it had probably tickled her half to death. It always did.

The cackling hen seemed to awaken the silent hills. Birds started singing, squirrels started churring, and chipmunks started squeaking. In the underbrush close to the trail, I saw a little wren. It was hopping around and chirping. I wondered if it was the same wren I had seen in the red oak tree.

Papa stopped and started looking around at the hills. With a smile on his face, he said, "Now, this is more like it. This is the way it's supposed to be. If you take the music out of these hills, they're not the same."

Just as we reached the house, Mama turned to Daisy and said, "Why don't you go to the garden and pick some fresh tomatoes and cucumbers? We'll have them for dinner."

"Sure, Mama," Daisy said. "After that rain last night, I bet I can find some dandies."

Papa and I went to the blacksmith shop to finish our work.

While Papa and I were working, I kept thinking about the fairy ring and the wishes we had made. I couldn't get them out of my mind.

"Papa," I said as I stopped turning the handle on the blower, "do you believe that the wishes we made at the fairy ring will come true?"

Papa didn't answer me right away. I could see by the expression on his face that he was having trouble finding the right words. Then, looking at me, he said, "Son, that's a pretty hard question to answer. But I do believe that any wish you make can come true if you help the wish. I don't think that the Lord meant for our lives to be so simple and easy that every time we wanted something, all we had to do was wish for it and we'd get it. I don't believe that at all. If that were true, there would be a lot of lazy people in this old world. No one would be working. Everyone would be wishing for what they needed or wanted."

"Papa," I asked, "how can you help a wish?"

"Oh, there are a lot of ways," Papa said. "Hard work, faith, patience, and determination. I think that prayer and really believing in your wish can help more than anything else."

"I sure hope the wish I made in the fairy ring comes true," I said. "I'll do everything I can to help it."

After Papa had explained about helping wishes, I still had one more thing I wanted to ask him.

"Papa, has Daisy said anything to you about the Old Man of the Mountains?" I asked.

"No, Daisy hasn't said anything to me about him," Papa said, "but your mother has."

"Do you believe that she really sees that old man?" I asked.

Papa frowned as if he were in deep thought. Before he answered, he laid his hammer down on the anvil, turned, and started stirring up the fire in the forge.

"Yes, son," he said. "I believe that Daisy does see the Old Man of the Mountains. It may be just her imagination, but I believe that she does see something. There is one thing I know. All little children who are crippled can see things and hear things that you and I can never see or hear. I think the Lord has something to do with this. It could be his way of showing them mercy."

"That's what Mama told me," I said. "She thinks that the Old Man of the Mountains is a spirit. Do you think he's a spirit?"

Papa thought a second. "Your mother could be right," he said. "What Daisy is seeing could be the spirit of Christ. Lots of people have seen his spirit; especially, those who are in pain or deep trouble. It happens every day somewhere in the world."

I was so startled by what Papa had said, I couldn't say a word. I even got scared a little. Right then I decided that never again would I tell my little sister that she wasn't seeing the Old Man of the Mountains.

I was thinking about the way Daisy had described the Old Man to me when she poked her head out the back door and yelled, "Come and get it, or we'll feed it to the chickens."

Papa chuckled. "It looks like we'd better go in for some dinner or we won't get any," he said.

15

We were sitting at the table eating, when Papa looked at me and said, "If you find the monkeys, are you going to try to catch them?"

"No," I said, "I just want to see if they are all right. Then I'm going to the store and have a talk with Grandpa. I hope he has something figured out."

As soon as I had finished eating, I walked out in the yard and called Rowdy. "Come on, boy! Let's go!" I said.

The storm had raised Cain in the thick timber of the river bottoms. Trees had been blown down. The game trail we were following was littered with broken limbs and leaves. Puddles of water were still standing in it. Several times Rowdy and I had to work our way around a big tree that had blown down across the trail.

"Boy, Rowdy," I said, "I don't think a ghost could have lived through a storm like that, do you? I bet those monkeys were drowned or got blown away."

About every fifty yards I would stop and listen. Then I'd call in a loud voice, "Jimbo! Where are you? Come on, Jimbo!"

I'd stand still and listen to the echo of my voice die away in the distance. There was no answer from the monkeys—just that cold, damp silence all around us.

The first two or three times I called and got no

answer didn't leave me too discouraged. Then a numb feeling of doubt started creeping in on me.

Rowdy didn't help the situation at all. He was slipping along as if he were walking on porcupines. At every bend in the trail, he would stop and peek around it before going on. His ears were sticking up and he was watching both sides of the trail.

Every little way, Rowdy would stop and look up into the trees. He just knew that any minute a monkey would come flying out of nowhere, land on his back, and start chewing on him.

"Aw, Rowdy," I said, "I wish you'd stop acting that way. You're making me nervous. I don't think you have to worry about any monkeys jumping on you. After a storm like that, I doubt if there's a live one left."

All the way through the bottoms to the river bank. I called and listened, called and listened. I didn't hear a thing—not a sound.

On reaching the river, Rowdy and I stopped to watch a mother duck, with about a dozen little babies, working around an old drift close to the bank. I could hear her talking to her little ones. She was teaching them how to find food around the drift.

One little duck decided to do some exploring on his own. He didn't get ten feet from his mother when she let out a peculiar quack that must have scared the little one half to death. With a baby quack, he scooted back so fast it looked like he was walking on top of the water. On reaching his mother, he shook his little tail as if it was on fire and he was trying to cool it off.

I watched another little duck climb on his mother's back. He sat down and started scratching his neck with a tiny foot.

Across the river on a sand bar, a big blue crane let out a loud squawk. With wings flapping and long legs dragging in the water, he took off down the river.

Out in the middle of the river, a big old catfish rolled and boiled the water to a white foam. Instantly the mother duck quacked her alarm and herded her babies into the shallows. She knew all too well that a baby duck would make a good meal for a big old catfish.

Rowdy and I walked up the river bank for about three hundred yards and then cut back through the bottoms. It was the same thing all over again. I called and called, and got no answer. By the time we reached the rail fence around our fields, my doubts were getting stronger and stronger.

"Rowdy," I said, "it sure looks like our luck has run out. I don't think there's a monkey around here anywhere. I guess something happened to them in that storm."

The next thing that Rowdy and I tried wasn't easy. We followed a game trail until we were about halfway between our fields and the river. Then we left the trail and took off right through the middle of the bottoms.

It was tough going through the thick underbrush. The ground was wet, muddy, and slick. Once my bare feet flew out from under me and I sat down so hard I grunted. Every now and then the underbrush was so thick I couldn't make my way through it. I'd get down on my hands and knees and crawl until I could stand up again. Every time I shook a bush, water would shower down.

All along the way, I called and listened for the monkeys. The only thing I heard was my deep breathing, the thumping of my heart, and the panting of Old Rowdy.

Several times I tried to get Rowdy to go out on his own and do a little sniffing around, but he wouldn't do it. He wouldn't get five feet from me. Once I really got tough with him. I scolded him and even picked up a stick and made believe I was going to whip him.

Rowdy knew I was bluffing. He knew I would never hit him with a stick. He just whined a few times, sat down in the mud, and looked at me.

In every way he could, Rowdy seemed to be saying, "If you want to go monkey hunting, that's all right with me. I'll even go along with you, but I'm not going hunting for those monkeys by myself."

We worked our way through the bottoms for a good quarter of a mile. I kept calling and calling, and got no answer. Finally, I gave up. Wet, cold, and very discouraged, I sat down on an old sycamore log and buried my face in my arms.

Almost in tears, I started talking to myself. "All the monkeys are gone," I said. "I'll never see them again. I'll never have a pony or a gun—not ever."

Rowdy could tell that I was unhappy and this made him unhappy, too. He came to me and tried his best to cheer me up. He tried to push his nose up under my arms so he could lick my face. Then he started licking my hands.

I put my arms around my old hound and said, "It's not your fault the monkeys are gone. It's not my fault either. I guess we weren't supposed to catch them."

Feeling lower than I had ever felt, I got to my feet and started for home.

I hadn't taken ten steps when I thought I heard something. I stopped and listened. I didn't hear a thing. I looked at Rowdy.

Usually, if anything made a racket, Rowdy would hear it and he'd let me know. His ears would stand straight up and he'd point his nose in the direction of the sound.

In a low voice, I said, "Rowdy, I thought I heard something. Did you hear anything?"

If Rowdy had heard anything, he sure wasn't letting me know it. He was just sitting there on the cold ground, looking at me, and wagging his muddy tail.

With his friendly old eyes, he was trying to tell me, "No, I didn't hear anything. I wasn't listening for anything. Let's get out of these cold, wet bottoms and go home where it's warm and dry."

I decided I had just imagined hearing something, and once again I started for home. I hadn't taken three steps when I heard the noise again. That time there was no doubt I had heard something. It was a low, whimpering cry and sounded like a small animal suffering.

Rowdy had heard the noise, too. His ears were

sticking straight up and he was looking toward my right. I could see his nose twitching as he sniffed for the scent.

"What was that, Rowdy?" I whispered. "It sure didn't sound like a monkey. It sounded more like a little animal that's been hurt. Let's see if we can find it, and maybe we can help it."

With Rowdy in the lead, we started working our way toward the sound. We had gone about two hundred yards when I stopped again to listen. For several seconds, I didn't hear a thing. Then I heard the low, pitiful cry.

"Rowdy," I said in a whisper, "whatever that is, it must be suffering. I bet that storm blew down a den tree that had some baby coons in it and one of them got hurt."

Again Rowdy and I started boring our way through the underbrush in the direction of the cry. We had worked our way to the bank of a deep washout when I stopped and listened.

I heard the cry again and I could tell that it was coming from down in the washout. Catching hold of a tall cane growing on the bank, I bent it down and used it like a rope to let myself down to the bottom.

I could see a lot farther in the washout. No underbrush or trees grew there—just bunches of grass, cattails, and ferns.

I stood still for a moment. When I didn't hear anything, I whooped. I was answered by that low cry. By the sound of it, I could tell that I was close to whatever was making it.

I walked up the washout about a hundred yards and stopped to listen. When I heard the cry that time, I almost jumped out of my britches. It was coming from right behind me.

I turned around. At first, I couldn't see anything. Then I saw a small pocket under the bank. Rushing water had made the hole a long time ago.

Mumbling to myself, I said, "Whatever it is that's crying must be under that bank. That's the only place it could be."

I eased over to the side of the washout, dropped to my hands and knees, and looked under the bank into the pocket. I almost screamed. I was looking right in, Jimbo's face. I just knew he would come boiling out from under that bank and jump right in my face— but he didn't.

Jimbo didn't move or make a sound. He just looked at me and batted his eyes as if he were very sleepy. He was sitting there with his back against the wet, cold bank. All the little monkeys were there, too. They were huddled up against his body as close as they could get—trying to keep warm. He had his long arms wrapped around his little friends as if he were protecting them.

Right away, I saw that the monkeys were in terrible shape. They were sopping wet and their small bodies were quivering from the cold.

"Holy smokes, Jimbo!" I said. "What are you doing in there? The storm's over. You've got to get out of that cold place and start moving around. If you don't, you're not going to make it. Come on, let me help you."

Jimbo didn't move. All he did was open his big mouth and utter that low, pitiful cry.

I felt sorry for the monkeys and wanted to help them, but I didn't know what to do. I was afraid they would jump on me.

One little monkey looked as if he were already on his way to monkey heaven. He was off a little to one side, stretched out on the cold ground. At first, I thought he was dead. Then I saw his tiny mouth open as if he were gasping for breath.

I couldn't stand it. I almost cried.

Before I realized what I was doing, I reached in, caught hold of the little monkey's hind legs, and pulled him out from under the bank. Taking my handkerchief, I started drying him off. I laid him down on his back and started rubbing and working his legs.

I almost rubbed all the hair off that monkey, but I must have been doing a pretty good job, because about five minutes later, the little fellow started moving. He even squeaked a few times.

Still holding the little monkey in my arms, I eased over and started talking to Jimbo.

"Come on, Jimbo," I said. "Bring your little friends and let's go down where the sun is shining. They can dry out there and get warm."

Jimbo looked at me and then he looked at the little monkey I was holding in my arms.

I started rubbing the little monkey and talking to it. "It looks like you're going to make it now, little fellow," I said. "It's a good thing I found you when I did."

Jimbo must have realized that Rowdy and I meant him no harm. He came out from under the bank.

The little monkeys started crying. They didn't want Jimbo to leave them.

I set the little monkey down on the ground. Then I stood up and watched to see what would happen.

Rowdy came over and started licking the little monkey with his warm tongue. The little monkey seemed to like it. He closed his eyes and let Rowdy wash away.

For a few seconds, Jimbo stood there watching Rowdy. Then he did something that almost paralyzed me. He shuffled over to me, caught hold of my overalls, climbed up into my arms, and laid his head on my shoulder.

I swallowed a big lump that had crawled up in my throat, and put my arms around his cold, wet body. I started talking to him.

"Everything will be all right, Jimbo," I said. "You don't have to worry. I'll take care of you. Let's get your little friends from under that bank and take them down to where the sun is shining, so they can dry out and get warm."

I set Jimbo on the ground, went over to the pocket, and got down on my knees. I closed my eyes and gritted my teeth as I reached back under the bank and got hold of a monkey. I just knew that some needle-sharp teeth would sink into my hand, but nothing happened. The monkeys must have been too cold and stiff. There was no bite left in them.

Jimbo watched every move I made, but he made no effort to jump on me. He seemed to realize that I was trying to help his little friends.

Five times I reached under the bank and pulled out a little monkey. They were in worse shape than I had thought. They sat where I put them down—all humped up, crying and shivering.

Talking to myself, I said, "I think that's about all I can carry at one time."

Gathering the little monkeys in my arms, I started in a dog trot down the washout to a patch of sunshine I had noticed. Rowdy and Jimbo came with me. About thirty minutes later, I had all of them drying out in the sun.

I had kept count as I made each trip with an armload of monkeys. I could hardly believe it. There were twenty-eight of the little fellows and Jimbo—twenty-nine in all.

In no time at all, the warm rays of the sun had the monkeys pretty well dried out. I picked up one little fellow and rubbed his fur with my hand. He was as dry as Grandma's yarn.

The monkeys made no effort to bite either Rowdy or me. I couldn't understand it. In fact, they seemed to be happy that we were there. I could pick one up and pet it any time I wanted and it wouldn't bite me. The storm and the terrible night must have had something to do with it.

I was pretty sure if I could get Jimbo to go with me, I'd have no trouble with the little monkeys. They would follow him and that was just what I wanted. I decided I'd give it a try.

Taking Jimbo's paw in my hand, I said, "Come on, Jimbo, let's go to the house. We have a good corn crib that's warm and dry. I think you and your little friends will like it. It'll sure beat those cold, wet bottoms. You'll have plenty to eat, too. I promise you that."

Jimbo must have understood me, or had already

made up his mind to come along willingly. He made no trouble at all.

We climbed out of the washout and started down a game trail. I was afraid to look back to see if the little monkeys were following. If they didn't follow us, there was nothing I could do about it just then—absolutely nothing.

We hadn't gone far when a little monkey came zipping by us. With his skinny tail high in the air, he took off down the game trail as fast as he could run. The first thing I knew, the monkeys were all around us: in the underbrush on both sides of the trail, swinging through the trees, and hopping along on the trail.

They were following us. I couldn't help grinning to myself.

"Boy, boy," I said in a low voice, "if my luck will just hold out, I'll have my pony and gun."

I could almost feel them in my hands.

I was within a hundred yards of the house when Daisy came out on the porch. At first, she just stood there leaning on that old crutch of hers. I saw her close her eyes, shake her head, and then very slowly open her eyes again.

She started yelling, "Mama! Mama! Come and look! Hurry, Mama! You won't believe it! Jay Berry's coming home with a thousand monkeys."

I'd never seen twenty-nine monkeys grow into a thousand so fast.

Mama came flying out of the house. She had a tea kettle in her hand. I saw her mouth open and I thought she was going to say something, but she must have lost her voice because I didn't hear her say a thing.

I really couldn't blame Mama for being so surprised at what she was seeing. It's not every day that a boy comes home holding hands with a chimpanzee, and with twenty-eight little monkeys hopping around all over the place. Things like that just don't happen every day.

"Don't just stand there," I yelled. "Somebody—go and open the corn-crib door for me."

Mama and Daisy started running at the same time. Mama still had the tea kettle in her hand. I had never seen my little sister run so fast. That old crutch of hers didn't seem to touch the ground at all.

I saw Papa come to the door of the blacksmith shop. He must have been sharpening something because he had a file in his hand. For a second or two, he just stood there, looking at me and all those monkeys. Then he dropped the file and came toward us in a long lope.

Mama and Daisy were standing off to one side of the corn crib when I came walking up. I couldn't help but smile at the look on their faces. I could see that Mama wasn't looking at me. She had her eyes glued on Jimbo. She was still holding the tea kettle in her hand.

"Jay Berry," she said in a frightened voice, "that thing's not a monkey. It looks like a young gorilla. You be careful."

"Aw, Mama," I said as I reached down and picked Jimbo up in my arms, "he's not a gorilla. He's a monkey and he's as tame as Old Rowdy is. Can't you see that he's not going to hurt anything?"

"No, I can't see!" Mama said in a loud voice. "Have you forgotten the day you and Rowdy came in, bitten all over?"

"That wasn't their fault, Mama," I said. "That was our fault, mine and Rowdy's. They thought we were going to hurt them. That's why they bit us."

"Jay Berry," Mama said in a firm voice, "I don't care what you say, you put that monkey, or whatever it is, in the corn crib this minute. Lock the door and keep it locked!"

"Aw, Mama," I said as I started toward her with Jimbo still in my arms. "Why don't you pet him a little? Then you'll see how friendly he is and you won't be scared of him. He won't hurt you."

I had never seen my mother move backward so fast. Her face turned as white as a hen's egg.

"Jay Berry Lee," Mama yelled, "you get that thing

away from me. I don't want it close to me. If you don't, you're going to get the whipping of your life, and I mean it."

From the tone of her voice and the look in her eyes, I knew she meant what she said.

"Aw, Mama," I said, "I don't see why you're so scared of Jimbo. He's not going to hurt you."

Just then Daisy came over to me and said, "Jay Berry, do you think Jimbo would let me pet him?"

"Sure," I said. "Do you want to hold him?"

Daisy nodded her head and held out her arms.

I passed Jimbo over to her. He wrapped his long arms around her neck and whimpered as if his feelings had been hurt.

Turning her head to look at Mama, Daisy said, "Oh, Mama, he's such a friendly little thing."

Seeing Daisy with Jimbo in her arms did Mama more good than anything. She lost a lot of her scare; but not quite all of it.

She said, "It does look like he's friendly. I didn't know monkeys got that big."

Papa came over. "How did you catch them?" he asked. "It couldn't have been very hard. You weren't down in the bottoms long."

"I can't understand it, Papa," I said. "I didn't have any trouble at all. I think they wanted to be caught. They sure acted like they did."

I told Papa everything that had happened from the time Rowdy and I entered the bottoms until I found the monkeys under the bank.

Papa said, "I think that storm had more to do with your catching them than anything elese. These monkeys are tame. They've lived in cages all their lives. They've never been out in a storm like that and it probably scared them half to death. It's no wonder they wanted to be caught."

"It's a good thing that Jimbo knew where that hole was," I said. "I don't think they could've made it through that storm if they'd stayed in the trees. They almost didn't make it anyhow."

I turned around to see what the little monkeys were doing. I couldn't see one anywhere. I got scared. I just knew they had gone back to the river bottoms.

"Where did the little monkeys go?" I shouted.

Papa laughed and said, "They all hopped up in the corn crib."

I hurried to the door of the corn crib and looked in. The little monkeys were sitting all over the place. Each one was holding a big ear of corn. They were tearing at the shucks with their needlesharp teeth.

Daisy brought Jimbo over and set him down in the crib. Right away he got an ear of corn and joined his little friends.

By this time, Mama had gotten over most of her scare. She came over to the corn crib and looked in at the monkeys.

"Why, the poor things are starving to death," she said, all concerned. "I'll go and heat a pan of milk for them. I bet they'd like that."

All excited, Daisy said, "I'll go and get them some apples."

Right then I saw a good chance to get back at my little sister.

"Daisy," I said, trying to act very serious, "if you don't stop feeding our apples to those monkeys, we're not going to have any apples left."

Daisy smiled and said, "Aw, Jay Berry, you're just trying to be cute now."

"That's what you told me," I said. "Remember?"

Papa said, "I think I'll get a bale of straw and make them a bed to sleep in. After a night like they had out in that storm, I'll bet they could use some sleep."

Just as Papa turned to be on his way, he stopped and looked at Mama. "There's something I'd like to know," he said.

"What's that?" Mama asked.

Papa smiled and said, "What are you going to do with that tea kettle?"

Mama looked at the tea kettle and I could see the surprise spread all over her face. From the way she was staring at it, you would've thought that she'd never seen it before.

Then she laughed and said, "Oh, for heaven's sake, what am I doing with this thing?"

All of us had a good laugh.

Daisy squealed, "Oh, look at Rowdy!"

Rowdy had hopped up in the crib and had sat down right in the middle of all the monkeys. His old tail was really making a racket as it swished back and forth in the corn shucks.

"Rowdy," I said, "I'm going to the store and tell Grandpa about catching the monkeys. If you're going with me, you'd better come out of there."

For once, Mama didn't say one word to stop me. All she said was, "Jay Berry, you hurry back because I don't want you out late."

16

Rowdy and I had made a lot of trips to Grandpa's store. Sometimes I would start out running as fast as I could to see if I was man enough to make it all the way before I ran out of steam. I never could make it. It was just too far. I always ran out of steam. But the day I caught the monkeys, I made the fastest trip to Grandpa's store I had ever made. I ran all the way and even had a little steam left when I got there.

As I came in sight of the store, I saw the mail buggy at the hitching rail. As Rowdy and I came bounding into the store, I saw Grandpa and the mailman standing at the counter, looking at a catalogue.

Almost shouting, I said, "Grandpa, I caught the monkeys! Every one of them! Even the hundred dollar one!"

"You caught them?" Grandpa said, as he jerked his glasses off and stared at me.

"I sure did," I said. "They're locked up safe and sound in our corn crib."

"How many did you catch?" Grandpa asked.

I reared back and said, "Twenty-eight little ones and Jimbo."

"Twenty-nine!" Grandpa said, all excited. "I knew you could do it. I knew it all the time. A man can do anything if he puts his mind to it."

The mailman looked at me. "Are those the monkeys

your grandpa was telling me about?" he asked. "The ones that got away from that circus train—the ones they're offering a reward for?"

I nodded my head.

The mailman looked up toward the ceiling and I could see his lips moving as if he were counting. Then he smiled and said, "Son, you're just earned yourself a lot of money. What are you going to do with all of it?"

"I'm going to get myself a pony and a gun," I said, very proudly. "That's what I'm going to do with it."

Grandpa looked at the mailman. "I know you're in a hurry," he said, "but as long as you're here, could you wait until I write a letter to those circus people? It won't take me five minutes. I'd like to get it in the mail."

The mailman said, "Go ahead but make it snappy. I'm running late and it's going to be after dark when I get back to town."

Grandpa hurried behind the counter, opened a drawer, and started fumbling through some papers. I heard him mumble, "Now what did I do with the letter that had that address on it? I thought I put it in this drawer."

My old grandpa was so excited he had forgotten all about his glasses. He was still holding them in his hand.

The mailman said, "Maybe if you put your glasses on, you could see what you're doing. They do help, you know."

I had to bite my lower lip to keep from laughing out loud.

Grandpa mumbled something that no one could understand, put on his glasses, and again started looking through the drawer.

Grandpa was still searching the drawer when the mailman suddenly spoke up and said, "Hey, wait a minute! Maybe you won't have to write that letter. I heard some fellows in town talking yesterday and they said that the circus is in Tulsa now. If it would help

any, I could send a telegram over there soon as I get
back to town."

I could see the relief on Grandpa's face.

"Help any!" he exclaimed. "I'd say it would help.
How much will it cost to send it?"

"Oh, I don't think it'll cost over fifty cents," the
mailman said. "It's not very far. What do you want
me to say in the telegram?"

Grandpa thought a second, and said, "Just tell them
that the monkeys have been caught and we're waiting to hear from them."

Grandpa and I followed the mailman out to his
buggy and watched as he took off down the road.

We were back in the store when Grandpa said, "Tell
me how you caught those monkeys. I want to know.
I was beginning to think they couldn't be caught."

"Grandpa," I said, "those monkeys were so easy to
catch, it's still hard for me to believe that I caught
them. If it hadn't been for that storm, I probably never
could have caught them. Papa thinks they wanted to
be caught."

"What did the storm have to do with it?" Grandpa
asked.

I told Grandpa all about catching the monkeys;
from the time I found them until they were locked
in the corn crib.

Grandpa chuckled. "Well, it makes no difference
how they were caught," he said. "You caught them
and that's that. Another thing, I don't think we'll have
to wait very long to hear from those circus people.
They want those monkeys pretty bad. I bet we hear
from them in a day or two."

"You think so, Grandpa?" I said, all excited.

Nodding his head, Grandpa said, "If they get that
telegram tonight, I don't think they'll fool around.
From what they told me, those monkeys are really
valuable to that circus."

"Boy," I said, "in a day or two! Wouldn't that be
something!"

I had never seen my old grandpa so pleased and

happy. He didn't know what to do with himself. He stepped behind the counter, picked up a good-size paper sack, handed it to me, and said, "Here, help yourself to the candy."

I was so surprised I didn't know what to say. This was the first time that Grandpa had ever told me to help myself to the candy. I opened the sack and looked inside it. I asked, "How much do you want me to put in it, Grandpa?"

"Fill it up," Grandpa said. "All the way to the top."

As I headed for the candy counter, I said, "Boy, if I eat that much candy I'll probably have a bellyache for six months."

Grandpa chuckled and said, "Oh, I don't think so— I've never heard of a boy having the bellyache from eating candy. I don't think that's possible."

Rowdy followed me and watched while I filled the sack with gumdrops, jawbreakers, peppermint sticks, and horehound candy. I didn't take any of the penny suckers. I figured that the sticks would take up too much room in the sack.

Rowdy knew that practically every time Grandpa gave me some candy, he was supposed to get something to eat, too. He turned, walked over to Grandpa, and sat down right in front of him. With begging eyes, he looked him straight in the face.

Grandpa didn't say a word. He shoved his hands down in his pockets. With a grin on his whiskery old face, he just stood there staring back at Rowdy.

Rowdy couldn't stand to have anyone stare at him and not say anything. His tail started beating the floor and he whimpered a few times. Then he raised his old head straight up and bawled. Never before had I heard such a bawl come out of my old hound.

Grandpa started laughing. He reached down, patted Rowdy on the head, and said, "All right, old fellow, I understand. I've been saving something for you. We had company yesterday and the women cooked a big ham. I saved the bone for you, but you'll have to take it outside to eat it."

That was the biggest bone I had ever seen Grandpa give to Rowdy. It had meat all over it.

When I saw Grandpa give that ham bone to Rowdy, I thought of the fairy ring and the wishes.

"Grandpa, did you ever see a fairy ring?" I asked.

Grandpa frowned, looked at me for a second before he said, "No, I've never seen a fairy ring. From what I understand, very few people have ever seen one. Why did you ask?"

"I saw a fairy ring this morning," I said.

As if he couldn't believe what he had heard, Grandpa said, in a rather loud voice, "You saw a fairy ring this morning?"

"I sure did, Grandpa," I said. "Daisy found it."

"Daisy found it!" Grandpa said. "Where did she find it?"

"Up on the hillside," I said. "Right in front of her playhouse."

Grandpa was flabbergasted.

"Did you make a wish?" Grandpa asked.

"All of us made a wish, Grandpa," I said. "Even Old Rowdy sat down in the fairy ring and acted like he was making one. If he did, it's a cinch he wished for a bone and it looks like his wish has just come true."

"What about your wish?" Grandpa said. "Hasn't it come true?"

"No, not yet," I said, "but I sure hope it does."

Grandpa frowned and said, "I don't understand. Didn't you wish you'd catch those monkeys so you could get that pony and gun? I thought you wanted that more than anything."

"I do want a pony and gun, Grandpa," I said, "but I didn't wish for that. I started to, but I changed my mind."

"Changed your mind," Grandpa said. "I thought catching those monkeys was all you could think about. It's all I've been thinking about. What did you wish?"

"Oh, Grandpa," I said, "I can't tell you what I wished. The legend says that if you tell anyone, the wish won't come true, and I really want my wish to come true."

Grandpa fidgeted a little. "Things like this bother me," he said. "I don't like to be left hanging on a limb. Maybe if you whispered and told me what you wished, no one would hear and everything would be all right."

"Oh, no, Grandpa," I said. "I don't want to take the chance. I want my wish to come true."

Grandpa grinned and said, "I was just kidding you. I don't want you to tell me what you wished. I just wanted to see if you were man enough to stick with it. I'm proud of you."

"Grandpa," I said, "if my wish comes true, I won't only tell you, I'll tell the whole world."

"I'm going to hold you to that," Grandpa said. "You can't ever tell, maybe your wish will come true."

Grandpa looked at his watch and said, "I think you and Rowdy had better hightail it for home. I'm going to lock up the store and make a trip up the road."

"Where are you going, Grandpa?" I asked.

"I'm going up to Indian Tom's place," he said.

"Do you mean Indian Tom, the horse trader?" I asked.

"That's right," Grandpa said, nodding his head.

"What are you going there for, Grandpa?" I asked.

"Indian Tom has been trying to get me to keep a couple of his horses here and sell them for him," Grandpa said. "I think this is a good time to make a deal with him. I'll tie them behind my buckboard and bring them home with me. When you come up tomorrow, you can pick the pony you want."

I was so surprised by what Grandpa had said, I dropped the sack of candy I was holding in my hand. My old heart gave one big thump and then it really took off. I wanted to say something but I couldn't. I just stood there with my mouth open; looking at Grandpa and not even seeing him.

Grandpa grinned and said, "Well, say something. Isn't that what you've been wanting—a pony?"

I swallowed a couple of times, nodded my head, and said, "Sure, Grandpa, I want a pony and a gun real bad, but I don't have any money yet."

"You will have," Grandpa said. "In a day or two, you'll have plenty of money. You can buy that pony and gun and have money left over."

"Boy, Grandpa," I said, "it's hard to believe all of this is happening to me. It's like a dream coming true."

"If a fellow didn't dream and have hope," he said, "life would sure be miserable."

"Grandpa," I said, "why can't I go with you to Indian Tom's? I might learn something about buying horses."

Grandpa frowned and said, "I thought about that, but I don't think it's a good idea. When two old horse traders get together, you might hear some words I wouldn't want you to hear; especially, if you're doing business with Indian Tom. He's the most bull-headed Cherokee I've ever run into. He's smart, too. When it comes to trading or buying horses, he's as smart as a two-headed fox."

"Aw, Grandpa," I said, "I don't think Indian Tom could ever get the best of you in a deal, could he?"

"I'm not too sure about that," Grandpa said. "I've been buying and trading with Indian Tom for a long time now and I always seem to come out on the short end. I can't see how that Indian can be so smart. I don't think he ever saw a schoolhouse."

"Grandpa," I asked, "how much does a pony cost?"

"I don't know," Grandpa said, "but if I know Indian Tom, it won't be cheap. Horses and mules are really bringing a price. Everything else is dirt cheap, but not horses and mules. I'll do the best I can."

"Grandpa," I said, "tomorrow will really be a big day for me—the biggest day of my life."

Grandpa smiled and said, "When you get to be as old as I am, you'll have a lot of memories. I can still remember my first pony. Someday when we have time, I'll tell you about it."

I thanked Grandpa for all he had done for me and I was walking on a cloud as I started for home.

When I reached home Daisy was sitting at the kitchen table where she was putting a new dress on a corn-shuck doll. With the sack of candy in my hand, I walked over and handed it to her. "Here, this is for you," I said.

"What is it?" Daisy asked as she opened the sack.

"It's candy," I said. "Grandpa gave it to us."

Daisy looked down into the sack and her eyes lit up like a match in the dark. "Boy, howdy!" she exclaimed. "Grandpa must really be feeling good today. A whole sack full of candy!"

"I think I'll go have a look at the monkeys," I said. "They may need something."

"I wouldn't bother them, Jay Berry," Daisy said. "They're sleeping now. After they had eaten all they could hold, they crawled down in the straw and went to sleep."

Just then Papa came in from doing his chores, carrying a bucket of milk. As he set the bucket on the washstand, he chuckled. "Just before I left the barn, I peeked in the corn crib," he said. "Those monkeys are all wadded up in that straw bed, sound asleep."

"I think we can forget about those monkeys for a while," Mama said. "Right now we're going to have some supper."

While we were eating, I told them about my trip to the store.

"Jay Berry," Daisy said, "what kind of pony are you going to pick out? What color will it be?"

"I don't care what kind of pony it is," I said, "or what color it is—just so it's a pony."

Mama got up from the table and started stacking the supper dishes.

Daisy said, "Mama, I'll help you with the dishes."

Papa looked at me and said, "While they're doing the dishes, let's go check on the monkeys."

"Sure, Papa," I said, "I'd like to see how they're getting along."

"Don't forget what night this is," Mama said.

"I haven't forgotten, Mama," Daisy said. "It's Bible-reading night."

In our home, three nights a week we read the Bible. It made no difference if we had company, or if one of us was sick, Mama would still read from the Bible. After she had finished reading, she would hold a question and answer period with Daisy and me.

Daisy was always full of questions.

It was different with me. I couldn't always keep my mind on what Mama was reading. Sometimes it would take me down to the river bottoms with Rowdy, chasing rabbits; or back in the hills messing around; or sitting on the river bank with a fishing pole and a can of worms. My mind had a mind of its own and all I could do was go along with it.

It had gotten dark while we were eating. I got the lantern, lit it, and Papa and I walked out to the barn. Before we opened the corn-crib door, we stood still and listened. We couldn't hear a thing—not even a mouse running around in the corn.

In a whisper, Papa said, "Everything must be all right. I don't hear a thing."

As quietly as I could, I opened the door, held the lantern up, and looked in. Jimbo raised his head out of the straw and looked at us for a second. Then he made a sleepy little noise and laid his head down again.

Papa whispered, "They're doing fine. Let's not bother them."

With as little noise as possible, I closed the crib door, locked it, and we went back to the house.

Mama and Daisy were in the front room when we got back. Daisy was sitting on the floor holding a small mirror in her hand and combing her hair.

Mama was sitting in her rocking chair close to the lamp, turning the pages of our Bible. "Jay Berry," she said, "it's your turn to choose what you want me to read."

"Oh, boy, here we go again," Daisy said. "It'll be Daniel in the Lion's den, or David and the Giant, or when Samson took that jackass bone and killed all those people. It'll be one of those three. It always is."

It seemed that every Bible-reading night, Daisy and I got into an argument. I never did figure it was my fault.

"Aw, Daisy," I said, "I like those parts of the Bible. What's wrong with that?"

"Nothing's wrong with it, Jay Berry," Daisy said, "but I've heard those parts so many times, I have them memorized. There are a lot of other good stories in the Bible. Why can't you choose something else?"

"All right, I will," I said, looking at Mama. "Read that part where God opened up the river and all those people walked across and didn't even get their feet wet."

Daisy said, "It wasn't a river—it was the sea."

"What difference does it make?" I grumbled as I walked over and sat down by Daisy's side. "It's all water."

As she turned the pages, Mama said, "Let's see—that will be in Exodus."

After Mama found the place in the Bible, she made herself comfortable in her chair and started reading. Mama was a good reader; especially, if she was reading from the Bible. For a good hour, we sat and listened to Mama read about how the Lord opened up the sea and let the good people walk over to the other side.

I really liked that part of the Bible. I thought it was wonderful how the Lord had opened up the sea. Many times while Rowdy and I were prowling the river banks I would stop and, with my arms folded, I'd stare over the river and wonder how He did it. I never could understand it.

After Mama had finished reading, and the question and answer period was over, Papa got up from his chair, stretched his arms, and yawned. "It's bedtime," he said. "I want to get a good night's sleep. It should be dry enough to work in the fields tomorrow."

I was in my room, getting ready for bed, when Daisy poked her head in the door. "Jay Berry," she said, "when you came back from the store, what was Rowdy carrying in his mouth?"

"It was a bone," I said. "Grandpa gave it to him."

Daisy smiled and said, "That's what I thought it was."

I heard her humming a happy little tune as she went to her room.

That was a miserable night for me. I must have had a dozen dreams—good ones and bad ones.

I dreamed that the corn crib was on fire and the monkeys were screaming for help. Then I dreamed that Jimbo had opened the door and all the monkeys got out. I could see them with their tails in the air, running back to the river bottoms.

I dreamed that I was riding a beautiful pony, up and down the country roads, and far back in the green rugged hills; even way up in the clouds—riding, riding, riding.

Once I fell out of bed and it scared me half to death.

Along in the wee hours of morning, I fell asleep. The next thing I knew I was awakened by Daisy, poking me with that old crutch of hers.

"Jay Berry," she said, "you'd better get up. Breakfast is almost ready, and things are liable to start happening around here today."

"All right," I said, "you don't have to poke a hole in me with that crutch. I'm getting up."

I heard Daisy giggle as she left my room.

When I walked into the kitchen, yawning and rubbing the sleep from my eyes, Mama looked at me and said, "Jay Berry, you look terrible. Your eyes are red and you look a little pale. Are you sick?"

"No, Mama," I said, "I'm not sick. I dreamed all night and I didn't sleep very good."

Papa and Daisy were already sitting at the table.

Daisy said, "Mama, maybe you should make him stay in bed for four or five days and let me doctor him."

"Oh, no, you won't," I said. "I'm not staying in

bed and I don't need any doctoring. I've waited a long time for this day. I'm going after my pony and I don't want anything to mess that up."

Papa said, "Wash your face in some cold water. That always helps. At least, it'll wake you up."

Our well water was as cold as a plow point in January. I poured some of it into the wash pan and washed my face. It almost took my breath away but I did feel better.

While I was drying my face, I saw that Mama was dishing up some oatmeal for me. "Mama," I said, "I think I'll go check on the monkeys before I eat breakfast."

"You won't have to do that," Papa said. "I took care of them while I was doing chores. I gave them a fresh pan of water and some more vegetables. They're doing fine."

I thanked Papa and sat down at the table.

I was so nervous and excited about getting my pony, my oatmeal didn't even taste the same that morning.

We had just about finished eating when all at once Rowdy came tearing out from under the porch, bawling his head off.

Papa looked at Mama and said, "Must be somebody coming."

"This early in the morning?" Mama said. "I wonder who it could be."

"Listen! What's that?" Daisy said.

Then we all heard it, the chugging of a motor.

"Why, that sounds like a car," Papa said.

"I think it is a car," Mama said.

To see a car pass our home was just about as rare as seeing a white blackbird. I had seen very few of them up until then and those I had seen had passed by in a cloud of dust.

We hurried out to the porch.

Rowdy was standing in the middle of the road, with every hair on his back standing straight up, and bawling for all he was worth.

It was a car, but not like any I had seen. It had one

seat and the back of it was nothing but a big box about ten feet high and ten feet long. The box was almost as wide as the road and was painted white and green.

I heard Papa say, "It's a truck, but I've never seen one like that."

"I haven't either," Mama said. "It looks like a house built on the back of a car."

"I know what it is, Mama," Daisy said. "I've seen pictures of them. It's a circus truck."

When I heard Daisy say that, a funny feeling came over me. My skin started crawling around on my bones.

Chugging and squeaking, the big truck wheezed up in front of our house and stopped.

Rowdy must have thought the truck was a booger and he didn't want it messing around our home. Growling and showing his teeth, he darted in and bit one of the tires.

I heard Mama say in a low voice, "That crazy dog."

On the side of the truck facing us was a picture of a huge gorilla fighting with a big snake. Above the picture, in a half-moon design, large red letters said "Johnson Brothers Circus."

Two men got out of the truck and came over to us. One of them said, "Good morning!"

Papa nodded his head and said, "Mornin'!"

The man said, "I'm Ben Johnson. This is my brother, Tom. We're looking for the Lee farm."

"You've found it," Papa said. "I'm Bob Lee. This is my family—my wife, Sara; my daughter, Daisy; and my boy, Jay Berry."

The Johnson brothers were very polite. They took off their caps and nodded to Mama and Daisy. Then they shook hands with Papa and me.

I had never shaken hands with a man before and it gave me a wonderful feeling. I felt like I had grown about a foot straight up.

Ben Johnson smiled and said, "So you're Jay Berry. Your grandpa says that you have some monkeys for me."

"Yes, sir," I said. "They're out in the corn crib."

"Could we have a look at them?" Ben Johnson asked.

"Sure," I said.

"It didn't take you fellows long to get here," Papa said.

"When we got that telegram, we didn't lose any time," Tom Johnson said. "We jumped in our truck and drove all night."

With Rowdy in the lead, we started for the barn. On the way, Ben Johnson explained how valuable monkeys were to a circus. He said a circus just wasn't a circus without monkeys.

When I opened the corn-crib door, we saw Jimbo sitting on top of the corn, eating an apple. The minute he saw Ben Johnson, he dropped the apple and started grunting as he hopped up and down on his short legs. Then he raised his long arms in the air and started toward us. He jumped from the corn-crib door right into Ben Johnson's arms.

Mr. Johnson wrapped his arms around Jimbo and buried his face in his fur. In a choking voice, he started telling him how happy he was to see him, how much he had missed him, and how much he loved him.

Jimbo whimpered like a little puppy.

I thought Mr. Johnson was going to cry.

Mama said, "I didn't know that animals could have so much love for anyone."

I looked at Daisy. She was leaning on that old crutch. There were tears in her eyes.

Ben Johnson looked at his brother and said, "Tom, do you think you could back the truck up to the corn crib?"

"Sure," Tom said, "that would be easy, but I don't know about getting through the gate. It looks a little narrow to me."

"We can take out one panel of the rail fence," Papa said. "You'd have plenty of room then."

"You wouldn't mind?" Ben Johnson said.

"Naw," Papa said. "That's one thing about rail

fences—they're easy to tear down and easy to put up."

After the truck was backed up to the door, it was no trouble to load the little monkeys.

Mr. Johnson locked the truck door. He turned to me and said, "Well, Jay Berry, I guess it's payday."

He reached in his back pocket and got his money poke. He opened it and took out the biggest wad of money I had ever seen.

My eyes almost popped out of my head.

"Let's see," he said, "two times twenty-eight is fifty-six, and one hundred for Jimbo—that comes to one hundred and fifty-six dollars."

I held out both hands and stood speechless while he stacked the money into my trembling hands. In a voice choked with emotion, I thanked him. I folded the money and crammed it down in my pocket.

I heard Daisy say in a low voice, "Mama, he's really going to be hard to get along with now that he's rich."

Tom Johnson walked over to Papa with four small blue cards in his hand. "Mr. Lee, I'd like you and your family to have these," he said. "They're lifetime passes to our circus."

Papa thanked him for the cards and said, "We're poor folks and don't get out of these hills very often; but next year when your circus comes to Tulsa, we'll try to be there."

"You do that," Tom Johnson said. "Look me up and I'll see that you don't miss anything."

Mama said, "Would you fellows like a cup of coffee or something to eat?"

Ben Johnson turned to Mama. "Thanks, Mrs. Lee," he said. "We'd like that fine but I'm afraid we don't have the time. We're in a terrible hurry. Our circus is leaving Tulsa for Arkansas tomorrow and we have to be there."

The Johnsons said "Good-bye" to Mama and Daisy, and shook hands with Papa and me. Then they got in their truck and took off down the road in a cloud of dust.

As I stood there in our barn lot and watched the truck disappear in the distance, a strange feeling came over me. I should have been very happy but I wasn't. I felt a little sad and a little lonely.

"There go the monkeys," I said. "I wonder if I'll ever see them again. I hope so—but even if I don't ever see them again, I know I'll never forget them. I'll always remember this as the summer of the monkeys."

Papa said, "I don't think any of us will ever forget those monkeys."

While still standing there, I thought of something. I ran my hand down in my pocket and pulled out the wad of money. I peeled off a five dollar bill and the one dollar bill.

"Here, Daisy," I said, offering her the money. "I want to pay what I owe you."

As if she couldn't believe what she was seeing, Daisy looked at the money and then at me. "Six dollars, Jay Berry!" she said. "You don't owe me that much."

"I know, but I want you to have it," I said. "You fed the monkeys for me."

Daisy took the money and smiled. "Jay Berry, you beat anything I've ever seen," she said. "I can't figure you out. I should kiss you."

"Kiss me!" I said as I backed up. "No, you won't! You're not going to do anything like that. I don't want any girls kissing me."

Mama and Papa were watching us. Papa laughed. Mama just stood there, smiling.

"I've waited a long, long time for this day," I said. "I'm going to see Grandpa right now. I'm going to get my pony."

"I don't think you have to be in that big a hurry, do you?" Mama said. "Can't you wait until after dinner?"

"I don't want any dinner, Mama," I said. "I don't want anything but that pony."

Mama looked at me for a second, then she smiled and said, "I guess you've earned that right. Go ahead. Get your grandpa to help you pick out a good pony."

"I will, Mama," I said.

17

Just as Rowdy and I started for Grandpa's store, Daisy yelled, "Jay Berry, if you're going to be running, you'd better be careful. You might lose your money."

This scared me. Daisy was right. I ran my hand down in my pocket, and took a firm grip on my money before I started running. I learned on that trip that it's not easy to run for three miles with one hand in your pocket, but I did it.

Grandpa must have been looking for me, because he was standing in the doorway when I came puffing up.

"When I saw you coming, I thought you had lost an arm," he said. "I couldn't see but one."

"I was afraid I might lose my money, Grandpa," I said, grinning, "so I held onto it all the way."

"Oh, I see," Grandpa said.

As we walked into the store, I said, "Did you get those ponies, Grandpa?"

"They're out in the barn lot," he said. "Two of them—a roan gelding and a paint mare. They've been broken and they're gentle."

As I stood there looking at my old grandpa, I had a feeling that something was bothering him. He just wasn't acting natural. He was too serious. He didn't seem to be the least bit excited about the ponies.

Thinking maybe I was just imagining things, I

asked, "Grandpa, how much is the pony going to cost me?"

"He wants a hundred dollars for the roan," Grandpa said, "and seventy-five dollars for the paint. That's what that Indian wanted when I got there and that's what he still wanted when I left. I've sworn a hundred times that I wouldn't deal with that Cherokee any more—and I mean it this time."

I couldn't help grinning, for I knew that Grandpa didn't mean what he was saying. The truth of it was that he and Indian Tom were very good friends—unless they were making a deal for horses.

"Grandpa," I asked, "will you help me pick my pony?"

Grandpa frowned. "I've been thinking about that," he said. "The way I look at it, this is your first pony and I think you should pick the one you want all by yourself. I don't think you should have any help from me or anyone else. This will be something you will always remember—your first pony. I don't think you should share this with anyone."

"All right, Grandpa," I said. "I hope I don't pick the scrubbiest one."

"You won't have to worry about that," Grandpa said. "They're both good ponies."

I thanked Grandpa, and with Rowdy bouncing along at my side, I walked out to the barn lot. Before I opened the gate, I peeked through a crack and saw two of the most beautiful ponies I had ever seen.

The ponies had heard us. They were standing with their heads raised and their ears pricked up, looking toward the gate. Horse flies were bothering them. They were stomping their feet and swishing their tails.

Right off I saw that the roan didn't stand as high as the paint. He was chunky and solid. His coat was so glossy it glistened in the sun.

"Rowdy," I said in a low voice, "that roan is built for power. He could go all day and night and never get tired."

The paint was almost too pretty. She was more white than black, and more streamlined than the roan. The dark black patterns looked like they had been painted on her. Her legs were long and slim. She had a perfect head, small and dainty.

"Rowdy," I said, "that paint is built for speed. I'll bet she could run like the wind."

I opened the gate, walked up close to the ponies, and stopped. What I knew about judging horses, you could have put in a snuff can. All I had to go by was what I liked.

As far back as I could remember, in every dream I had had of owning my own pony, it had always been a beautiful paint.

Not taking my eyes from the paint, I said, "Rowdy, I won't have to look at that roan, I've always made up my mind. I want that paint. That's the pony for me."

Rowdy seemed to realize that this was one of the biggest days of my life. He was so happy he was wiggling all over the place.

To make the ponies move so I could see how they walked, I stomped my foot, clapped my hands, and shouted, "Hey!" in a loud voice.

The roan snorted and bolted to the other side of the lot. The muscles in his legs and shoulders knotted and quivered as he ran. He was a beauty.

The paint didn't move from her tracks. She just stood there with her head up, looking at us.

I liked that. I didn't want my pony to be nervous and jumpy. I walked over to her and held out my hand.

The paint wasn't the least bit nervous or scared. With her small ears pointing at me, she lowered her head. I felt her hot breath on my fingers as she nuzzled my hand. Then she raised her head and nibbled at the brim of my old straw hat. I noticed that her eyes were light brown, warm and soft.

I almost cried as I laid my face against her head. "I've waited a long, long time for you, little girl," I said. "Now you're mine. I'll always be good to you."

I backed up about ten feet from the paint and snapped my fingers. "Come on, little girl," I said. "I want to see you walk."

She came to me willingly, but what I saw hurt me all over. She was limping in her right hind leg.

"What's the matter, little girl?" I asked as I walked around to have a look at her leg. "Do you have something in your hoof?"

When I knelt down, I saw why the pony was limping. My old heart dropped clear down to the bottom of my stomach. I didn't want to believe what I was seeing.

In the fetlock, just above the hoof, my beautiful pony had a deep, raw, red wound. Flies and gnats were swarming around it. I jumped back and said, "Oh! Oh, no!"

Not taking time to open the gate, I flew over the rail fence and ran to the store.

"Grandpa," I shouted as I darted through the door, "that paint pony has a bad cut on its leg."

Grandpa looked over his glasses at me. "I know that pony has a cut on its leg," he said. "She got it caught in a barb-wire fence, but it's not as bad as you think. The tendon hasn't been hurt at all. With the right kind of doctoring, that pony will be as good as new in four or five weeks."

"Four or five weeks!" I exclaimed. "Grandpa, I don't want to wait that long for a pony to ride. I want a pony I can ride right now. I'd like to ride it home."

"What about the roan?" Grandpa said. "He's a good pony. He's just as good as the paint—maybe even better."

"He sure is a beauty," I said, "but I wanted the paint. I've always wanted a paint pony, but I don't want one that's crippled."

"Why don't you have another look at that roan," Grandpa said. "You might change your mind."

"All right," I said, "but I sure wanted that paint."

With a heavy heart, I went back to the barn lot to look at the roan gelding. I must have walked around him at least fifty times. I liked everything I saw but I just couldn't make up my mind. Something seemed to have gone out of my pony-wanting.

Every step I took, the paint followed; limping along

beside me. Time after time, she would push me with her head. She nibbled at my clothes. Once she even nickered. She seemed to be begging me to take her.

More disturbed than I'd ever been, I went back to the store to have another talk with Grandpa.

"Grandpa," I said, "I like that roan—I like him a lot—but I can't make up my mind. I just wish that paint wasn't crippled."

"I'd like to help you," Grandpa said, "but I'm afraid I can't. You'll have to make up your own mind."

"Grandpa," I said, "are those the only ponies Indian Tom had to sell?"

"No," Grandpa said. "Indian Tom had about sixty head he wanted to sell; all kinds—horses, mules, ponies, and even a few donkeys."

"He did!" I exclaimed. "Then how come you brought that crippled one home? Why didn't you bring one that wasn't a cripple?"

"Oh, I don't know," Grandpa said very seriously. "You know, there's a reason behind everything. Maybe I felt sorry for that little mare. I feel sorry for anything that's crippled, don't you?"

"Oh, sure, Grandpa," I said, "I always feel sorry for crippled things. I really feel sorry for that little mare. She's so pretty I'd take her in a minute, but I don't want to wait four or five weeks to ride her."

"It's tough for anything to be crippled—animals, human beings, even little birds," Grandpa said. "You know, a lot of cripples could be helped if someone would just take the time to help them."

The way Grandpa kept talking about crippled things started me thinking that he wanted me to take the paint pony.

Because I'd have done anything for my grandpa, even if it hurt me, I said, "Grandpa, do you want me to take the paint? If you do, I'll take her even if she is a cripple."

"No! No!" Grandpa said, shaking his head. "I'm not trying to make up your mind for you. I want you to do that. You pick the pony you want."

"I think I'll have another look at them," I said. "I just wish that paint wasn't a cripple. I'd be riding right now."

"If you do make up your mind," Grandpa said, "there's a halter hanging on the gate post."

I thanked Grandpa and walked back to the barn lot with Rowdy. I took the halter from the gate post, opened the gate, and stepped inside.

The ponies were standing at the far end of the lot, about ten feet apart. They were watching us.

As I stood there with the halter in my hand, looking from the roan to the paint and from the paint to the roan, I said, "Doggone it, Rowdy, I don't know which pony I want. If I take the roan, I know I'll never forget that little mare. If I take her, I'll have to wait before I can ride her. If I had enough money, I'd just buy both of them."

I had about decided to have another talk with Grandpa when suddenly Rowdy trotted across the barn lot and sat down right in front of the little mare. With his old tail stirring up the dust, he looked up at her.

The little mare wasn't the least bit scared of Rowdy. She just stood there looking down at him with her small ears pointing forward. Then very slowly she lowered her head and sniffed him. I saw Rowdy's long tongue reach out and lap her nose. She threw up her head and snorted but didn't move from her tracks.

Rowdy's old tail went crazy. I couldn't hear him but I knew that he was whimpering happily.

I could tell by the surprised look on the little mare's face that it was the first time she had been kissed on the nose by a hound dog. She must have liked it because she lowered her head and had another sniff.

Rowdy went absolutely crazy. He wiggled and twisted all around the little mare. Once he even pranced under her.

The little mare never moved. She just stood there, favoring her crippled leg, swishing her tail, and watching Rowdy's happy actions.

All at once Rowdy left the little mare and came bounding back to me. He almost knocked the breath out of me by rearing up and hitting me in the chest with his front paws.

I put my arms around my old hound. "Aw, Rowdy," I said, "what did you want to do anything like that for. Are you trying to tell me to take the little mare? She's crippled. Can't you see that? I don't want a crippled pony."

I still had my arms around Rowdy and was trying to dodge his lapping tongue when I saw a movement from the corner of my eye. I looked up and saw the little mare come limping across the barn lot. She came right up to me and gave me a push with her head.

Up until then everything that had happened had made my old heart as heavy as lead, but when the little mare gave me that push it just hauled off and melted.

With one arm around my old hound dog and the other arm around the neck of the little mare, I said in a choking voice, "All right, little girl, you win. You've got yourself a home and I've got myself a pony. I think I would have picked you anyway."

I could have sworn that she lowered her head to make it easy to put the halter on. I led her out of the barn lot and was tying her to the hitching rail when Grandpa came out of the store. His hands were shoved down in his pockets and he had a serious look on his face.

"Is that the pony you want?" he asked.

"It sure is, Grandpa," I said. "I've waited this long for a pony to ride, I guess I can wait another four or five weeks."

Grandpa frowned and started digging at his wiry whiskers with his fingers. "I hope you haven't made a mistake," he said. "Sometimes a fellow can do things in too much of a hurry. Later on, he may regret what he's done."

"I won't ever regret buying this little mare, Grandpa," I said. "I won't ever regret that."

"I hope not," Grandpa said.

"Do you think I should have taken the roan?" I asked.

"No," Grandpa said, "I didn't mean that at all. I just want you to be sure of what you're doing. I wouldn't want you to be hurt later on."

Just then Grandma came out on the porch of the house.

"Jay Berry," she hollered, "is that the pony you're going to buy?"

"It sure is, Grandma," I hollered back. "What do you think of her?"

"She's a beauty," Grandma said, "but I thought I saw her limping."

"She has a cut on her leg," I said. "Grandpa says it'll be all right in a few weeks."

"You let your little sister doctor that crippled leg," Grandma said. "She'll have her well in no time."

Before I could say anything, Grandpa said, "By golly, your grandma's right. Daisy probably knows more about crippled legs than anyone in these hills. She's been walking around on one all of her life."

"If I know Daisy," I said, "I won't have to ask her to doctor my pony's leg. She'll put on that Red Cross uniform and take over. She always does."

"Maybe I should have another look at that leg," Grandpa said.

He came over, knelt down, and fingered the cut with his gentle old hands. Clicking his tongue and shaking his head, he said, "That is a nasty cut but the tendon hasn't been hurt at all. I hate to see anything crippled like that. It's pitiful."

On hearing a rumbling noise, I looked down the road and saw a wagon coming. There were five Cherokee Indians in it.

"Grandpa," I said, "it looks like you have some people coming to the store."

Grandpa stood up, looked down the road, and said, "That's John Comingdeer and his family."

Then Grandpa turned to me and said, "Maybe you

should go home and think more about buying this pony. Talk it over with your mother and father, and your sister. You might want to change your mind."

I could hardly believe what Grandpa was saying. "Change my mind!" I said. "Oh, no, Grandpa, I wouldn't ever do that. I want this little mare more than anything. I won't ever change my mind about that."

"I know how much you want that pony," he said. "I went through the same thing when I was a boy. But sometimes a fellow can want something so bad he will overlook things that are more important. When that happens it can really hurt a fellow. I know. I've had it happen to me."

Knowing my old grandpa as I did, I had the feeling that he was trying to tell me something but I couldn't figure out what it was. He knew how much I wanted a pony and a .22.

"Grandpa," I said, "I couldn't be overlooking anything. Owning my own pony and a .22 are the most important things in my life. That's all I've ever wanted. I don't want anything else."

"All right," Grandpa said. "I guess your mind is made up. If a pony is what you want, a pony is what you'll have. You've earned that right. I won't say any more."

Just then the wagon pulled up in front of the store and the Indians started getting out of it.

"Oh, yeah," Grandpa said, "I almost forgot. You'll need a saddle. I know a fellow down the river has a good used one he wants to sell. I think we can get a pretty good buy on it."

"I'll take it," I said before I thought. "That is, if I have enough money. If I have to, I can do without that .22 for a while."

"You won't have to do without anything," Grandpa said. "You have a hundred and fifty-six dollars, don't you? That's more than enough to get the pony, saddle, and gun."

"Grandpa, I gave Daisy six dollars," I said. "I just

had to. She's always doing things for me. She even fed the monkeys for me."

"That's all right," Grandpa said. "You still have enough, and you should have some left over."

I ran my hand down in my pocket, pulled out my money, and handed it to Grandpa.

"Grandpa," I said, "will you take care of my money, and pay Indian Tom for the pony? If I have any left after I buy that saddle and gun, I'll give it to Mama."

"I'll take care of it," he said. "Don't worry about a thing."

I was untying the halter rope from the hitching rail when Grandpa said, "On your way home, I'd take it easy with that mare. Don't walk her too fast. In a few weeks, you'll have one of the finest little ponies in these hills."

"Grandpa," I said, "without you, I don't know what I'd do. I really don't. You're always helping me."

Grandpa grinned. "That's what Grandpas are for, isn't it?" he said.

I thanked Grandpa and, with my heart singing, I started for home.

As I walked along the country road leading my pony, no boy on earth could have been happier. All my dreams had finally come true. I had my own pony.

I couldn't remember a day when the sky looked so clear and blue, or the sunshine so bright. Every bush seemed to have a bird singing its head off. From down in the bottoms I heard the shrill call of a bobwhite and the clammering cry of a kingfisher in flight.

At the top of an old dead tree close to the road, a mockingbird started singing. I stopped to listen. He mocked every bird in the Ozark hills; from a red-headed woodpecker to a screaming blue jay.

On that walk, my old hound wouldn't get a foot from my side. He never had done that before. About every ten feet, I would feel his warm tongue lick my hand. He acted like he was jealous of the little mare.

I stopped, knelt down, and put my arm around him. "Aw, Rowdy," I said, "you don't have to be jealous of my pony. I'll always love you. You know that. Why, I couldn't live without you."

Rowdy was so pleased he went all to pieces. He started running circles around us. He found an old corn cob laying by the side of the road and started playing with it. Holding it in his mouth and slinging his head, he bounded down the road. He dropped the corn cob in the middle of the road and started to growl and dig at it.

I laughed out loud at his playful actions.

As I walked along, I decided I'd try something. I threw the halter rope over my pony's neck and kept walking without looking back. I hadn't gone twenty feet when I heard the clopping of her hoofs. She was following me. I was so proud of her my old heart came close to jumping right through the bib of my overalls.

As I neared our farm, I saw Papa plowing way down in one of our fields. He stopped his team, jerked his battered old hat from his head, and waved it at me. I waved back—feeling as proud as I ever had in my life.

About fifty yards from our house, I stopped. With my fingers, I combed my pony's mane and straightened out the long hair in her beautiful tail. I rubbed the dust from her coat with my handkerchief. I wanted her to look pretty before Mama and Daisy saw her.

Just as I took hold of the halter rope to be on my way again, I heard Daisy humming. She was in her playhouse up on the hillside.

I wasn't too surprised when she started singing. I stopped and listened. She was singing my favorite song —a song I had heard my mother sing many, many times, "The Old Master Painter from the Far Away Hills."

As I stood there listening to her clear voice ring out over the valley, I happened to glance down to the raw, red wound in my pony's leg. Like a bolt of lightning, it hit me. I knew then what my old grandpa had been trying to tell me.

I was so shook up, I dropped the halter rope. Closing my eyes and shaking my head, I said, "Oh, Grand-pa, how could I have been so dumb? Dear God, how could I have been so stupid?"

In a daze, I stumbled to the side of the road. I sat down on a rock and buried my face in my arms. I remembered everything my old grandpa had said; from the time I got to the store until I left.

"Don't be in too big a hurry about buying this pony. Talk it over with your mother and father. Be sure of what you are doing. I don't want you to do something you'll be sorry for later on."

Rowdy must have sensed that something was wrong. He came to me and tried to push his head up under my arms so he could lick my face. I put my arms around him.

In a voice choked with emotion, I said, "Rowdy, I can't buy this pony. I just can't. If I did buy her, I could never ride her. Every time I got on her back, I'd think of my little sister and that old crippled leg of hers. That's what Grandpa was trying to tell me. He wanted me to give the money to her so she could go to the hospital and get it straightened out. How could I have been so dumb. I guess I just couldn't think of anything but the pony."

I got up, took the halter rope in my hand, and started back to the store."

I saw Papa stop his plowing. He didn't wave his hat at me that time. He just stood with his hands on the plow handles, watching me as I walked back up the road.

That was a long, long walk for me. The longest walk I had ever taken in my life. I didn't see any blue sky or hear any birds singing. My mind was numb. I couldn't think. I felt like I was lost in deep, dark timber and didn't know which way to go or what to do.

As I came in sight of the store, I saw my old grandpa sitting in his rocker on the porch. As usual, he was just sitting there looking off across the country; with a fly swatter in his hand and rocking away.

With my head bowed, and not even looking at him,

I walked by within ten feet of him. He never said a word. I didn't either.

When I heard the squeaking of his old rocker stop, I knew he was watching me. I opened the gate, led my little mare into the barn lot, and took the halter from her head.

With tears in my eyes, I patted her on the neck and said, "Good-bye, little girl. I guess we can't have everything we'd like to have. We have to give up a few things now and then. I'll never forget you, and I'll always love you."

I was hanging the halter on the gate post when something way down inside me busted wide open. Placing my hands on the post, I buried my face in my arms and cried.

If tear drops could have made a fence post sprout roots and grow, that post would have grown twenty feet tall.

After I had had a good cry, I felt a little better—but not very much. With my handkerchief, I dried my face the best I could, walked over, and sat down on the porch by my grandpa.

He was just sitting there with a pleased look on his friendly old face; rocking away. Neither of us said a word.

I thought that the slow squeaking of Grandpa's old rocker was going to make me bawl again. It would have, too, if Grandpa hadn't started talking.

He coughed and squirmed around in his chair. In a low, soft voice, he said, "What's the matter? Have you changed your mind? You going to take the roan this time?"

"I'm not going to take either one of the ponies, Grandpa," I said. "I can't."

"Neither one of them?" Grandpa said. "I don't understand. What happened?"

"I can't buy a pony, Grandpa," I said. "If I do, I'd always feel guilty. Every time I climbed on its back to go riding, I'd think of my little sister and that old crippled leg of hers. I'm going to give my money to her so she can go to the hospital and get it fixed up.

"I think you were trying to tell me that all the time. That's why you brought the crippled mare home with you, so I could see it and maybe it would wake me up. But I was so blind I couldn't see anything but the pony."

Not saying a word, Grandpa ran his hand down in his pocket, pulled out the money I had given him, and handed it to me.

In a voice that quivered with emotion, he said, "Son, I've always been proud of you, but right now, no grandpa on this earth could be as proud as I am—though I'm not very proud of myself."

"Why, Grandpa?" I said. "You haven't done anything."

"Oh, I don't know," he said. "I think there's a passage in the Bible that could explain it better than I could; where it says 'O ye of little faith.' "

On hearing a door slam, I turned and saw Grandma coming over from the house. She was carrying a small cloth sack in her hand. She walked up to us.

Holding the sack out to me, she said, "Here, Jay Berry, take this to your mother."

"What is it, Grandma?" I asked as I took the sack.

"It's the money your grandpa and I have been saving for Daisy's doctor bill," she said. "That's what you're going to do with your money, isn't it?"

"Sure, Grandma," I said, very surprised, "but how did you know?"

Grandma smiled and said, "Oh, I knew. Us old grandmas know a lot more than you boys give us credit for."

"Aw, Grandma," I said, "I should have known. You always could read my mind."

"Say," Grandpa said, all excited, "I just thought of something. Your grandma's been wanting to go to town. Tomorrow is a good day for it. Now—if you and your father can come up and take care of the store for me, your mother and Daisy could ride in with us. The train that runs from Tahlequah to Oklahoma City doesn't leave until the middle of the afternoon. We'd get them there in plenty of time to catch it."

"I'll tell Mama as quick as I get home," I said.

"It's getting late," Grandma said. "You'd better be on your way. Tell your mother, if she wants to ride in with us, to be ready first thing in the morning."

I thanked Grandma and Grandpa and lit out for home.

Mama, Papa, and Daisy were just sitting down at the supper table when I came flying into the house.

I walked up to Mama, handed her the sack of money, and said, "Here, Mama, this is for you."

"What is it?" Mama asked.

"It's the money I got for catching the monkeys—and all that Grandpa and Grandma have saved. We want you to have it so you can take Daisy to the hospital and get her crippled leg fixed."

I saw Mama's face slowly turn grayish-white. Her mouth opened but no words came out. She looked at the sack and then across the table at Daisy. She looked again at the sack and then at Papa.

It was so still in our kitchen you could have heard a dream walking. The only sound I heard was the slow hissing of the tea kettle on the cook stove.

Mama closed her eyes. I saw the tears when they squeezed out of her eyes and ran slowly down her cheeks.

In a low whisper, Mama said, "Oh, thank you, dear Lord. Oh, thank you. I'll be forever grateful."

Daisy went over to Mama and put her arms around her. She started crying. Something that felt like a big old wasp's nest got all wadded up in my throat and darned if I didn't bawl a little, too.

Papa got up from the table and walked into the front room. When he came back, he had what little money he and Mama had saved.

Daisy hurried to her room and got her money.

I never saw so much money. There was money all over the place.

"Papa," I said, "Grandpa and Grandma are going into town tomorrow. He said if you and I would take care of the store, Mama and Daisy could ride in with them and catch the train."

Papa looked at Mama and said, "As long as we have waited for this day, I can't see any reason to put it off. What do you think?"

"What do I think?" Mama said, all excited. "Why, I'd go this very minute if I could."

"Then start packing," Papa said. "Don't worry about Jay Berry and me. We'll make out all right."

Mama and Daisy were off in another room packing their clothes when Papa said, in a low voice, "Son, I wanted to say this before but I didn't want your mother and Daisy to hear. I didn't want them to know that you had almost gotten home with your pony. You grew ten feet tall today. I'm proud of you. I'd like to shake your hand."

I shook hands with Papa for the first time in my life. It felt like all his strength came right up my arm and spread through my body.

18

For the first time in a long time, I slept all night without waking up. I was still asleep the next morning when Grandpa and Grandma drove up to our house.

That was a very busy morning around our place. Both Mama and Grandma were giving me orders at the same time. "Don't forget that. Bring this. Hurry now, we don't want to miss that train." I never saw anything like it.

The last part was the worst. Mama, Daisy, and Grandma were all bawling at the same time. I didn't think Mama would ever turn loose of Papa.

Daisy was bawling and kissing everything that got close to her. She kissed Papa four or five times. She tried to kiss me but I got away from her. She caught Rowdy and kissed him right between the eyes.

The last thing I put in the buckboard was Daisy's old crutch. I cried a little when I saw them disappear down the road.

Papa and I took care of Grandpa's store that day and I made myself sick—I ate so much candy. By late evening, I was the sickest boy in those Ozark hills. I was still sick when I went to bed that night.

The next morning while we were having breakfast, Papa said, "Now that Mama and Daisy are gone, things are going to be a little different. You and I will have to take care of everything. If you can do the

cooking and take care of things around the house,
I'll take care of the fields. How does that sound to
you?"

"It sounds fine to me, Papa," I said.

"Do you think you can do it?" Papa asked.

"Oh, sure, Papa," I said. "I won't have any trouble
with the cooking. I've watched Mama do that a
thousand times."

Papa laughed. "I don't know," he said. "You may
find there's more to cooking than you think."

"Naw, Papa," I said. "I won't have any trouble with
it. Every time you come in from the field, I'll have
some food on the table just like Mama does."

To have a little company, I propped the kitchen
door open so Rowdy could come and go. This pleased
him very much because only on special occasions was
he allowed in the house. I figured that this was a very
special occasion.

With Mama's apron tied around me and humming
a happy tune, I got started. The first thing I tried to
cook was some beans. I got a pot and filled it about
two thirds full with beans. I poured in a little water,
dropped in a chunk of salt pork, and set it on the
stove.

Then I peeled three potatoes and sliced them. I set
a skillet on the stove, waited until it was hot enough
to fry nails, and dropped the potatoes and a scoop of
hog lard in it.

While the beans and potatoes were cooking, I figured that I'd make some flour gravy.

All this time, I was still humming that happy little
tune.

It didn't take long to find out that I knew absolutely
nothing about cooking. I was setting the table when
things started happening. First, it was the beans. They
hadn't been boiling very long when they started crawling out of the pot as if they were alive. In no time, I
had beans all over the stove and all over the kitchen
floor. Some even fell off the stove into Mama's wood-
box.

Then the potatoes went crazy. They started burning

and smoking at the same time. Before I knew it, the house was full of smoke. I opened every door and window to let it out.

Rowdy got scared, ran outside, and crawled under the porch.

When I tried to pour the gravy out of the skillet into a bowl, it wouldn't pour. It just plopped out like a pancake.

I had no trouble getting rid of my messes. Our chickens and Sloppy Ann, our hog, would eat anything.

I tried to get Rowdy to come back in the house so I'd have someone to talk to, but he wouldn't do it. I threatened to whip him but it did no good.

When Papa came in from the field for his dinner, he said, "Boy, I'm hungry. What are we going to eat?"

"Papa," I said, "I'm afraid I'm not much of a cook. Everything I put on the stove either boiled over or burned up. There must be more to this cooking than I thought there was."

Papa laughed. "I was afraid of that," he said, "but don't let it bother you. We'll make out all right. I'll help you with the cooking."

For dinner, we had cold cornbread that Mama had baked, sweet milk, honey, and butter—that was all.

We made out all right, but it wasn't easy. Papa couldn't cook any better than I could. I would have starved to death if it hadn't been for Grandma. About every two or three days, I'd pay her a visit and she would fill me up.

The mail buggy made one trip from Tahlequah to Grandpa's store each week. We never knew what day it would come. Each time the buggy came there were two letters from Mama: one for Papa and one for Grandma and Grandpa.

Papa and I would read Mama's letters over and over.

Mama wasn't very happy about staying in the big city. She told us how lonesome she was and how much she missed us. Daisy was getting along fine. They had operated on her leg and she had a cast on it. The doctor told Mama that he felt sure the operation had been successful. If everything went as they thought it would, Daisy wouldn't need her old crutch any more. They wouldn't know for sure until they took the cast off.

I thought it would be fun with no one around but Papa and me. There was no one to give me orders or tell me what to do. But the fun didn't last very long. I began to miss Mama and Daisy. The days got longer and longer, and the nights were almost unbearable.

By the end of the third week, it seemed as if a gloomy silence had settled all around our home. Everything seemed to have changed.

Our chickens had all but stopped laying. We were getting about half as many eggs as we had been. Sally Gooden had dropped off in her milk until she was barely wetting the bucket. One day I went to get a bucket of water and almost cried when I noticed that our well was going dry.

Papa tried to explain these changes by saying it was that time of year when everything around a farm changes. Summer was almost gone and fall was coming on. It happened every year, and it wasn't anything to worry about.

The way I was feeling I wasn't worrying about our farm. Right then I didn't care what happened to it. I was lonesome. I wanted Mama and Daisy to come home.

Rowdy didn't help at all. He had stopped following me around and didn't have any more bounce to him than an Ozark flint rock. He couldn't understand why I didn't go prowling any more.

As the days passed, Papa started moping around as if he didn't have any life left in him. Some nights he would sit in his rocker on the porch, and smoke his pipe until way in the night. It got so bad that sometimes he would go all day and not say one word to me.

It was worse around Grandpa's store. He got so grumpy he couldn't get along with himself, much less anyone else.

In the middle of the fourth week, we got a letter from Mama that cheered us up for a few days. Mama said that the doctor had taken the cast off Daisy's leg. The operation had been a success, and Daisy was learning to walk. She said that Daisy was walking all over the hospital.

After hearing this, Papa and I felt pretty good for a few days. Then that lonely feeling crept in on us again. It seemed to be ten times worse than it had been before.

Six, long, miserable weeks went by. It got so still around our home, it gave me a scary feeling. I went out of my way to find things to do. I kept the weeds hoed out of Mama's garden. I cleaned the barn. I swept the floor in our house so many times it was a wonder I didn't wear out the floorboards.

I couldn't forget the little mare. There was hardly a day went by that I didn't think of her. It was the dreams that hurt worst of all. I would dream that I could hear her nickering but I couldn't see her. When I would see her, I couldn't put my hands on her. She was always just out of reach. In ghostly slow motion, I could see her running with mane and tail blowing in the breeze. Sometimes I would try so hard to catch her but I never could quite make it. Oh, I'd get close— so close that I could almost touch her with my hand, and then I'd wake up.

It hurt—oh, how it hurt.

One day about the middle of the afternoon, I took a broom and a bucket of water and walked up to Daisy's playhouse. I gave it a good sweeping and I watered all of her flowers. I noticed that the wind and rain had unwrapped some of the tinfoil from the grapevine cross.

I was rewrapping the crossarm of the cross when I thought of the Old Man of the Mountains. With tears in my eyes, I knelt in front of the cross and asked him to help me.

"Old Man of the Mountains," I said, "I know you're here somewhere. Daisy says that you're always around. She says that you see and hear everything that goes on in these hills. I hope you hear me today. Please send Mama and Daisy home. I miss them so much. I don't think I can stand it any more. If you do this one thing for me, I promise to be good for as long as I live."

The Old Man of the Mountains must have decided that I did need help. The very next day something wonderful happened.

Papa and I were sitting on the porch of our home in the twilight of evening. Rowdy was lying at my side. Thousands of lightning bugs had just started their flickering dance. They looked like tiny flashlights going on and off, on and off.

In one of the big red oaks, a small screech owl started his eerie twitter. Across the river at the Mose Hobb's farm, an old milk cow was mooing and an old hound was baying in his deep voice. Down in the river bottoms, an old hooty owl started singing his hoot-owl song to the silent night.

I saw when Rowdy raised his head, pricked up his ears, and looked down the road. "Papa," I said, "somebody's coming."

Papa stirred in his chair and said, "What makes you think someone's coming? I don't hear anything."

"I don't either, Papa," I said, "but Rowdy does."

Papa looked at Rowdy. "I believe he does hear something," he said.

Then we heard the jingling of harnesses and the fast clopping of horses' hoofs.

Papa got up from his chair. He said, "I wonder who it could be this late in the evening."

It was Grandpa. In a cloud of dust, his buckboard pulled up in front of our home. Grandpa started talking as he got out of it.

"I've been trying to get down here ever since the mailman came," he said, "but I couldn't get away from the store. I never saw so many people."

He came over and handed Papa a letter. "They're coming in tomorrow," he said. "On the noon train. That's what she said in our letter."

Papa never said a word. He turned and walked into the house. Grandpa and I followed him.

Papa opened the letter. In the glow of our coal-oil lamp, he started reading it out loud.

The letter was short. Mama said that she and Daisy would be on the noon train and wanted us to meet them. She said there were a lot of things she wanted to tell us but it would be better to wait and let us see for ourselves.

Grandpa said, "If you're busy with your farm work, I'll be glad to go in and pick them up."

"No, we'll go in," Papa said. "I think it would do us good to get away from here for a day."

I knew that I was going to bawl so I went to my room and lay down on the bed. With my face buried in a pillow, I said, "Thanks, Old Man of the Mountains. Thank you very much, and I'll keep my promise."

I didn't sleep every well that night. I kept waking up. Papa must not have slept at all. Every time I woke up, I could hear him stirring around in the house.

The next morning, Papa was up before daylight. He had opened the door and let Rowdy in the house.

Rowdy came flying into my room and jumped right up in the middle of my bed. I tried hiding under the covers but it did no good. With his paws, Rowdy dug the quilts off me and started licking my face.

I put my arms around him and said, "Boy, you'd better be glad that Mama's not here. She'd wear the broom out on you."

In the kitchen, Papa was chuckling as he built a fire in the cook stove.

All the time Papa and I were doing the chores that morning, Rowdy stayed so close to me I could hardly walk. Several times I almost stepped on him. Even while we were eating breakfast, he sat where he could look right in my face. He wiggled and he twisted. He whimpered and he whined. His old tail was going in all directions.

Papa laughed and said, "What's the matter with that old hound? He's sure acting funny."

"He knows we're going someplace," I said, "and he's begging me to let him go with us."

Papa said, "Why, we'll have to take him. We couldn't leave him here all alone. He'd die a thousand deaths. Just be sure that we have a rope with us."

"Watch this, Papa!" I said.

Looking at Rowdy, I said, "It's all right, boy. You can go with us."

Rowdy was so pleased he had a running fit. He bounded into the front room, made a U-turn, and came flying back through the kitchen and out the door. He ran all the way around the house and came back in. He sat down, raised his old head, and bawled.

I thought everything in the house would come down.

Papa and I laughed and laughed.

That was the first good laugh we had had since Mama and Daisy had gone away.

While I was doing the dishes, Papa hitched our mules to the wagon. Both of us put on clean overalls and shirts. I even went out to the watering trough and washed my feet a little—but not very much.

All the way to town Papa kept our old mules a-stepping.

When we got to the depot, Papa drove around behind it and tied the team to a hitching rail. While he was taking care of the team, I took the rope and tied it to Rowdy's collar.

A lot of people were milling around the depot. They didn't pay much attention to Rowdy and me. Oh, some of them looked at us and nodded their heads. A few spoke, but that was all.

Papa walked over to where a group of men were talking, and joined in on their conversation.

While Papa and the men were talking, Rowdy and I took a walk along the track. That was the first time I had walked a steel rail of a railroad track. It was fun.

Not to be outdone, Rowdy got up on the rail and walked it, too.

Rowdy did all right with his rail-walking but I didn't do too well. It's not easy to walk a rail if you're holding onto a rope with a hound dog tied on the end of it. Believe me, it's pretty hard to do.

Rowdy and I were a good way down the track when I heard the train whistle in the distance. It was coming from the other direction. We hurried back to the depot.

I had never seen a train before and I was all excited about seeing my first one.

The track made a bend about five hundred yards from the depot. I glued my eyes to the bend and held my breath. I waited and watched. The rails started clicking and the ground started trembling. With its bell ringing and black smoke rolling, the engine came around the bend.

When Rowdy saw the big, black, noisy engine coming toward him, he got scared. He tried to get between my legs, but I wouldn't let him.

I was scared, too, and I didn't want a hound dog and a rope wound around my legs if I decided to have a runaway.

Rowdy must have gotten so scared he didn't know what he was doing. With every hair on his back standing straight up, he growled and showed his teeth. He ran out to the end of the rope and started to bawl at the train.

Behind me, I heard someone say, "If that boy would turn that old hound loose, I think he'd tie into that train."

All around me people started to laugh.

Just before the train got to the depot, it whistled. I all but jumped out of my britches. I had never heard anything like it in my life.

That whistle was too much for Rowdy. With his tail between his legs, he came scooting back to me and tried to get between my legs again.

"Rowdy," I said in a quavering voice, "if you don't sit down and behave yourself, I'm going to whip you."

I didn't mean what I said, but I was so scared I had to say something.

Jarring the ground with its big pounding wheels,

the engine chugged by us. It pulled past the depot a little way and, with steam hissing and brakes squeaking, it stopped. A passenger coach was right in front of us.

For several seconds, a silence settled over the people waiting on the depot platform. All I could hear was the hissing breath of the engine.

The door of the coach opened and a black man with a small stool in his hand stepped out. He was wearing a dark green uniform and a round hard-top cap with a long bill.

That was the first black man I had ever seen and I couldn't take my eyes off him. He must have noticed me staring at him. As he set the stool down on the platform, he looked at me and then at Rowdy.

With a friendly smile on his face, he said, "Will that hound tree anything?"

I swallowed and said, "Yes, sir, he'll tree anything."

The smile spread all over the black man's face. His white teeth flashed. He said, "That's the kind of dog to have. When I was a boy, I had an old hound just about like him. I still remember that old dog. We had a lot of fun together."

I liked the black man. He was so friendly and I could tell that he liked boys and dogs.

Two cowboys were the first ones off the train. They were carrying their saddles over their shoulders.

In a loud voice, someone in the crowd said, "Hey, Larry! How did the rodeo go?"

Larry laughed and said, "It went all right for me, but Old Henry here, he didn't do so good. He got bucked off everything he got on."

Henry said, "If you had drawn the buckers I drew, you would have been in the air so much you would have sprouted wings."

Everyone around roared with laughter.

Then two drummers got off. Each one was carrying two suitcases. No one said a word to them.

The next person to get off was a big, stout woman. She had about a dozen kids bunched up behind her. It sounded like every one of them was bawling. The woman was jerking and shoving kids and giving orders.

Then I saw Mama and Daisy at the door of the coach.

Mama was carrying her suitcase in one hand and Daisy's old crutch in the other. She saw me and smiled. Tears flooded her eyes.

Mama didn't waste any time getting off the coach and coming to me. She dropped the suitcase and the crutch, threw her arms around me, and kissed me. She squeezed me so tight I could hardly get my breath. Then Mama turned me loose and, with a low choking sob, she went right into Papa's arms. I never saw so much hugging and kissing between Mama and Papa.

Daisy was the last one to get off the train. She was still standing in the door of the coach and was looking at me. She had her suitcase with her and some bundles. I had never seen such a warm, tender smile on her face. Her blue eyes were as bright as a bluebird flying into the sun. Two big tears were sliding slowly down her cheeks. The tears stopped about halfway down and held there as if by some invisible force.

I let my eyes travel from Daisy's face down to that old crippled leg. I sucked in a mouthful of air and stared. I just couldn't believe it. Daisy wasn't crippled any more. I kept staring from one leg to the other. If I hadn't known which one had been crippled, I never would have been able to guess. There was no difference in either leg.

As I stood there, looking at Daisy, I knew that I would never regret giving up my pony. It was all worth it. My little sister wasn't a cripple any more.

Daisy must have seen that I was staring at her leg. Very slowly she raised her foot and wiggled it. Never before had my little sister been able to move her foot like that.

To let her know that I understood, and was happy for her, I smiled and nodded my head.

With no limp at all, Daisy came down the steps and over to me. She stopped about three feet from me, set her suitcase down, and piled the bundles on top of it. For a second, she just stood there, looking at me. I could see the tears glistening in her eyes. Then she just kind of jumped, and wrapped her arms around me.

I didn't know my little sister was so strong. She was hugging me so tight her small arms felt like steel bands around my neck.

"Jay Berry," she whispered, "I love you so very much. I won't ever forget what you did for me."

Then she kissed me right on the mouth.

I felt the blushing heat as it crawled up my neck and spread all over my face. "I love you, too," I said in a low voice, "but you didn't have to kiss me like that— not right here in front of all these people."

Daisy smiled and said, "I don't care what anyone thinks. You're my brother and I'll kiss you any time I want to."

I wanted to argue with Daisy about that but I didn't think it was a good time to start an argument.

Papa came over and hugged and kissed Daisy. It was the first time in my life I saw tears in his eyes.

Just then the deep voice of a hound dog rang out over the depot platform. In his own way, Rowdy was telling the whole wide world that he was a happy hound. The family was together again.

All around us people started laughing. I was feeling so good that I laughed a little, too.

We were putting the suitcases and bundles in our wagon when Papa looked at Mama and said, "Why did you bring Daisy's old crutch home? She doesn't need it now."

"I know," Mama said as she climbed to the wagon seat, "but I don't care. I brought it home anyway. I want it hung on the wall in our home where I can see it every day—and be thankful."

Papa never said a word as he laid Daisy's crutch in the wagon, but I could tell by the look on his face that he was thankful, too.

19

As we rode along in our bouncy old wagon, Daisy
talked up a storm. She had so many things to tell
me. She told me all about her operation and her stay
in the hospital. She said that the first day she walked
without her crutch was the happiest day of her life.

Rowdy would ride in the wagon for a while. Then
he'd jump out and go sniffing along the road. He had
so much hunting blood in him, he couldn't stay in
the wagon for very long.

When we came in sight of our home, Papa said, "It
looks like we have company."

"Why, that's Grandpa's buckboard," Mama said.
"Bless his old heart! He just couldn't wait—he wants
to see Daisy."

Papa stretched up to see better. "What's that I see
in our barn lot?" he said. "I'm sure it wasn't there
when we left this morning."

I stood up in the wagon so I could see over the rail
fence around our barn lot. My mouth flew open and
my eyes all but popped out of my head. I got warm
all over and my old heart started pounding like a
sawmill.

Standing in the center of the lot, with her head up
and looking in our direction, was the little mare.

Daisy grabbed the back of the spring seat to steady

herself and stood up in the wagon, too. "What is it, Jay Berry?" she asked.

I wanted to answer Daisy but I couldn't. I couldn't do anything but stare at that beautiful paint pony.

Just then the little mare shook her head and snorted. She trotted over to the rail fence. With her small ears pointing straight up, she looked at me and nickered.

The nicker jarred me out of the trance I was in. "It's the little mare!" I shouted. "It's the little mare!"

"Oh, it's a paint!" Daisy said. "Isn't she beautiful!"

The little mare was all excited. With her mane and tail flying, she galloped around the lot. Now and then, she would stop, toss her head, and nicker.

I could see that she wasn't limping at all.

Daisy said, "Jay Berry, that pony acts like she knows you. Have you ever seen her before?"

"She does know me," I said. "I saw her at Grandpa's store."

I was still looking at the little mare when Papa drove up in front of our house and stopped the wagon.

Grandpa was sitting on the porch in Papa's rocker. He was just sitting there with a grin on his whiskery old face; rocking away and looking at us.

I jumped down from the wagon and ran to him. "Grandpa," I said in a loud voice, "the little mare—did you bring her?"

"I sure did," Grandpa said. "She's all yours—she's your pony."

I was so stunned I couldn't even thank Grandpa. I just stood there with my mouth open, looking at him and not even seeing him.

From behind me I heard Daisy squeal with excitement. "Oh, Mama," she said, "it came true! It really did! The wish I made in the fairy ring has come true. I wished that Jay Berry could get his pony and .22."

On hearing the rustling of paper, I turned around just as Daisy walked up to me. She had one of the packages in her hands and was hugging it to her.

With a serious look on her face, she said, "Jay Berry, this is your gun. But before I give it to you, I want you to promise me something. I want you to promise me that you won't ever shoot any of the little things that live in these hills. I mean little birds, squirrels, chipmunks, and bunnies. They don't hurt anything. If you just have to shoot something, there are plenty of old rattlesnakes, chicken hawks, wolves, and wild cats around. You can shoot them—but not the little things. Will you promise me that?"

Things were happening so fast I couldn't think straight. My mind went completely blank. I wanted to promise Daisy but I couldn't talk. All I could do was nod my head.

Daisy said, "Don't just nod your head, Jay Berry. I want to hear you say it out loud."

I took a deep breath and said, "All right, Daisy, I promise that I won't hurt any of the little things— not ever again."

As Daisy held the package out to me, she smiled and said, "Mama and I walked all over Oklahoma City looking for this .22. I think it's just like the one I saw you looking at in our catalogue."

With trembling hands, I tore the paper from the package. There it was—my own .22. It was a single-shot Hamilton—the very gun I had always wanted.

I turned the gun over and over, and ran my hand along the dark walnut stock and the slick metal barrel. I put the stock to my shoulder and drew a bead on a fence post.

As I stood there with the .22 in my hands—one of the most precious treasures a country boy can own—I looked over to the pony in our barn lot. The little mare was standing with her head over the rail fence, looking at me. She nickered, tossed her head, and started pawing the ground.

It was so still on the porch of our home, you could have heard a worm breathing. Visions started flashing through my mind. I saw Daisy's playhouse and all her treasures—the cross she had made from grapevines wrapped in tinfoil, and the face of Christ she had molded from the dark red clay of the Ozark hills. I could see the wild mountain flowers peeking from the tin cans—rooster heads, violets, and daisies. I saw the fairy ring and remembered the wish I had made when I knelt in the center of that snow-white circle.

I felt the hot tears in my eyes. I tried not to bawl, but I just couldn't help it. I bawled anyway.

I wiped the tears from my face with the sleeve of my shirt. "Daisy," I said, "there's something that I want to tell you. The wish I made in the fairy ring has some true, too. I wished that you could get your crippled leg fixed up."

Whimpering like a pup under a tub, Mama buried her face in Papa's chest.

Papa put his arms around Mama. Looking at me, he said, "Son, when your mother and I made our wishes, we wished for the same thing you did. We wished that Daisy could get her crippled leg taken care of. Our wishes came true."

In a choking voice, Mama said, "It's a miracle! All four of our wishes have come true. It was the work of the Lord. It couldn't have been anything else."

With a low cough, Grandpa cleared his throat. He got up from his chair and said, "You know, when your grandma and I first came to this country, I did a lot of walking. I don't do much walking any more—not since I opened the store. But from this day, I'm going to walk all over these hills and river bottoms, and I don't care where I walk I'm going to look for a fairy ring. I'd sure like to find one. There are a lot of things I'd like to wish for—a lot of things."

Grandpa seemed to be so serious in what he was saying, it was funny. All of us started laughing.

Grandpa got a little upset. He said, "I mean it. I mean every word I said."

All excited, Daisy turned to me and said, "Jay Berry, let's go look at your pony. I'm dying to see her."

"All right," I said as I set my gun down and leaned it against a porch post. "She's a dandy."

With Rowdy bouncing along with us, Daisy and I hurried to the barn lot. We had no more than opened the gate, when the little mare tossed her head and came trotting to us.

While Daisy was petting her, I went to the barn and got a currycomb. As much petting, rubbing, and grooming as my pony got, it was a wonder she had any hair left on her.

The little mare loved the attention she was getting. She nibbled at our clothes and pushed us with her head. Once she got so excited she whirled, and galloped all the way around the lot.

Daisy laughed and said, "Look at her. She's a regular little show-off."

I felt sorry for Rowdy. The poor old fellow was so jealous of the little mare he could hardly stand it. In every way that a hound dog could, he tried to keep his body between us and the pony. He didn't want my pony to get all the attention and petting. He wanted to get a little of it himself.

Right out of a clear blue sky, Daisy said, "Jay Berry, what are you going to name your pony?"

"Oh!" I said. "I haven't even thought about a name for her."

So many things had happened to me, I hadn't even thought about naming my pony.

Daisy said, "She's as sweet as a doll, I don't think it would be hard to find a name for her."

When I heard Daisy say "doll," I shouted, "That's it! It's perfect! I'll name her Dolly."

Daisy looked at me and started repeating "Dolly" over and over. Then her eyes lit up and she said, "Oh, Jay Berry, it's the perfect name for her. You couldn't have thought of a better one."

Rubbing the soft velvety nose of my pony, I said, "Little girl, from now on your name is Dolly. Someday I may write a story about how I got you.

"Daisy," I said, "do you want me to get a bridle and put it on her? You can be the first to ride her."

"No, Jay Berry," Daisy said. "I'd love to ride her, but we'll have plenty of time for that. Right now, there is something else I want more than anything."

"What's that?" I asked.

"I want you to run with me," Daisy said. "I want that more than anything I've ever wanted."

I was so surprised I couldn't believe what I heard Daisy say. "Run with you!" I said.

"Yes," Daisy said. "All through the years when I've been up in my playhouse and watched you and Rowdy running in our fields, I could hear you laughing and Rowdy barking. You seemed to be having so much fun. I wanted to be running with you. Oh, how I wanted to be there—but I couldn't. Sometimes it hurt so much I cried. Now, I want to run and run and run. Please, Jay Berry, run with me this one time."

My little sister wasn't just asking me to run with her, she was pleading with me. I could see it in her eyes and hear it in her voice. It almost broke my heart.

"All right, Daisy," I said. "I'll run with you. I'll run all over these hills with you if you want me to."

We climbed over the rail fence and walked out to the edge of our fields. I took my little sister's small hand in mine and we started running.

Rowdy seemed to know that this was a special day. He ran ahead of us and he bawled. He zigged and he zagged. Then he turned and came flying back.

Hand in hand, Daisy and I ran through the clover, the alfalfa, and the timothy—through a field of shocked corn and a pumpkin patch. We leaped high in the air as we jumped over the big yellow pumpkins. We ran all the way down to the river bottoms.

As we ran, I glanced over at Daisy. She had her head thrown back and her face was flushed with excitement. Her long hair was flying and her eyes were as bright as morning glory blossoms. She was squealing with laughter.

I had never seen my little sister so happy. It made me feel good all over.

I was still a boy when I left the Ozarks, only sixteen years old. Since that day, I've left my footprints in many lands: the frozen wastelands of the Arctic, the bush country of Old Mexico, and the steaming jungles of Yucatán.

Throughout my life, I've been a lover of the great

outdoors. I have build campfires in the Rocky Mountains of Colorado, and hunted wild turkey in the Smoky Mountains of Tennessee and the Blue Ridge Mountains of Virginia. I have climbed the Grand Tetons of Wyoming, and hunted bull elk in the primitive area of Idaho.

I can truthfully say that, regardless of where I have roamed or wandered, I have always looked for the fairy ring. I have never found one, but I'll keep looking and hoping. If the day ever comes that I walk up to that snow-white circle, I'll step into the center of it, kneel down, and make one wish, for in my heart I believe in the legend of the rare fairy ring.

Lose yourself in award-winning teen fiction from Laurel-Leaf books!

Robert B. PARKER

"The toughest, funniest, wisest private-eye in the field."*

☐ A CATSKILL EAGLE	11132-3	$4.95
☐ CEREMONY	10993-0	$4.50
☐ CRIMSON JOY	20343-0	$4.95
☐ EARLY AUTUMN	12214-7	$4.50
☐ GOD SAVE THE CHILD	12899-4	$4.50
☐ THE GODWULF MANUSCRIPT	12961-3	$4.50
☐ THE JUDAS GOAT	14196-6	$4.50
☐ LOOKING FOR RACHEL WALLACE	15316-6	$4.95
☐ LOVE AND GLORY	14629-1	$4.50
☐ MORTAL STAKES	15758-7	$4.95
☐ PALE KINGS AND PRINCES	20004-0	$4.50
☐ PROMISED LAND	17197-0	$3.95
☐ A SAVAGE PLACE	18095-0	$4.50
☐ TAMING A SEAHORSE	18841-5	$4.95
☐ VALEDICTION	19246-3	$4.95
☐ THE WIDENING GYRE	19535-7	$4.50
☐ WILDERNESS	19328-1	$4.50

*The Houston Post